DEADLY PURSUIT

MISTY EVANS

ROMANTIC SUSPENSE AND MYSTERIES BY MISTY EVANS

The Super Agent Series
Operation Sheba
Operation Paris
Operation Proof of Life

The SCVC Taskforce Series
Deadly Pursuit
Deadly Deception
Deadly Force
Deadly Intent
Deadly Affair
Deadly Attraction
Deadly Secrets
Deadly Holiday

The Justice Team Series (with Adrienne Giordano)
Stealing Justice
Cheating Justice
Holiday Justice (novella)
Exposing Justice
Protecting Justice
Missing Justice
Defending Justice

SEALs of Shadow Force Series
Fatal Truth
Fatal Honor
Fatal Courage
Fatal Love
Fatal Vision
Fatal Thrill
Risk

ACKNOWLEDGMENTS

As Cooper and Celina would tell you, it takes a team to pull off a successful undercover op. Writing, publishing, and promoting a book is also a team effort. Without my friends, family, and editors, this book would still be unfinished, languishing on my computer.

Thank you, Dianna and Adrienne, for asking me to include this story in a boxed set. You provided the motivation to finish the book and the perfect outlet to publish it. Many thanks, also, to Amy R., the best and fastest beta reader in the world. You were the first to see the finished product, and I'm so grateful for your accurate and timely feedback.

Undying gratitude to Nana, who cheered for this book since the day I ran the plot by her five years ago, and who is my source for all things Southern California.

And as always, I'm grateful to my husband and sons for understanding when I'm up at four a.m. typing away…and still going at it after bedtime. For all the times you asked what you could do to help, and all the times you just did it—laundry, dinner, walking the dogs—I love you and appreciate the team work. I can't wait for our next vacation to Carlsbad.

DEDICATION

To Mark and the real-life Thunder…
you are the inspiration for this story.

CHAPTER ONE

Celina Davenport looked out at the dark sky, the even darker ocean on her right, and the track of highway flying under the belly of the Porsche. The high pressure sodium freeway lights and the stars shining overhead did nothing to reassure her. The all-consuming view was like a sci-fi movie when the starship hit warp speed and the stars turned into streaks of light.

Warp speed. Her mind was flying in tandem with the car. This was no sci-fi movie. Weirdville, yes, but still planet Earth and still part of her job.

What awaited her on the other end of this crazy ride was either death at Emilio Londano's hands or the successful end to her first undercover case. A year out of the academy, she'd managed to stay alive so far, due more to her wits than her training. Spending the past two months with the head of the San Diego mafia had taught her more than her training at Quantico ever could. More about flirting with danger while never losing sight of her goal.

At that moment, odds weren't in her favor that she'd live to see the sunrise only a few hours away.

Time to do something about those odds.

Taking a discreet deep breath, she turned her big, brown eyes to her companion. In the light from the dashboard, Emilio caught and held her gaze. He loved her eyes. Loved her petite frame with its Cuban curves.

He smiled. The cat about to eat the canary.

She gave him a full-on, sexy smile back. The canary about to become the tiger.

Emilio Londano was a man too handsome for his own good. His Latin roots were evident in every hair, every smile, every polite command. His predictable self-confidence came with a self-deprecating charm. The power he held in every pocket of his skin overcame any and all resistance.

No one, man nor woman, said no to him. The legions of employees he directed, from his drug cartel to his housekeeping staff, were more than happy to make Emilio happy. His generous philanthropy and good citizenship wooed the everyday world of executives who clamored to do business with him through his legitimate organizations while they recruited him to be on their community boards.

The man driving Celina into the dark sleeve of the night was irresistible.

But so was she.

He had flirted, charmed, and tried to seduce her for the past two months. She had flirted, charmed, and seduced in return, stopping short of sleeping with him. That she would not do, not only because it would effectively destroy her job as an FBI agent, but because even handsome, charming criminals made her skin crawl. While Emilio and his lieutenant, Petero Valquis, checked into her past and watched her for any sign of deceit, Celina covertly collected information on the Londano operation and fed the damning evidence to her bosses in Carlsbad and L.A.

To Emilio and his mafia world, she was Celina Mendez, photographer and graphic design artist. She took photographs, fed them into her computer, and made art with them. Some of her designs resembled Warhol. Others were more Picasso. Celina Mendez made a comfortable living selling artwork to commercial venues as well as private parties. Emilio himself had a collage she had created of the infamous Che Guevara hanging in his home office.

Finding nothing in her cover background to give him pause, Emilio was in full conqueror mode, every move in his book in action tonight in order to get her into his bed. Generous amounts of flirting aside, the most Celina had offered him was a kiss. A sensuous meeting of her mouth with his that she knew had left the mafia leader weak in the knees.

Never had a beautiful woman said no to him or his advances.

Never had he wanted anyone more than he did her.

"You are quiet tonight." Emilio down-shifted the Porsche as he brought it to a stop at a red light. They had entered Carlsbad. Nearing two a.m., most of the shops and restaurants that lined the divided highway were closed.

A man, tall and filling out a Billabong sweatshirt to the max, crossed in front of them walking a Chihuahua. The hood of the sweatshirt was up and his face shadowed, but a familiar prick of recognition made Celina's pulse quicken. Military straight back, self-assured gate. He hit the sidewalk and turned south, the tiny legs of the dog double-timing it to keep up with his long stride.

Checking up on me, are you, Mr. Boss Man?

Time to initiate her plan. A plan DEA Special Agent in Charge of the Southern California Violent Crimes (SCVC) taskforce, Cooper Harris, wasn't going to like.

Celina continued to watch the straight back while she nudged her fingers in between Emilio's on the gear shift. "The Pacific Highway does that to me. The rocks, the ocean, the open expanse of night sky. It's beautiful." She let go of a soft sigh. "Makes me feel happy and carefree, like I might dare anything."

Squeezing his hand, she gave him a knowing smile. A smile that said she might be willing to give him what she knew he wanted.

One side of his mouth tilted up. His dark eyes penetrated hers. "Then I'm glad we chose it over the interstate."

The light changed. As Emilio shifted the car into first gear, Celina teased open the lapel of his crisp, white shirt. He'd ditched his jacket and tie before they'd left the parking lot of the theatre. The fundraising benefit for one of his favorite charities had given Celina the perfect set up for this take down. She needed him away from the tight security of his home as well as getting him to lower his guard while Petero Valquis was taking care of business elsewhere. Tonight's date had secured all three.

"You look very handsome," she murmured, leaning toward him and pressing her breast against his arm. She stroked her fingers across his collarbone.

"We were a perfect pair tonight, then." He glanced admiringly at her cleavage as he shifted the car. "You've never looked more beautiful."

The dress Celina was wearing was Marc Jacobs, a gorgeous flesh-pink silk and gauze combination with a beaded halter that showed off every inch of her assets to full advantage. When she'd met Emilio at the door of her apartment, he'd been speechless for the first time since she'd met him. Speechless was good.

She hoped Cooper would be speechless when he saw her too.

The first part of her plan a success at the apartment, she'd kept the distaste off her face and smiled as Emilio twirled her around, ogling every inch of her body. It had worked. He did not have his security goon search her, because he was either so enthralled with the merchandise that his mind went blank, or he was so sure she wasn't anything other than a beautiful woman in a slip of a dress who would finally share his bed tonight.

His mistake. The microphone she wore was a cordless number she'd sewn behind the large jewel centered at the cusp of her cleavage. The transmitter, a small, square, plastic box, was tucked into the left cup of her bra. Off-balanced breasts would have been too noticeable in the dress, so she'd sewn a thick layer of Kleenex between the fabric and the lining of the other cup to even things out.

Which did a great job of hefting her boobs into outer space.

"Oh, look at the sky." Celina tilted her head to look through the open moon roof. "Let's stop at the boardwalk and go down to the beach."

Emilio frowned before looking back at the road. "It's late. Too late. Parking anywhere along here—" he waved his hand at the empty parking lane next to the concrete sidewalks "—will get my car towed. Let's go back to my place."

"Please," Celina begged. She shifted her pleading eyes to his face and again brushed her boobilicious upper body against his. "A walk on the beach would be the perfect ending to this night."

She scooted as close to him as the seats allowed and mentally morphed him into her fantasy man before she ran her right hand around his stomach. Her fingers touched leather. Gun holster. One that held a mean Glock.

Nothing like reality to interrupt her fantasy.

Sliding her fingers under the gun, she gave him a small hug and resuscitated the image of Cooper. Sexy, serious. *Beast* in the urban slang so widely used in the surf shops and outdoor restaurants she frequented when not on duty. She'd started calling him that behind his back, and the other taskforce members had picked it up. Cooper hated it. She loved that he hated it. He was no beast. In fact, he was two hundred and thirty pounds of sexy. And she wanted to be his Beauty.

Probably a lot of women in the DEA, FBI, and CIA had their own particular fantasies about him. Women all over Southern Cal as well. Too bad for them, she played hard and never gave up. He'd be hers. And soon.

While Cooper and Emilio were at opposite ends of the spectrum, running her fantasy-man mental movie always worked when she had to deal with Emilio. That particular mind game was the only thing that had kept her seduction act even close to believable the past few weeks.

She placed a soft kiss on Emilio's neck, still pretending he was Cooper. Which took a superior imagination. "One of your men could drive the car around for a few minutes while we walk the beach." She nipped the lobe of his ear. "If you're scared of getting towed."

Emilio's two bodyguards were behind them in a black SUV.

They were characteristically big, bad and ugly. To arrest Emilio without endangering anyone, Celina had to ditch them and get him totally alone. If one bodyguard had to drive their vehicle and one had to drive the Porsche, she'd have Emilio all to herself.

The key to success. Easy on paper. Hard in reality.

Time for the big guns. Or boobs, in this case.

"The night is dark and the beach is unlit," she said softly. Emilio leaned toward her and she teased his lips with hers as she spoke. "The rocky walls and concrete boardwalks will hide us. You don't need your security detail."

She switched her lips to his earlobe, and still envisioning Cooper, she whispered, "You'll love this dress even more when it's wet."

That sealed it. Emilio's hand came off the gear stick and grabbed her by the back of the head. He drew her to him, bringing his mouth down on hers even as he drove the car.

Forcing herself not to recoil, Celina shifted her imagination into high gear. It was Cooper whose tongue was now in her mouth. Cooper holding her captive while they sped down the road ten miles over the speed limit, playing a dangerous game of make-out roulette.

She forced herself to return Emilio's ardor with her own.

CHAPTER TWO

You'll love this dress even more when it's wet.

Cooper Harris wanted to hit something. Hard.

FBI Special Agent Celina Davenport—sexy siren of his daydreams as well as evil temptress of his night dreams—was sucking face with the biggest drug cartel leader in California and there wasn't a damn thing he could do about it.

Her soft voice coming through the mic as she taunted Londano to have sex with her on the beach gave him an instant headache of giant proportions. But it was the silence that followed, broken only by the sound of them kissing, that made him want to slam the wall of the surveillance van with his bare fist.

Sucker punched. That's what it felt like.

It's her job, idiot. She knows how to handle herself.

Didn't make him any happier. Which showed what a total sexist he really was. Sure, he felt protective about all the guys on his squad, but he never second-guessed them or their skills. He never went apeshit if they kissed a mark or led her on in order to get the information to take someone down.

Celina was female and a little one at that. Short, underweight, except for a few well-placed curves, and she had a soft, almost Southern Belle persona that totally belied her fiery Cuban roots. Push her buttons and you'd see that fire, but it took an ungodly amount of button-pushing for it to surface. He knew. Out of everyone on the SCVC taskforce, he'd managed to tweak every hot button she had at least once. Most of them he'd not only pushed, but punched into the stratosphere.

He loved it when the real Celina came out. Not the professional FBI agent she'd polished to perfection, but the holy shit amazing woman underneath. The one whose emotions rose up and took over, blasting him with her clever wit and overwhelming logic even as she flushed with anger and made gestures with her hands he'd never seen before.

Yeah. *That* was the Celina he'd fallen for.

But he couldn't ever let her know that. How she tied him up in knots. How absolutely gone he was every time he was around her. He was her boss. Head of the taskforce.

He was also fourteen years, six months and four days older.

She was a baby. A rookie. A Feebie, for Christ's sake. DEA agents did not play well with FBI agents.

And he was The Beast after all. His reputation would hardly hold up under the pressure if he robbed the cradle *and* got the female rookie Fed on his team hurt in the line of duty.

So he didn't cut loose and punch the wall of the surveillance van, didn't give into the surge of acid in his stomach. Instead, he scratched Thunder's tiny square head and batted away the image of Special Agent Celina Davenport kissing Emilio Londano.

FBI agent Dominic Quarters' gaze was heavy on Cooper's neck. Fucker had the hots for Celina, too. Cooper shot him an accusatory glance. Fucker could eat shit. "What the hell is your girl doing to our op, Quarters? This wasn't the takedown we had planned."

"Pull your shorts out, Harris." The shorter man eased back in his plastic chair and shrugged. The San Diego Mafia had been formed in the early 1970s by Jose Prisco. Thirty years later, his twin nephews, Emilio and Enrique Paloma-Londano took over the business. While most cartels gained international reputations for brutality and murder, the San Diego traffickers posed as legitimate businessmen. Their unique criminal enterprise involved itself in counterfeiting, kidnapping, and drug trade, but Emilio and Enrique passed off as law-abiding citizens, investing in their country's future and earning the respect of their neighbors and the general public. The Feds wanted them gone. The DEA wanted them gone. Even the CIA thought it was a good idea. Too bad it wasn't one of the spies he'd worked with before instead of Quarters sitting next to him. "She saw an opportunity and ran with it."

An opportunity? That's what this asshole called it? "She's going to get herself killed."

Quarters did the shrug thing again and Cooper's hand balled into a fist. Punching Quarters would be way more satisfying than punching the van's side panel.

The van slowed, following a discreet distance behind Londano's car and bodyguards' vehicle. "Perp is pulling off highway and parking approximately one-quarter klick from here," announced Thomas, a West Point grad who'd held a high profile position with the Department of Defense before defecting to the DEA. The T-man was Cooper's right hand man on this takedown.

Two keystrokes of Thomas's fingers and a night-vision view of the boardwalk appeared on the screen in front of Cooper.

The surveillance van wasn't the only vehicle in the area. A few diehard surf heads always parked near the beach overnight, only moving when the cops harassed them. There were plenty of cops in the area tonight, but none would be visible until after the sting took place, thanks to Cooper's friendly relationship with the police units from L.A. to San Diego. They all wanted Londano out of business and they knew Cooper's taskforce was about to do it.

"Perp is exiting car."

Like he couldn't see that. On screen, Londano and Celina headed to the beach. Thunder, in Cooper's lap, whined. Cooper was petting the dog too hard. "Sorry, hot rod," he murmured, never taking his eyes off the screen. He wanted to watch Celina.

But years of intense training and experience told him to keep his attention on Londano. "Radio the other units in the area that this is going down here and now."

Thomas made a sound of acknowledgment and began notifying their backup.

Celina kicked off her high heels and strolled into the rolling Pacific Ocean. The moon and stars lit the beach with a surreal light that even the night-vision view couldn't compete with. Cooper could only shake his head at her stupid courage and undeniable sensuality. She glowed like a beacon.

A beacon that only reminded him he was trapped in a hell of his own making.

"What is she doing?" Done with notifying the local units, Thomas leaned closer to the screen as if he could decipher Celina's plan by getting face to face with the video. "She gets that mic wet and it's all over. We won't have jack squat of a confession to bring to court."

They all watched Londano plant his feet in the sand and observe Celina with a predatory posture that made adrenaline burn in Cooper's veins. He set Thunder on the van floor, littered with empty disposable coffee cups and torn candy wrappers, and stood up as best he could. The van ceiling was higher than most to accommodate their equipment, but still not tall enough for his large frame.

"That's what you get with rookie Feebies," he said, moving to the back of the van. *One step closer to Celina.* "I'm going in before she winds up shark meat."

Quarters and Thomas protested. Cooper ignored them. Raising the hood of his sweatshirt, he jumped out onto the pavement. Good thing he'd worn his boots instead of his running shoes. They'd hurt a lot more and leave an unforgettable impression when he kicked Celina's butt back to Quantico.

CHAPTER THREE

An ocean wave hit her and Celina sucked in her breath. The water was freezing. If only she had on her wet suit instead of the gauze dress.

But everything was in place. Dumb and Dumber cruised the side streets while their boss watched her from the dark deserted beach. He was waiting for her to drench herself in the ocean and reveal what only his mind had imagined. She wondered if he would try to take her right there under the stars, but it didn't matter. She wouldn't let things get that far. The high wall of rock and concrete behind him did exactly what she'd told him it would. It shielded them from the traffic on the street above, while giving her the opportunity to arrest him quickly and quietly.

Another wave drove into her thighs and rolled up to her waist. With her back to Emilio, she pulled the jeweled pin out of her cleavage and carefully brought it to her lips. "Billabong, this is Switchfoot. Initiating beach cleanup in three. I repeat, initiating beach cleanup in three. Over."

She had no way to know if Cooper received her message clearly over the sound of the waves, but he was nearby along with the rest of the cleanup crew. They'd been waiting for her. Cooper had shown himself at the traffic light to let her know everything was a go. She hadn't talked to him in almost a month, only received small signs here and there that he and his taskforce of agents from the Southern California Violent Crimes

Division were getting her packages and watching her back. Her assignment had been straightforward: Get the proof needed to put Emilio and his cartel out of business for good. Bring him in alive.

And don't get killed.

Like *that* wasn't obvious.

A rookie Feebie, known in FBI vernacular as the FNG or "fucking new guy", Celina had joined Cooper's elite group of agents before a random encounter with Enrique Londano's girlfriend had landed her inside the mafia the SCVC and Mexican officials had been trying to infiltrate for four years.

Celina had stumbled into their private circle quite literally by accident. Danita, the girlfriend of Emilio's twin brother, Enrique, had found Special Agent Celina Davenport photographing whales, her hobby, on a whale-sighting expedition and asked Celina to photograph her and her group of friends. The situation had given Celina the chance to buddy up with the young, naïve woman whose picture was contained in a blue folder on Celina's desk at FBI headquarters in Carlsbad. It hadn't taken more than a few compliments for Celina to convince Danita she was destined to be a model. Celina Mendez, the photographer, found herself the newest member of Danita's social club before the boat returned to shore. Emilio and Enrique ran an art gallery that covertly laundered money and was always looking for fresh, cutting edge artists to fill its walls. Within days Celina had attracted Emilio's attention.

And the entire Southern California task force working on the San Diego Mafia case had cheered.

Cooper had been both pleased and worried. She could either nail this guy and prove his taskforce's worth or completely ruin their chances of ever stopping the elusive Londanos.

Wanting more than anything to prove her value to the team and to Cooper, Celina threw herself into the assignment. She would end Emilio's cartel, and in the process, impress the hell out of Cooper.

With her phones bugged, her email monitored, and one of Londano's men watching her day and night, Celina had become ultra paranoid. She'd only risked delivering evidence against Emilio to Cooper twice, packaging the proof they needed in pictures sent to fictitious customers, but apparently it was enough. She'd gotten the go ahead to arrest Emilio in the form of a red surf board appearing in the window of the local surf shop by her apartment. That was her signal from Cooper to bring it home.

Celina took a step deeper into the water. Dominic Quarters, her FBI superior on assignment with her for this sting, had insisted on a verbal confession tonight, but Celina knew they didn't need one to nail Emilio, and he was too suspicious of everyone and everything. No way was she blowing this mission. Not only would the Londano operation get off scot-free, the taskforce would never get close to the brothers again. Any type of leading question about their black market business was sure to tip Emilio off and blow the takedown.

Time to take the plunge. The salt water would cripple the mic and make the dress stick to her breasts, but there was no backing out now. This was the moment she'd been planning for two months. This arrest would rocket her into FBI stardom and secure her place on Cooper's team. The poor little girl from Miami was about to show everyone exactly what she was made of and what she could do.

Running the next minute through her head, Celina walked further into the ocean and braced herself against the sharp push and pull of the cold water. The water and sky blended into one immense black wall, dotted only with stars. The full moon hung low, its shadow reflecting in the ripples of the ocean.

Still conscious of her audience, Celina raised her arms to the sky, dropped her head back, and let the ocean carry her on the next wave. God it was cold.

But she was tough. Too tough to let a little cold water get in the way of her plans. Too tough to let Londano see her shaking, not from the frigid Pacific Ocean but from nerves.

Sufficiently wet, the dress clung to her breasts. Celina made her way back to the shore.

She had no gun, no weapon. Emilio was a black-belt in karate and carried his gun at all times, although he rarely used violence himself. He was wearing his suit jacket to conceal the weapon hanging under his left arm. The muscles he constantly worked in his private gym gave him a seventy-pound advantage.

But Celina had the element of surprise and could win a wet T-shirt contest hands down. As the water turned loose its hold on her legs, she scanned the beach that was still empty before locking her sights on her quarry. Under the moonlight, his heavy gaze rested on her breasts. Emilio was thinking with his dick at that moment instead of his calculating brain, and that's exactly what she was waiting for.

Conjuring up Cooper once more from the depths of her imagination, she smiled at the man in front of her and moved slowly and seductively into his waiting arms.

With his lips forcing hers to part, Celina opened her mouth, and, at the same time, ran her hands over his shoulders, pushing his jacket off and down his arms. It dropped to the sand behind him. Then she slid her hands down his chest and stomach, tugging his shirt free from his waistband. Emilio's hands found her breasts, and *shit!* She couldn't stand him touching her so intimately.

Shrugging out of his grasp, she laughed seductively, teasing him. He chuckled low and deep, his hands on her upper arms, dragging her back to him, lips assaulting hers once more.

Pushing the straps of her dress off her shoulders, Emilio once again went for her breasts. In one swift movement, Celina shoved at his chest with one hand and grabbed the heavy Glock from his shoulder holster with the other. Glocks. She'd qualified with the standard .22 but went on to qualify with an assortment of others as well. She knew the lovely Glock family as well as she did her own.

Taking two steps back, she pointed the gun at his chest. "Emilio Paloma-Londano, you are under arrest by the United States government for charges relating to the organization and running of the San Diego Mafia." She took a deep breath and one more step back as she watched Emilio's face transform from utter confusion to pure anger. "Drop to your stomach and put your hands behind your head."

He stood stock still, effectively refusing to lie down on the ground, but all hell broke loose around them. FBI, DEA, and local police officers emerged from the nearby lifeguard house and descended from the boardwalk. Spotlights came on, illuminating Emilio, still standing, and Celina, who managed to return her dress straps to her shoulders while never moving the gun sight from Emilio's heart. Their eyes locked on each other and though he didn't move or say a word, Celina felt the intensity of his hatred penetrating every cell of her body.

Special Agent Quarters came up beside her and took the Glock from her grip while she watched two police officers force Emilio face down in the sand. Within seconds, his hands were cuffed and his rights read. She stood there shaking, teeth chattering, arms crossed over her very wet, cold breasts. The officers raised Emilio back to a standing position, and again the dark eyes she knew well snapped to hers. Again she saw the depth of his anger. And then he took her by surprise.

He ignored Quarters and spoke to someone behind Celina. "Give her my jacket so she can cover herself."

As Celina watched Emilio be led away, a soft warmth fell over her shoulders and enveloped her. Instinctively she pulled it closer, stuffed her arms into the sleeves. It was not Emilio's jacket, but a red Billabong sweatshirt.

She smiled as she turned to face Cooper. "Thank you," she said, forgetting the past few months of fear and manipulation the moment she saw his face.

It was a beautiful face. Not in the pretty L.A. boy actor way. Those types of faces she saw all the time and they were fake.

No, Cooper's was a rugged beauty, deeply tanned and handsome. It was the controlled face of a man who lived with danger every day for several decades.

His gaze was as serious as always as he stared down at her. "You all right?"

"Better than fine." *Now that you're here.* Every time she stood next to the DEA agent, she felt like she'd just downed a triple mocha latte with whipped cream. Warm, buzzed, and ready for seconds. "How'd I do?"

He was silent for a moment, studying her. "You went off the rez and we need to talk about that, but…you did okay, kid."

Celina's smile faltered. Kid? *Kid?* "I'm not a kid, Cooper. I'm twenty-four years old." She held his stern gaze. "I did better than okay and you know it. I just nailed Emilio Londano."

Said out loud, those words seemed to vibrate in the air. The moon smiled down at her and she drew her first fearless breath in months. She felt a sudden hot rush in her veins, a tingling sensation shooting through every cell of her body.

Letting her head fall back on her shoulders, she let it come, this rush of accomplishment instead of fear. It roared through her.

Laughing up at the sky, she sang out, "I did it! I arrested the Lord of the Cartel World!" She took a few steps back, staring at the sky, and held out her arms. Twirling, she let her herself enjoy the sweet tingle of relief and success racing through her body.

God, she was beautiful.

And young, Cooper reminded himself for the hundredth, possibly thousandth, time since she'd joined his team. Too young. For him anyway.

But as he watched the beautiful agent twirl herself around in unabashed joy on the sand, with the spotlight on and an audience of horny males watching her, Cooper would have sold his vintage Fender guitar collection to be even five years younger.

And not her boss.

Celina was so alive and so beautiful and so completely crushing on him, it made him want to turn in his badge and chuck his very last moral into the garbage can just so he could touch her. Just once. He would touch that smooth, soft, creamy skin, take her full bottom lip between his and…

Die.

Die and go to heaven.

Hypnotized by her blissful twirling and the idea of a heaven filled with her, Cooper let himself feel what she was feeling. Pure rush. Total adrenaline. Joy. He'd felt it with his first major bust too. A long time ago, when he was still fresh and eager and hungry. The rush of taking out a bad guy was a drug, making the hunger intensify. That hunger had added a lot of notches to his DEA belt and catapulted him to his current position, but he'd had an epiphany on this last assignment. He was worn out.

At thirty-eight, he still loved his job. Loved protecting his country and meting out justice to assholes like Emilio Londano. His taskforce was the best in the country, a machine, just like him, apprehending cartel leaders that trafficked drugs, weapons, and people. In the past year, they'd extended their reach. He and Thomas had gone to Colombia back in the fall, trying to figure out Londano's operation in the Southern Hemisphere in order to help them deal with this one in the Northern.

Thomas and a couple of the other guys on the taskforce had been with him since the early years, taking out several large drug rings while always trying to get the Londano operation that stayed consistently out of their reach. But when the latest addition to his team, this twirling rookie Fed, was handed a personal invitation into the Londano den of lions, Cooper almost pulled the plug on the whole operation.

She'd turned him. A couple of months with his group and

she'd made him feel less like the cartel-eating machine he'd made himself into and more like a human. A man.

A man who wanted her.

A man who realized that if she walked into the den of lions, he couldn't keep her safe.

Celina stopped and walked toward him, off balance and laughing. An unbidden smile crept to his lips—after all she was safe now and Londano was headed to federal prison—but then she was standing right in front of him and looking like she was about to throw her arms around him, and *whoa*—

She threw her arms around him and kissed him. Right on the lips.

Her lips were so soft and she smelled like the ocean and, *holy mother*. Cooper jerked his head back, pulled her arms from around his neck, and stepped back.

Quarters, the fucker, cleared his throat, looking displeased and jealous at the same time. Celina dropped her arms, the happiness fading from her face and replaced with fear as it dawned on her that they were spotlighted on the beach with a significant audience, some of whom were now clapping and whistling.

Quarters, eat your heart out.

"Sorry," she murmured. "I don't know what came over me."

It hurt to watch her lose that carefree joy and Cooper averted his eyes to the water, regaining his own balance. Best to pretend that hadn't happened. "Go change your clothes, Switchfoot, and meet me at headquarters. I'll buy you a cup of coffee and you can tell me all about your experience with Londano."

"I don't drink plain coffee." Celina scanned his face, trying to read him. Read what he was thinking. "At least I don't mainline it like you do. But Starbucks opens in an hour." She smiled, hope in her eyes now. "You can take me to my apartment, I'll shower and change my clothes, and we'll be their first customers."

Her recovery was quick. And she was ignoring Quarters as effectively as he was.

Score one for The Beast.

She was so bold, Cooper almost chuckled. She'd invited him six times—now seven, not that he was counting—up to her apartment. *Wish I could shove that in Quarters' face.*

If the situation were different, he would take her up on her offer. The real one she was hiding between *shower* and *clothes.* He'd peel that dress off her beautiful body and mainline her instead of his favorite dark roast.

The thought made him dizzy, especially after that kiss, and he shook his head, more to clear it than to tell her no. "I have to follow the uniforms. Make sure they don't inadvertently screw up Londano's booking. Can't have him getting off on a technicality after all your hard work." He put his thumb and his pinky between his lips and whistled, signaled to Thomas up on the boardwalk, and waved him down. "T-man'll run you home so you can change."

Celina piqued one eyebrow at him as Thomas ran down the boardwalk steps toward them, nearly tripping over his feet. "Gee, thanks," she said, so totally not thankful Cooper again had to stifle a chuckle.

He picked up her high heels from the sand and handed them to her. Damn things had heels long enough to skewer a steak. "As soon as you're cleaned up, meet me at headquarters. I want to debrief you before the upper echelon chiefs get their hooks into you."

Quarters cleared his throat in that demanding way he had. "I will be in charge of debriefing Celina." He held out a hand to her. "Congratulations, SA Davenport. I'll be happy to escort you home so you can change."

Ignoring the man and his outstretched hand, Celina put her hands on her curvy hips. "What about Starbucks?"

Cooper's last moral hovered an inch above his mental trash can. Coffee at the local and very public coffee house wouldn't be that bad. Screwing over Quarters would be a bonus.

But looking at Celina wrapped in his sweatshirt, and

remembering the soft touch of her lips against his, sent his libido into overdrive. Which sent a clear message to his brain.

You cannot lead her on in any way, shape or form.

Could not, would not, lead *himself* on. She was too young and she was in his care as a new agent. He'd already risked her life by letting her go undercover to trick Londano. He would not risk her career or his because of a silly, school-girl crush. "I don't do Starbucks, Celina, and even if I did, there's no Starbucks in our future."

Message sent.

Celina's mouth curved down and she started to say something, but Thomas arrived, accidentally kicking sand on her. She sent Cooper a *please, don't leave me with him* look as Cooper took her elbow and handed her off to his buddy. "Take her home, T."

"Yes, sir," he said, all smiles at Celina. She didn't smile back, didn't even glance at Thomas. Instead she shot daggers at Cooper. "Where's Bobby? Why can't he take me home?"

Quarters sighed over the noisy crashing waves. Cooper almost sighed with him. Celina constantly used Bobby Dyer to worm her way around Cooper's resistance. Dyer was Cooper's best friend and second in charge of the SCVC taskforce. "Dyer's in L.A., covering a few things there. I'm sure he'll want to hear all about your takedown as soon as he gets back."

He left her standing there, hands on hips, but she still had to get in the last word.

"I'll meet you in your office in one hour," she called to his back as he crossed the sandy beach toward the boardwalk. "And I'll bring the Starbucks."

Cooper, head down, let go of the chuckle he'd been suppressing, glad it was muffled by the sound of the waves. "Plain, black and hot," he called over his shoulder, and then he added, "kid", emphasizing it just to make sure he pissed her off royally.

Message dittoed.

CHAPTER FOUR

Six months later
Des Moines, Iowa

Cooper Harris put his eye to the sniper scope in the upstairs bedroom window of 1621 Boylston Avenue and looked up the street to a pigeon-gray duplex he was surveilling. The house was a mirror image of the one he was standing in except the perp's girlfriend's needed a new front stoop. The concrete steps were crumbling and beginning to sag from the landing. The wrought iron railings on each side of the stairs leaned out like a pair of woman's legs. He would have to remember to watch his footing when he and his teammates rushed the house.

Cooper and his group of DEA agents had been tracking Dickie Jagger for the past thirty-six hours. This particular SoCal criminal had a rap sheet as long as Cooper's leg, including armed robbery, drug trafficking, rape and assault. He also had information Cooper needed about an upper level lieutenant in the Palermo-Londano operation who'd managed to escape arrest. Like most of the criminals Cooper went after, Dickie considered himself above the law.

Cooper felt it was his duty to show the guy otherwise.

"Heads up, Coop," Thomas said. He was sitting in a chair next to Cooper with binoculars growing out of his eyes. "We've got company."

Cooper took his eye away from the scope and squinted through the gauzy curtain at the street traffic. The only thing that stood out was a turd-brown Ford inching its way down the street. Cooper grabbed Thomas's binoculars. "Local or Feds?"

Thomas stood and grabbed his flak vest off the chair back. "The only people in Des Moines who'd be caught dead in a POS Fairmont are Feds. Even the poorest of drug dealers wouldn't drive that."

"Suits?" Cooper lowered the binoculars. "What the hell are they doing here?"

Thomas secured his vest and pulled on his black windbreaker. DEA was spelled out across the back. "Must have gotten your bulletin that Dickie was in town. I'm sure they want to talk to him as badly as we do."

"Yeah, they want their fingers in the pie." Cooper swore under his breath and raised the binoculars. The Fairmont turned into the driveway and he saw the driver hesitate a moment before opening the door.

A pair of red leather boots and jean-clad legs finally emerged. A second later, the rest of the woman materialized and a warning bell rang in Cooper's head—instant certainty, he knew this woman.

Petite, with long, dark hair, a hint of mocha in her skin, and curves in all the right *thank-you-Jesus* places...

Cooper shook his head. It couldn't be her; had to be someone else. Probably not even a Suit. Probably just another of Dickie's gun-toting, get-away-car-driving girlfriends.

The woman hesitated again, eyes glued to the front of the house while she stood behind the open car door. Cooper scanned her backside looking for the bulge of a weapon. Her hair spilled down the back of her red jacket. The hair and the jacket ended just above a very nice heart-shaped ass.

His gut flashed a wave of certainty even though her backside was devoid of a tell-tale bulge. "No way," he grit out between his teeth. "No *goddamned* way."

"What?" Thomas asked, his eyes bouncing between Cooper and the Fairmont.

Cooper stood silent as he watched the woman's gaze leave the house and then, very discreetly, scan the street. Yep, gun or no gun, she was definitely FBI.

Celina.

The Fed of Cooper's nightmares.

Time magazine's "New Face of the FBI".

Thomas leaned toward the window. "Is that who I think it is? Isn't she supposed to be laying low?"

Media darling or no, Celina Davenport didn't know how to lay low. Wasn't in her DNA.

"Shit, shit and more shit." Cooper tossed the binoculars on the nearby bed, picked up his radio from the dresser. "FBI has joined the party," he said, alerting his other men scattered throughout the house and down the street. "Deal's going down now. Everybody in position."

As he led Thomas out of the bedroom, Cooper grabbed his own flak vest and black jacket, running the scenario of the next few minutes through his mind. He'd get his man, all right.

And maybe if he was lucky, he'd find the opportunity to shoot Special Agent Celina Davenport right in her perfect ass.

———

"Take your gun, Davenport." Chief Forester's voice was low and ominous, rising out of the back seat of the car where he was hiding. Not an easy thing to do, Celina figured, with so much body mass.

Bending down, she motioned at her partner Ronni in the passenger seat and shucked off her mittens. "Give me your bag."

Celina rarely carried handbags to work. She hung her badge on her belt like her male counterparts and carried her ID in her back pocket. Her gun was always in a shoulder holster. Now her gun, ID and badge were lying on the Fairmont's floor. "Avon ladies don't carry guns," she murmured to her boss. "At least not in Iowa."

Ronni handed Celina her brown leather purse and the Avon catalog. "Right behind you," she said, giving her a wink.

"Take. Your. Gun," the chief ground out again. His voice carried as much threat in its low volume setting as it did at its ear-piercing level. "You want to end up a goddamned hostage?"

That was her plan. Celina knew when she approached the door, Annie would immediately sense something was up. *Something* in Annie's world always involved police. Celina could see no other outcome but a dangerous hostage situation. She doubted Annie would even open the door, but if she did, Celina was going to offer herself as a trade for Annie's kids. Any mother, even an outlaw one, would look for a way to save her children. Celina was prepared to give it to her.

Slinging the strap of Ronni's bag over her shoulder, she shut the car door, defying the chief's direct orders. Not the best idea, but he'd stuck her in a no-win situation and therefore, Celina decided, she was calling the shots. For a split-second she wondered if he and Quarters would transfer her like Cooper had after the Londano case. Where would she end up this time? South Dakota?

Probably.

Not the end of the world. If I can get the kids out safely, that will be enough.

Shifting her shoulders, Celina forced her feet to walk up the cracked sidewalk toward the steps of the duplex. She loved her job, wanted to serve her country, but if there was anything she'd learned in the past year, it was that she didn't always get what she wanted.

Ronni's car door slammed and Celina glanced at her partner. Her hair was a bright apricot color, her skin darker than Celina's but no less smooth. As they walked down the sidewalk, the sun popped out, glaring off the new fallen snow. Celina started up the stairs, shielding her eyes against the glare and trying to keep her breathing even. There were fifteen of her counterparts hidden around the block, watching the apprehension and scrutinizing every move she made.

Annie was one honest to God bad girl. Having been on the run for more years than Celina had been legal, Annie was an experienced fugitive. The woman had once shot her partner in his nether region in the middle of a bank robbery because he wouldn't let her carry the bag of money.

Clearing her mind, Celina tried to think positive. Ronni was by her side and definitely carrying. Chief Forester was right behind her in the car for immediate backup with his Remington, and the other guys were scattered up and down the block. All had extensive training in marksmanship and deadly-force decisions.

Voices from a television filtered through the door. Muffled laughter drifted down from upstairs. Little girl laughter. She had to do this right, not to prove that she was as good as any of the men in the unit, but to keep those little girls safe.

Glancing at Ronni, Celina mouthed *Ready?* Ronni gave her a nod. *Do it.*

Celina knocked sharply on the door. "Avon calling," she said, trying to mimic the singsong voice Ronni had used earlier when they'd decided to approach the house under this outdated guise.

At first nothing noticeable changed inside the house. Then the TV went silent and Celina heard a man's voice, low but commanding. A man? No one had reported a man being inside the duplex.

Before she could consider who or what she was now up against, Celina saw a drapery move in the window to her right. Instinctively, she shifted her weight and her hand went for her gun.

And came up empty.

Before she could curse her poor judgment, the door handle turned and her eyes dropped to it. *Watch their hands,* the words of her Quantico instructor echoed in her head. *Not their eyes.* No one could shoot you with their eyes.

"Don't want no Avon," a man's voice said as the door opened a notch.

A fragment of sun bounced off metal. Instinct had Celina moving before she could think. "Gun!" she yelled, pushing Ronni to the side.

The sawed-off shotgun boomed in her ears and the iron railing gave out as Ronni and Celina toppled off the porch and into the dead evergreens by the house. They landed with a thud on hard ground next to the concrete foundation. A thousand prickly evergreen needles showered down on them as they rolled in unison away from the porch.

Before the spent shells hit the concrete, Celina was hauling Ronni up by her jacket. "Run!" she yelled, hearing the distinctive click of the shotgun snapping back into place.

BOOM!

The sound sent her to her knees, but adrenaline had her back up in the blink of an eye, her legs moving like a runner taking off out of the blocks. More gunshots cracked through the air. Celina heard the Fairmont's windshield explode.

Crouching with her arms thrown over her head, she ran for the edge of the house where Ronni had disappeared. She rounded the corner at full speed.

And ran smack dab into a wall.

Bouncing back as her feet scrambled for purchase on the late season ice and snow, she grunted when her butt hit the ground. Glancing up, black Magnum boots were in her line of vision. Big boots, laced military tight.

She hadn't run into a wall. She'd run into a man.

A hulk of a man with very broad shoulders. Celina followed the line of his body up to his face. The sun was reflecting off the house and snow and blinding her. She could make out a few things: a black baseball cap with the letters DEA across the front pulled down low on his forehead, a mean-looking semiautomatic gun in his left hand. His scowl made her already-racing heart shift into warp speed.

When did the Terminator arrive in Iowa?

He shifted his gaze down to her and the look of disgust in it made her, if only briefly, entertain the idea of taking her chances with the sawed-off shotgun.

"Get up," he ordered, and the sound of his voice and the impatient tone clicked in her brain, but her ears were ringing from the shotgun blasts and she wasn't sure she'd heard him correctly. He reached down and grabbed her by the knot in her knitted scarf. Hauling her to her feet, he pulled her with him as he backed up against the side of the house. Her legs wobbled and her feet skimmed on the ice. She lost her balance and fell face first into his chest.

His bullet-proof vest was hard, but under it, she sensed a wall of pure, solid muscle. Just like his arms and his legs and everything else hidden under his DEA-approved wardrobe. Celina knew once her adrenaline slowed down, she was going to ache all over, not from falling off the porch but from hitting the Terminator at full speed.

The machine-like DEA agent pulled her closer. "You all right?"

"Cooper?"

There was a spurt of gunfire from the street and then the sound of more glass breaking. Cooper drew her in tighter. She flinched at the sound of the shotgun booming again. It sounded like a small explosion.

But then Cooper pushed her away, pushed her against the house. She mimicked his position, wishing she could have stayed in the protective embrace of his arms and knowing why she couldn't. Ronni was a few feet away, sitting on the ground, back against the house with her gun out. Leaning her head back against the siding, Celina let out a breath. They were both a little shook up, but otherwise unscathed.

The gunfire stopped and total silence descended on the

street. No birdsong. No traffic noise. Cooper had his eyes on her, sizing her up from top to bottom. "What the hell did you think you were doing?"

On one hand, she was excited to see him. On the other, the tone of his voice and his general man-handling pissed her off. Celina knew the silence around them meant her FBI counterparts were regrouping, while they tried to figure out their next move.

"I was doing my job," she said to him. She let her eyes run over him in the same sizing-up he'd given her. He looked good. Solid and handsome, and serious as ever. "What are you doing here?"

"Where's your gun? Or do female Feds in Des Moines carry Avon books as weapons these days?"

Celina shut her eyes for a moment. She had fantasized relentlessly about her reunion with Cooper. Never had her fantasy involved the current scene. Ronni cleared her throat and Celina glanced at her. Her partner was watching the exchange and had a questioning look on her face. Celina mouthed *Cooper*, and Ronni raised her brows and nodded her *nice, very nice* look of approval.

"Dickie Jagger is mine, Celina."

"Dickie Jagger? Annie's ex-boyfriend?" Celina scanned her memory. Richardson and Jagger had been tight in the early 90's, pulling off more than their fair share of petty crimes together before Jagger had joined a gang in L.A.. It was probably Jagger who'd fathered at least one of Annie's kids. "That's who answered the door?"

"You were expecting the Great and Powerful Oz?"

"I was expecting Annie Richardson or her mother."

Cooper grunted. "You can have Richardson, but Jagger's mine."

Turf war coming up. The FBI and the DEA often overlapped each other's jurisdictions with criminals, which is why taskforces like Cooper's SCVC were created. But even though they were supposed to be working together, they were more interested in trying to one-up each other.

Think Big Picture, Dominic Quarters always preached. His Big Picture was now clearer to Celina. Her boss and her boss's boss wanted jurisdiction over everything and they'd do whatever it took to keep all other agencies in the dark.

She wondered what Forester was doing in the Fairmont, and if he was okay. If he was, she was going to give him and Quarters a piece of her mind when this operation was over. They had sacrificed children and two agents in a hurry to beat the DEA to the house.

"I'm sure Chief Forester would like to talk to you about that," she said, when what she really wanted to say was, "Where have you been? Why didn't you call me?"

For months after her transfer, Celina had analyzed Cooper's behavior out loud while on stakeouts with her partner. Ronni had put it in six easy to understand words: *he's just not that into you.*

Cooper did a quick scan of the area again. "Where is he, your chief?"

"In the car."

His eyes snapped back to hers and the brim of his cap rose with his eyebrows. "The car in the driveway?" He shook his head. "What kind of half-assed FBI unit is this?"

"You should know," Celina retorted, mad all over again. "You sent me here."

"I didn't send you here," Cooper corrected her. "That was Quantico's orders after your face was splashed all over *Time* magazine as the New Face of the FBI."

"But you kicked me off—"

"This is not the time, Celina."

Before Celina could reply, Cooper cocked his head, picking up noise inside the house. His hand came up to silence her. For several seconds he stilled; a freeze frame of anticipation. Not even a breath escaped his body, only a prevenient energy radiating from every inch of him. A cat preparing to pounce on a mouse.

Another noise inside the house—this time Celina heard it too—voices and the sharp snap of a shotgun locking into position. Cooper pulled a mouthpiece out of his cap and spoke into it. "Assume take down positions," he announced quietly to whoever was listening. "We're going in."

"There are three innocent people in that house. Kids." Celina's voice sounded too loud in her ears. "You can't just bust in there. Someone could get hurt."

Cooper pointed one of his fingers at a spot next to Ronni. "Have a seat, Agent Davenport. This take-down no longer concerns you. You shouldn't be here and if you and your buddies hadn't screwed this up to begin with, we wouldn't have this problem."

"Now, wait a minute," she started, but Cooper grabbed her shoulder, twirled her around and pushed her down hard on her butt. She gasped from the impact and his incivility.

"Everybody move on my count," he said into his radio.

Walking to the corner of the house, he locked his gun into firing position under his arm. "One, two, three." His voice rose. "*Go! Go! Go!*"

And then he was gone.

Celina looked at Ronni, whose eyes were still on the spot where Cooper had disappeared. "So that's The Beast, huh?" A silly grin split her face. "That gun powder and Wheaties diet is working for him."

"Yeah," Celina huffed, sarcasm blowing out with her breath, "and he definitely wants me. Did you notice how he was practically falling all over himself to see if I was okay?" She pushed herself off the ground to follow him. "Asshole."

CHAPTER FIVE

FBI Headquarters, Des Moines

Feeding a dollar into the candy machine, Celina pressed the F8 button. The bag of peanut butter M&M's pushed up and over the edge and fell to the bottom.

She knew the drill. Forester and Quarters would no doubt both receive commendations for a successful bust. Both perps had been smoothly apprehended by Cooper and his team with just-for-show backup from the other agents in Forester's unit. Annie's daughters and mother were unhurt and none of the FBI or DEA agents on the scene were injured. Forester and Quarters would work a deal with Cooper that looked like the combined efforts of both agencies won the day for society. The FBI scored Annie. The DEA got Jagger.

And Celina and Ronni got three dozen required pieces of internal paperwork stacked on their desks. They were waiting to start on them until after their follow-up interviews with Forester and Quarters, who were now holed up in Forester's office prepping the "You Screwed Up" speech. More than likely, Celina would be returning to her desk in the office with a reprimand. No more field work until Hell froze over or she received a transfer. Neither seemed likely.

At least the kids are okay, she consoled herself, if ending up in child services could be considered okay. She pushed the door of the candy machine open and reached in to grab her version of Valium.

She'd ignored Cooper's instructions during the takedown and followed him into the house. He and his group had done a quick and efficient arrest of Jagger and Richardson while making sure Annie's kids were never in the line of fire. Locating the two children, Celina had stayed with them through the arrests, and when the worst was over, she'd packed some clothes and a stuffed animal for each into two garbage bags and introduced them to their new case worker. It was the kids that always got to her. Innocent kids with no chance to escape the life their parents had forced on them.

Plopping more change into another vending machine, Celina bought a Diet Mountain Dew, cracked it open, and took a sip.

"You're one lucky Avon lady," Cooper said from behind her.

Celina glanced over her shoulder. He looked so damn good even if she was irritated with him for being such a selfish bastard. "You were here in Des Moines and you didn't call me?"

He was silent, standing in the doorway just staring at her. He wasn't quite expressionless, but Celina couldn't read what he was thinking. Other than, of course, he didn't want to have this discussion because *he wasn't that into her.*

She crossed the room, set her pop on the counter, and opened the bag of candy, fishing out a blue M&M. "Congratulations on your arrest." Her voice sounded completely insincere and she didn't care. "Why didn't you notify us that you were tagging Jagger? Could have saved duplication on the take-down."

Cooper broke his stillness and sauntered to the candy machine, putting his back to Celina as he dug a ratty dollar bill from his jeans pocket. "Your office was notified." The machine whined and Cooper punched his selection.

Celina watched him, feeding herself one M&M at a time. "There was no posting on the Current board this morning. I would have seen it and known…" *you were here.* She couldn't finish the sentence. Chocolate was caught in her throat. Crap. She coughed, trying to clear it.

Cooper glanced at her, removing a Snickers bar from the machine. King Size, of course.

Tossing the candy bar on the table, he pulled out a chair, flipped it around, and sat down. "You working field ops again?"

Swallowing a sip of her soda, she eyed him suspiciously. If she answered yes, would he take her back? Probably not after witnessing today's sorry fiasco. "Why?"

"I thought you were supposed to be lying low. Keeping off the streets until the media circus blew over."

She leaned her butt against the counter and sucked a few more candies into her mouth. "I have been, but I'm bored out of my mind. Ronni too. Forester only gives us cold cases, and I do mean cold, as in colder than the wind chill outside, to work on."

He chewed his candy bar, challenge in his gray eyes. "Solved any?" A small smirk played at the corner of his mouth and Celina knew he was betting she hadn't.

"Three," she told him, pride in her voice. "One murder, in fact. The other two, child abductions."

Cooper nodded, approval in his eyes now. "So why were you going after Richardson today?"

Celina sighed. "Ronni and I were on our lunch break and happened to be in the area when the call came in. We sort of invited ourselves to the party."

"And the Avon lady routine? Please tell me that wasn't your idea."

"I suggested an alternative, but Forester and Quarters didn't like it. Quarters told me I didn't see the *big picture*"—she made air quotes—"and to follow orders."

"Following his orders almost got you decapitated."

Celina nodded, happy to be having a conversation with Cooper. "I knew the Avon routine wouldn't work, but I had hoped to offer myself as a trade to Annie for her kids. That's the only reason I went up to that door unarmed. We believed the only other adult in the house was Annie's mother."

Cooper went very still. "You were going to let Richardson take you hostage? On purpose?"

"I didn't want those kids to get hurt."

Cooper looked away, rubbed a hand over his face. "Jesus, Celina. Didn't you learn anything from me when you were in the SCVC?"

Yes, Celina thought. *Fidelity. Bravery. Integrity.* The guiding principles she had cut her teeth on at Quantico Marine Corps Base. After thirteen weeks of new agent training, she'd held up her hand, taken an oath to defend the Constitution against all enemies, foreign and domestic, and accepted her gold shield with a sense of pride and honor.

She had breathed, ate, and lived them under Cooper's guidance. Working the L.A.-San Diego pipeline with Cooper, she'd absolutely nailed bravery.

"I didn't have a lot of time with you," she said, purposely letting the double meaning hang in the air for a moment. "Maybe I should come back and take a few more lessons."

Cooper threw the end of the candy bar in his mouth. "Sorry." He shook his head. "Not my call. Director Dupé's the guy you need. It's probably too soon for you to work undercover anyway after that *Time* article. Your face is so..."

He trailed off while he stared at her for several beats and Celina's pulse kicked up. This time the expression on his face was familiar...like he couldn't quite take a deep breath....she'd seen that expression on his face before. She knew he felt exactly what she was feeling. Heat. *Not into me, huh?*

"So *what*, Cooper?" she prompted, giving him a small, and she hoped sexy, smile.

Bingo. Pushing his chair back abruptly, he returned to the candy machine. For a half second he just stood there and she watched the muscles in his back as he drew in a deep breath.

There *was* something between them. Something that looked, smelled, and felt like pure sexual tension. Continuing to watch the muscles in his back as he drew out another dollar from his pocket and fed it into the slot, Celina smiled to herself. Every muscle, every pore was brimming with unspent sexual emotion. And it was all aimed at her.

A King Size Payday dropped into the bottom of the machine and Cooper reached in and grabbed it. Leaning against the candy machine, he focused on tearing off the Payday's wrapper. "What's the big picture?"

Topic shift. He was scrambling for safer ground. "You. Your team. Quarters must've known you were in town to grab Jagger." She shrugged. "He wanted to be sure he got Richardson and if he could preempt your take down, he might nail both of them."

"This unit having problems?"

"Des Moines is not high on the list for federal funding, except for counterterrorism. We're totally understaffed for all other criminal activities." But she didn't want to talk about the Des Moines unit. She wanted to talk about Cooper. The best way to bring things back to him was to talk about his job. The SCVC. "How's Thomas? Bobby? The other guys?"

Cooper stopped chewing, threw the rest of his candy bar on the table. All the color seemed to drain from his face.

Celina felt an uncomfortable tightening in her ribcage. "What happened?"

A nerve in Cooper's jaw pulsed. It was a long time before he answered, his voice low and rough. "Valquis got Dyer, Celina. The night you arrested Emilio. Remember how you knew Valquis was out of town on business? He found Dyer and beat him to a pulp while I was following you and Emilio. He didn't kill him, but he did so much damage to Dyer's spinal cord he's paralyzed from the waist down. Now he's living—if you can call it that—in a damned wheelchair."

A chill shot down her back. Not for the first time, she wondered how she'd pulled off betraying Emilio so completely without ending up in wheelchair, or possibly a grave, herself.

But Dyer? She couldn't imagine him paralyzed. Like Cooper,

he lived to be a DEA agent. He'd spent hours prepping Celina for her role as Emilio's reluctant girlfriend. And never even hinted that she was too young or inexperienced to pull off the sting. "Why didn't you tell me?"

"I didn't..." He looked at the floor, the muscle in his jaw continuing to jump. When he spoke again, his voice was controlled. "Valquis left Dyer behind a dumpster in Santa Cruz without ID. He was transported to a hospital and laid there for several days before I found him. Eliza was out of her mind with worry, and then we both lived at the hospital with him until he gained consciousness. I was there every day in the middle of trying to wrap up the paperwork on Londano, hunt down Valquis and Enrique, and still run the taskforce. A week after it went down, the *Time* article turned you into a media magnet and you were removed from my team and sent here. I was in Mexico tracking Valquis and Enrique and I never had a chance to tell you."

Celina was suddenly angry. Forget the fact that he'd never called to check on her. He could have at least called to tell her about Bobby. "Ever heard of a phone, Harris?"

She waited for him to answer. When he didn't, she shook her head. "How could you possibly not tell me this? How could Bobby not tell me? He emailed not more than a month ago to see how I was doing and never mentioned anything about it."

Cooper stood there, eyes glued to the floor. "Dyer insisted I not tell you, Celina. He didn't want your first major bust to be tainted by his accident."

This is what she got for refusing to tune into the gossip always going around. But most of the gossip had been about her after the Londano operation and that stupid article. *Time* had even put her face on the cover, causing an uproar inside the Bureau. "And he didn't think I would find out what happened eventually?"

Cooper lifted his head. "He wanted you to have your moment of glory for as long as possible."

Her moment of glory. So fleeting. So useless.

Celina pressed her eyes shut. She remembered the rush she'd felt on the beach after nailing Emilio. Remembered how high she'd felt. Since then, everything had gone downhill. Her career thrown completely off track because of the media blitz, and now finding out Bobby was paralyzed from the waist down, she felt like it had all been for nothing.

She should have been more observant. Should have tried to find out what Petero Valquis was planning that night. But she'd been so intent on fooling Emilio, she hadn't thought past her relief that Valquis was scheduled to be out of town. Guilt burned in her stomach.

Throwing the rest of the M&M's in the garbage, she followed them with the bottle of soda. "I was part of your team, Cooper. You and Bobby should have told me what happened, no matter the consequences of my feelings."

The pain on Cooper's face morphed into anger. "I did what I thought was best for everyone," he told her in his don't-argue-with-me voice. "You may not agree with that, Celina, because God knows you've never agreed with any of my decisions as head of the SCVC, but you don't have the experience I do. You haven't been the leader of a team. Seen your best friend and partner lying in a hospital bed with tubes and wires like mutant spider webs running in and out of his body."

Celina let her own anger wrap around her like a blanket. "You think I don't feel guilty about what happened?" She watched his expression change to confusion. He didn't get it. He didn't understand her at all. "You are unbelievable."

"Celina?" Ronni's voice interrupted from the doorway.

Celina immediately noted her partner's pale face behind her masklike expression. Ronni had been in Forester's office, giving him and the Special Agent in Charge her official version of Richardson's capture. From the tightness around her mouth, Celina knew Ronni had just had her butt chewed out in a royal way. The younger woman was, at that moment, trying to stay professional on the outside while her guts churned like a washing machine on the inside.

Celina knew the feeling. It wasn't every day you got double-barreled by both the bad guys and the good ones.

"Chief Forester would like to see you, now." Ronni's gaze darted back and forth between Celina and Cooper.

For a split second, Celina saw Ronni in a wheelchair and felt her stomach bottom out. She couldn't imagine what Cooper had felt over Dyer's injuries at the hands of Valquis. How something like that would leave him unable to call her and talk about it. "Thanks, Ronni."

As Ronni's footsteps faded, Celina returned her gaze to Cooper. The air around him was still vibrating with his anger and hers. The anger was mixed with guilt. She drew in a breath and let it out slowly, tired of being angry, tired of being left out. Just tired, period. And sorry for him and for Bobby. It didn't take Einstein to know that Cooper's anger was simply a shield of armor to hide his true feelings. Shock, rage, grief.

No wonder he hadn't called to check up on her. Knowing she would ask about Bobby and the other taskforce members, Cooper had blown her off to save himself from having to talk about the tragedy. How nice it might have been if he'd called and confided in her. She could have shared his anger and grief and helped him realize it wasn't his fault. Instead, he chose to ignore her and take on all the guilt himself. Deal with the grief alone.

Typical alpha male, just like her brothers.

"I have to go. I'll call Bobby later." She stopped in the doorway. "Congratulations on getting your man," she repeated, forcing more sincerity this time.

Cooper's eyes held hers. His anger was gone now too. Was that regret shining in them? "Always do."

Celina nodded, wishing he'd apologize.

But what she really wished was that she could draw a big red S on her shirt and turn back the Earth, turn back time, to the night of Emilio's arrest. If only she could change what had happened.

———

Cooper was halfway to the hotel when he drove off the street and parked the rental car next to a Kwik Trip. Sitting in the Durango with the heater on high—damn it was cold in Iowa—and a local vintage rock station blaring in his ears, he mentally kicked himself soundly in the ass.

He should have told her. Plain and simple. While she'd only known Bobby Dyer a few weeks before getting caught up in the Londano operation, the two of them had bonded. At first, Cooper suspected Celina was dogging Dyer because he was usually with Cooper, which made it convenient for her to flirt with him. Later Cooper realized Celina went to Dyer for advice because Dyer talked to her and listened to her and wasn't interested in getting in her pants. Unlike most of the other male members of his team.

Outside the Durango, teenagers enjoying a snow day pumped a few dollars' worth of gas into their rusting cars and grabbed Cokes inside the convenience store. Dickie Jagger was on ice at the local sheriff's department waiting for the judicial system to extradite him back to California, but the sense of satisfaction Cooper usually felt after nailing a perp was absent. While the rest of his team celebrated back at their hotel with pizza and Coronas, Cooper sat in the parking lot and gave himself one more mental kick. He'd screwed up. Royally.

How could he explain to Celina what he couldn't explain to himself? How he'd let Dyer go off on his own to track Valquis. How he'd never suspected that Val was leading his best friend and partner on a wild goose chase, just to send Cooper and the rest of the SCVC unit a message. How he wasn't there to stop the beating. How he hadn't found Dyer in that hospital for three days.

Three fucking days.

Seeing Dyer in that bed, helpless, paralyzed and one step away from life support, Cooper had lost it. His hatred for Petero Valquis and Emilio Londano had warred with his feelings of total helplessness over Dyer's condition. What he couldn't explain to Celina, then or now, was how he of all people had let Dyer get hurt.

And that he couldn't beg, bargain, or sell his soul to turn back time and make things right.

Cooper had picked up the phone a hundred times to call Celina, even when Dyer insisted he didn't want her to know. And every time he'd had the phone to his ear, his pulse raced and words had evaded him. Even now, he could do little more than simply gut out the facts to her.

Closing his eyes to fight off the memories, he listened to the Red Hot Chili Peppers gutting out their own angst. Dyer, being the man that he was, had told Cooper repeatedly to get over what had happened. Move on. He wasn't happy about the wheelchair, but he was damn glad to still be breathing. He was back at work for the DEA, albeit at a desk now, and continued to take physical therapy. Dyer had never let anything keep him down for long. He'd given himself a whole week to work through his anger, depression, and grief over the loss of his legs and then he'd told Cooper one day to get lost.

"I'm alive," Dyer had said, rubbing his hand over his newly grown bush of beard, "and I'm going to *live*, damn it. I'm not going to hold your hand and endorse your fucking guilt complex, Coop, so get the hell out of here and go save the world."

Cooper smiled, opened his eyes.

Three girls in their early teens jostled each other, laughing as they filed out of the convenience store's front doors. Each was dressed identically to her friends in tight jeans and puffy nylon coats. As they walked in front of the Durango, each carried a pop and a bag of M&Ms.

A high-def image of Celina's full lips sucking blue M&Ms

into her mouth rose up in Cooper's mind. Jesus, she made him crazy. He'd put himself on the Jagger team just so he could come to Des Moines and try to see her, knowing exactly how he'd react when he did. Even after all these months she could do the simplest thing and send his libido into overdrive. All that flawless skin and those righteous curves.

And a superhero complex bigger than his own.

"...I had hoped to offer myself as a trade to Annie for her kids."

A superhero complex channeling Mother Teresa.

"I just didn't want those kids to get hurt."

Shit. When he'd seen her, not in the rush of the adrenaline-fueled take down, but back at the Fed building, he'd so totally lost the ability for coherent thought, he'd stopped breathing and nearly grabbed her and wrapped his arms around her just to make sure she was okay. She looked so damned good in her simple black turtleneck and jeans. Those red boots. Her cheeks still rosy from the cold air...

Then, when she'd told him her plan to trade herself for Richardson's kids, he'd almost grabbed her to shake some sense into her. What was she thinking?

But the worst thing about their reunion was how she went from flirting with him to despising him in a heartbeat when he explained—tried to explain—why he hadn't told her about Dyer.

She was right. He was unbelievable. He should have told her. He should have called and checked on her.

Slapping the steering wheel, Cooper shoved the Durango in gear and pulled back out onto the highway. He couldn't go back to San Diego without setting things straight. Couldn't look at Dyer now without remembering the hurt and sadness and anger he'd seen in Celina's eyes.

Cranking the radio up louder, Cooper pressed the accelerator and gutted it out along with the Peppers.

CHAPTER SIX

Crossing the one-way downtown street, Cooper entered the complex that housed the FBI. The building was well-worn but architecturally interesting with gothic details all over the façade. He flashed his badge at the elderly black security guard and the man nodded, giving him a semi-salute with his hand. "Back for more?" he asked, his grin sporting a gold tooth.

"Can't get enough of this place," Cooper lied.

The guard chuckled. "Miss Celina makes it an attractive place to visit." He winked at Cooper. "Stay outta trouble."

At that moment, Celina burst out of the frosted glass door of the FBI office, a backpack on her shoulder and a box crammed to the brim in her arms. Her dark eyes were narrowed to slits and he thought, *uh-oh*.

Forester had his hand on her elbow, trying to keep up with her, but Celina walked faster, shaking off his hand. "I do not need an escort to walk twenty crappy steps out of this building." She bee-lined straight for Cooper.

Cooper stopped in his tracks.

Forester tried to catch her. "Enough crap, Davenport." His hand touched her elbow, grabbed for purchase, and somehow Cooper knew what was coming.

"You can't quit over this," the chief said.

Quit? "You quit?" Cooper echoed.

Celina's narrowed eyes glanced at and dismissed him all in one motion. She stopped and Forester barely avoided crashing into her. His face was puffed up like a bulldog and he was breathing hard. He righted himself, but left his hand on her arm.

"I'm not the one who messed up." Cooper recognized the dangerously low tone of her voice, and almost took a step back as she went for Forester's throat. "And I won't be the fall guy for you or Quarters. Your *big picture* mentality almost got two innocent kids killed today. I will be taking this to the Assistant Director in Charge and the Deputy Director, and if all else fails, by God, I'll take it all the way to D.C. and Director Moeller himself." She drew in a breath and let it out sharply, and Cooper was relieved that her hands were full. Her sidearm was in easy reach. "Now, get your hand off my elbow."

Forester stared her in the eye for a second before releasing her. "You walk out of here, Davenport, and your career with the FBI is over."

Oh, Christ. Don't challenge her.

Celina's chin raised a notch. She glanced at Cooper and back at Forester. "Then I'll go to work for the DEA," she said, and Cooper found himself taking the box from her arms as she shoved it at him.

Forester finally registered that Cooper was witnessing this exchange. The chief sent him a look that would have made a lesser man piss his pants.

Heading for the door, Celina hiked up the backpack sliding off her shoulder and blew a kiss at the security guard. "Take care, Lawrence."

"You ain't leavin' us, are you Miss Celina?"

"Afraid so. Don't forget to take your blood pressure medicine." She pushed the door open with her butt. "Have Ronni remind you, okay?"

"Yes ma'am," he answered, a hang-dog look coming over his face.

Celina waved at him as she walked out and shot one more round of daggers at Forester.

Forester stared at the closing door, then turned on Cooper. "Your supervisor's going to hear about this."

Cooper tried to raise his hands, found them full. "What did I do?"

"Go back to California where you belong, Harris, before you do something really stupid and find my shoe buried in your ass."

Forester disappeared behind the frosted glass, and for a split second, Cooper considered showing the chief his own shoe, but in his years with the DEA, he'd learned not to waste time on people and situations that did not further his purpose. Losing his temper with the Des Moines Unit Chief would only endanger his prestigious position with the SCVC taskforce. That did not serve his purpose.

Besides, karma was a bitch and it looked like Forester was due for a visit right along with that fucker Quarters.

Looking out the front door again, Cooper followed Celina's progress across the one-way street toward the parking garage. She'd just quit because her job had come in conflict with her personal ethics code. Cooper remembered a time when he'd almost done the same.

A wise mentor had showed him the value of balancing judgment calls while keeping his ethics and morals intact. Hard to do, especially after seeing the rot-gut shit of the underground world for years. His deep-seeded ethics and morals had sometimes taken a backseat to his all-encompassing desire to clean up that world. He rarely thought in terms of ethics anymore, just laws.

Like today. He hadn't given much thought to Richardson's kids. If he'd thought about them, it would have bothered him, and he couldn't perform his job properly if he was bothered over the ethical dilemma they presented. Arresting their mother and her boyfriend in front of them wasn't a day at the park, but letting the two criminals go wasn't an option. The damage they had done, and would continue to do to innocent lives, warranted definitive and immediate action. How could you balance that with two innocent children? It was a no-win situation.

"You goin' after her?" the guard asked, bringing him back to the here and now.

Cooper started for the door. "Yeah, I'm going after her." Using a shoulder, he pushed open the door. "God help me, I never could resist trouble."

Standing by her Civic hatchback in the parking garage, Celina waited for Cooper. Her cheeks were hot, even though she could see her breath puffing out in little white clouds. Her heart hammered in her chest and her palms were sweating. It wasn't bad enough she'd quit in the heat of the moment, but then she'd forced a showdown with Forester in front of Cooper. Not an impressive move for someone trying not to look inexperienced and overly emotional. Someone trying to prove her team-oriented approach to work so she could get back on his team.

Damn. This day was spinning further into the realm of unbelievable. Getting shot at. Running into Cooper. Finding out he had lied, if only by omission, about Dyer. Then Forester and Quarters trying to intimidate her during the debriefing and when she'd questioned their hasty and ill-thought-out take-down plan, they'd tried to stick her on administrative leave.

Administrative leave. The words stuck in her throat, clogging it.

Already on edge and emotional after her argument with Cooper, she'd let her temper get the better of her. Damn Cuban temper.

Cooper entered the parking garage and stopped, eyes squinting at the change in light as he scanned the area looking for her. When his face registered her presence, Celina didn't know what to do. Smile or cry? Apologize or demand an apology from him? Fall at his feet and beg him to take her back to California or grab her box and run from the lecture she knew was coming?

Undecided, she brought her hands up to her mouth and blew warm breath on them as he approached. His face was expressionless as she stretched out her arms to take the box filled with her scant personal stuff, but he stopped far enough back she couldn't reach it. "You ever do anything half-assed?"

Celina searched his eyes for any trace of humor but what she saw was unreadable. She shored up her backbone just in case he was going to start the lecture. "No."

It was at least a full thirty seconds before Cooper smiled. "Me neither." He bypassed her, opened the hatch of the Civic, and dropped the box into it. Shutting the door, he leaned a hand on her car. "Buy you a beer?"

Letting go of the breath she was holding, Celina's heart hammered in a different rhythm. Heat bloomed in her stomach as well as her cheeks. She decided to throw her last ounce of luck out as a wager. "Only if dinner's included, and only if we stop by Child Services and check on Annie's kids first."

This time Cooper extended the silence for a full minute before he answered her, and there it was again, that almost palpable sexual energy. "You know, Celina," Cooper started.

And then Celina heard her name echo off the concrete walls around her. "Davenport!"

Go away! Celina wanted to shout back. Cooper was just about to say something like *I've missed you* or *I'm sorry I didn't call you. Come back to the SCVC with me.* Celina didn't care if there was a full-blown blizzard and an all-out terrorist attack descending on them at that very moment, she didn't want to be interrupted.

As Cooper turned and Celina leaned around him to see who was calling her name, she closed her eyes in dismay.

Dominic Quarters, complete in parka and boots, jogged toward them.

She'd gotten out from under Quarters' thumb in California,

only to end up under it once more here. It was like career stalking. The man would not leave her alone.

But she'd just quit. Nothing he could do to her now.

"Celina," he said, as he came to a stop near them. He gave Cooper a dismissive once-over. "This has all been a terrible misunderstanding." He smiled at her; the same smile he'd given her earlier that afternoon in the Hy-Vee parking lot when he'd suggested she act as an Avon lady.

Unbelievable. Even after putting her, Ronni, and Annie's kids in danger, and sticking Celina on administrative leave, he still had hopes she'd get busy with him.

"Tensions are running high and, well, my god,"—he forced a sad face—"you were shot at earlier. You're stressed."

Reaching out, he tried to rub her arm, but she jerked it away. Cooper leaned back against a black Durango parked behind him and crossed his arms, open interest on his face.

"You're emotional right now," Quarters continued. "I understand that. Believe me, I do. But quitting isn't the answer." Moving so he could put his arm around her shoulders, he drew her away from her car. "Let's go back to my office and talk about this. I'll make some reservations at Luigi's and we can discuss your future over dinner."

Celina almost laughed. Instead she rolled out from under his arm, shoved him away. "No thanks. In case I haven't already made this clear, which I'm pretty sure I have, that scenario is never going to happen in this lifetime."

Opening her car door, she met Cooper's stare over the frame. "Mexican sounds good. There's a great little mom-and-pop restaurant a few miles from here. You want to ride with me or follow?"

He didn't miss a beat. Straightening, he uncrossed his arms and gave her a small salute. "I'll follow you."

Celina started the car and cranked the heater, relieved to be out of Quarters' reach. As she put the car in reverse and drove out of the parking spot, Quarters said something to Cooper.

Cooper's response was delivered with a finger to Quarters' face. Celina chuckled as Quarters stepped back and narrowed his eyes. Cooper smiled, patting him on the shoulder and walking around him to get in the Durango.

A minute later, at a stoplight, Celina snuck a look in her rearview mirror at Cooper idling behind her. Forget The Beast. The Terminator was back, his dark eyes hidden behind mirrored sunglasses, jawline set belligerently. One hand was on the wheel of his SUV and he appeared to be staring back at her, but she couldn't be sure.

She glanced away, convinced he looked more like a dangerous criminal than a man of the law.

Running her hands through her hair, Celina pulled it away from her face and secured it with a rubber band. As the light turned green and traffic started to move, she gave Cooper another glance and found she still couldn't decide if he was looking at her or not.

Reaching over to the passenger seat, she retrieved her sunglasses and slid them on before shifting the car. Looking up in the rearview the next time, she saw Cooper was smiling.

———

The restaurant was on the outskirts of town, set off the main road a hundred yards with a gravel parking lot and a trailer park atmosphere that made Cooper's skin tight. In ten years as a DEA agent and the three years before that as a street cop, he'd spent a fair number of nights in dives just like this one, hanging out with narks and drunks and losers in order to peg his criminal.

"You look like you're about to have a tooth pulled," Celina said, her boots kicking up little puffs of snow as she walked toward him. Her hair was pulled up in a ponytail and her full lips now sported pink lip gloss that matched her rose-tinted sunglasses. Between the clouds and setting sun, Cooper knew she didn't need the sunglasses. He also knew the lip gloss was for him.

Forcing his attention away from her lips, he scanned the rusting gutters, the lopsided sign claiming authentic Mexican food, and the peeling beige paint. The place was only one step below the Child Services building they'd just left. "Makes me want to get back on the first plane to San Diego."

"We're here for the food, not the décor."

"True, but if I didn't know better, I'd say you're afraid to be seen with me." He wished she'd lose the sunglasses so he could see her eyes. Those eyes that had been so much a part of his fantasies in the past year. "Afraid some of those suits in your office will see you having dinner with a DEA man?"

Celina removed her glasses like he wanted. Her brows flexed down as she tried to decide if he was joking. "There are only two things I'm afraid of, Cooper, and neither of those concerns what my coworkers think about my personal life. I admire and respect you and if you'd prefer a nicer building, I'll take you across town, but the food and the service won't be as good." She shrugged one shoulder. "Your choice."

He didn't give a rat's ass where they ate so long as he got to look into those eyes and feed another fantasy. She was still pissed about the Dyer thing, and, like Quarters had mentioned back in the parking garage, she had been shot at earlier. With a sawed-off double-barreled cop killer. That wasn't an experience most people shrugged off easily. Even experienced agents like him.

On top of that, she was still upset about her bosses'—former bosses, now—poor judgment calls. What she needed was a hot dinner and a cold beer. "Are we going to stand here in the freezing cold and yak at each other, Agent Davenport, or are we going to go in and eat?"

Cooper let her lead him between two pickup trucks and fell into step beside her. "I'll see what I can do about getting you a job when I get back to California."

She stopped and turned her gorgeous eyes on him. "Technically, I didn't quit."

"Could have fooled me."

"I only quit the Des Moines unit. Says so in my written resignation. Tomorrow I'll place a few calls, see where I can transfer to. This was never meant to be a permanent assignment and I'm done hiding. And just so you know, if there's an opening on your taskforce any time soon, I plan to fill it."

No doubt about it, Celina always gave it to him straight. Not an ounce of coyness when she knew what she wanted. "Look," Cooper started, but she cut in.

"I know what you're going to say. That I can't come back yet, but—"

Now Cooper cut in on her. "I apologize for being a rude ass earlier today," he said, before he could talk himself out of it. "And I'm sorry I never called and told you about Dyer."

Her surprise was genuine. One glossy corner of her mouth rose. "Really?"

Shifting his weight, Cooper tried not to appreciate the relief in her eyes too much. He'd said what he'd wanted to. If he were a smart man, he'd forget about having dinner with her and head back to the hotel. Time and distance hadn't changed the fact that she was still too young for him and he still wanted her too damn much.

If he were a smart man. "Yes, Celina, really."

"Okay then," she said, giving him a wink. "Are we going to stand here and yak all night, Agent Harris, or are we going to eat?"

The place was cleaner and neater than Cooper had expected. The smell of seared meat and stale beer mixed with cigarette smoke. A lone mariachi player strummed a guitar in the far corner, a man and a woman moving in time to the guitar player's rhythm on a miniscule square of floor in front of him.

There was a host, a guy who'd tried to make up for his lack

of stature by beefing up his biceps. Cooper gave him a back-off narrowing of his eyes after the guy looked Celina over. Leaving her name with the host, Celina motioned Cooper to the bar area. Finding a high table at one end of the room, they ordered drinks from a stocky waitress who left them a basket of freshly fried tortilla chips.

Celina shrugged off her jacket and hung it on the back of her chair before sprinkling salt liberally over the chips in the basket between them. "Have you ever been shot?"

Cooper helped himself to a chip and dipped it in the salsa bowl. "Twice. Knifed twice too. Twenty-seven stitches on top of the knife wounds. Took a nail in my foot from a pneumatic nail gun once. Broke a rib and bruised a couple others."

Celina stopped chewing. Swallowed, her eyes doubling in her face. "Jesus, Cooper. All in the line of duty?"

He shrugged. "Just doin' my job."

"Sounds like you're lucky to be alive."

He'd seen twilight a few times. Hated the thought of dying almost as much as he hated drug dealers and murderers. "I am."

The drinks arrived and he tried not to watch the way Celina licked salt off the rim of her margarita glass while she watched him over it. "Ever think about quitting?"

"Only after Dyer was injured."

"Because you felt responsible."

"Hell, yes," Cooper said. "I *was* responsible."

Celina started to argue, seemed to think better of it, and took a sip through her straw. "Ever had your boss insist you do something you knew was stupid?"

Picking up the bottle of hot sauce, he poured a generous amount into the salsa bowl, fished another tortilla chip out of the basket and tested it. Better. "Sure."

"And?" She gave him a *go on* look.

"First time, I was a rookie like you; only I was a street cop. I helped some detectives on my beat find a serial killer, big guy, ex-heavyweight champ, bigger than me. Abducted teenage girls in fast food parking lots and took them home. McKiller we dubbed him."

He chewed, swallowed. "Guy dumped their bodies in abandoned buildings around L.A. once he got his rocks off. We got evidence tying him to three murders, had an arrest warrant, but the detective in charge was a scrawny guy. Called me in for backup to take out the front door and McKiller at the same time. From the evidence I'd gathered, I thought McKiller might have another kid in his house, possibly still alive. If we busted in, the girl might die. I wanted to sneak in through a basement window and try to save the kid first. Detective axed the idea, told me if we didn't hit McKiller front and back doors, he might get away and more kids would end up dead. I took the front door, ended up chasing the guy to the basement. Took a healthy beating."

"But you caught him?"

"Yes," Cooper said, but hated admitting the rest. "But he killed the girl in the basement before I even got down the steps."

"Damn," Celina swore under her breath.

"Yeah."

They sat in silence for a minute, the music from the guitar player and the conversation of the few scattered diners rising and falling around them. "That's why you're such a good boss," she said. "You listen to your agents. Respect their gut feelings and don't put them in no-win situations."

It would have been easy to let her think he was the perfect boss she described, but it wasn't true. "I've learned a lot of lessons through the years, Celina. Some of them the hard way, but the School of Hard Knocks is an effective teacher. The Academy teaches you what to do in the field. Hard Knocks teaches you what *not* to do in the field. Both are important."

Celina tried out his salsa, spilling a drop on the table and another on her chin. She licked sauce off her bottom lip, and then reached for her drink. Taking a long sip, she blinked tears out of her eyes and wiped off her chin with a napkin. "Forester and Quarters put me on administrative leave when I questioned their motivation today."

"On what charges?"

She ticked the offenses off on her fingers. "Incompetence. Defiance of a direct order. Entering scene of a take-down unarmed. Endangering life of another agent. Failure to announce to criminal I was FBI. Failure to instruct criminal to put down his weapon." She grabbed another chip, pointed at the air. "That one really got me. When exactly was I supposed to instruct Jagger to put his weapon down? The moment he opened the door? The moment I jumped off the porch? I didn't even know he was in there, much less that he had a weapon the size of Forester's ass pointed at me."

Cooper laughed. And then sighed. "I know you don't want to hear this, but they're right on most of those counts."

She bristled. "If I had known Jagger was in the house—"

"You still would have tried to offer yourself as a hostage for those kids."

"Yes," she nodded. "But I would have been waving a Maxim magazine instead of an Avon catalog."

Her selfless bravery, even though misguided, impressed him. And equally scared the hell out of him. "Don't make logic calls based on emotions. It will get you killed."

"So save my own skin and let the kids become hostages."

He wasn't going to win this argument. Didn't stop him from trying. "You plan for the worst-case scenario but you don't walk in and cause it. Forget Jagger. What if Richardson had grabbed you, shot Ronni, and still held her kids in that house? Refused to let them go, knowing she had the upper hand, because now she had an FBI agent. She could have demanded whatever she wanted and, in the end, still killed you. The FBI and SWAT teams would've had to rush the house at some point and the kids might have died along with you. Your sacrifice would have been for nothing."

Celina's eyes were on the tabletop. She swirled her drink with the straw. Poked at the chips before teasing one out of the pile. "Okay, maybe I messed up. You've never done anything stupid based on emotion?"

Cooper didn't want to talk about what had happened after the doctors told Dyer he'd never walk again, but he knew Celina was smart enough and connected enough in the Federal world to find out. "I punched out my unit chief right after you left town."

Celina choked on her chip. "You punched out your unit chief," she repeated deadpan.

"She didn't take it well." Cooper shrugged. "Got a little miffed."

"*She*? Your unit chief is a woman?"

"Lana has a black belt and bench presses two hundred pounds without breaking a sweat. Don't cut her any slack because she's female." Cooper took a swig of his beer. "She didn't cut you any during the Londano operation. She had everyone convinced you were sleeping with Emilio to get the goods on him."

Celina's smile faltered and Cooper wish he'd kept that to himself. "It's my fault Dyer ended up paralyzed," he said, bringing the subject back on track. "From the information you forwarded to us from Emilio's e-mails, we had the details of loads and money shipments of all his cocaine and meth cells working in the United States. We knew the how, when, and where of every batch, right down to the markings on the packages. We even had the necessary search and arrest warrants. What we didn't have was the go ahead from above.

"As you know, it was a career-making case for people in both the FBI and DEA camps. The SCVC taskforce was ready to move in based on your first batch of information, but Lana wouldn't let us. She wanted more evidence to be sure there would be a successful prosecution. I got fed up hearing that. I was obsessed about the case and I was worried Valquis was going to dig deep enough to figure out you weren't Celina Mendez. After your second batch of info came through, I made the call to grab Emilio and I followed you instead of backing up Dyer. It was the biggest mistake of my life."

"But why did you punch out Lana?"

The beer from his next pull tasted flat in his mouth. "After the case was over, I was at the hospital with Dyer. We knew he was permanently paralyzed, and there wasn't much to say, but I went to sit with him, just to be there. I didn't know how to say I was sorry, you know? And I didn't want him to think I was deserting him.

"Anyway, not even ten hours after the doctors tell Dyer he'll never walk again, Lana shows up with your section agent, Quarters. They weren't there to see Dyer, to see how he was holding up. They walked into the room, Lana waving a piece of paper in my face and reading me the riot act. Seems my years of 24/7 work on the San Diego Mafia and the loss of my partner weren't enough to warrant any slack from her. She hunted me down that day to bust my balls for forgetting to fill out an expense form."

Celina made a face. "Ouch. Definitely insensitive on her part, but punching her out had to screw up your career plans, didn't it, Cooper? You're the best agent the DEA has in the Southwest quadrant in this century. You were on the fast track to becoming a unit chief yourself."

Cooper dug into the chips and salsa again, hiding his annoyance. Lana had been so embarrassed, she'd hid the incident for the most part, stabbing him in the back instead. "I never wanted to be a unit chief. The taskforce is where the action is." He chewed, swallowed. "And quit already with the brown-nosing. It's not going to get you back on my team any faster."

"Are you denying you're that good?" she teased.

"No," he answered. "I'm not denying that I'm good at what I do."

"Let me guess, you're gifted with some kind of primal gut instinct that never lets you down."

Picking up his beer, he pointed the neck of the bottle at her. "That's bullshit and you know it. Gut instinct only carries you so far. Discipline and constant training are the keys to staying alive out there."

The hostess called Celina's name and they gathered their drinks and followed her. She seated them in a booth at the far back corner, opposite the guitarist and near the back exit. Cooper maneuvered around Celina so he could sit in the booth with his back to the wall. "What's good?" he asked, surveying the menu.

"If you want Mexican," she said, picking up her own menu, "the arroz con pollo is pretty good, but since you're in Iowa, I recommend the steak. You don't get beef in California like you do here, no matter what the farmers claim."

After the waitress took their order, they listened to the guitar music and talked about restaurants they knew from Santa Cruz to San Diego, the new governor, and the Padres latest losing streak. "Sounds like you miss California," Cooper said.

She nodded. "Especially the ocean. I'd love to get back to Santa Cruz to see the migrating whales next year."

"So come back. Looks like you have some time off right now. Be a good time to buddy up to Director Dupé. He always needs desk help with his cold cases."

"Ha, ha." Celina sighed, then met his gaze head on. "I want to come back and work for you."

"I'm heading back to California tomorrow. It's still too dangerous for you to work with me, but I'll call Dupé if you want. See if I can at least help you get back to the area."

Those beautiful eyes lit up, but before she could comment, their food arrived. The waitress refilled their drinks and left them to eat.

Cooper's steak bled pink as he cut into the prime cut. "What are you scared of?" he asked, shoving a thick piece of the medium rare meat into his mouth. As promised, it was delicious.

Celina opened up her chicken wrap and stuck a strip of the grilled meat in her mouth. "What?"

"You said earlier there were only two things you were scared of."

"Oh." She licked her fingers. "That."

Cooper chewed slowly and cut another piece. "So? What are the two things?"

She played with her food for a minute, salting her refried beans and scraping the chopped tomato out of the wrap with her fork. "I'm scared that Emilio will kill me."

"He's in North Platte with a life sentence and no chance of parole."

Celina picked bits of jalapeño out of her rice. "Yeah, I know. But with his connections and his money, it wouldn't take all that much for him to break out of prison."

For someone with her Cuban roots, she sure shies away from the hot stuff. "Not his style," he said. "It'd be easier for him to just pay one of his goons on the outside to do it."

Mixing the doctored rice with her refried beans, Celina took a bite and shook her head. "I don't think so. He would want to do it himself. Make it personal, you know?"

He did know. Cooper wasn't afraid of Emilio, but he understood Celina's fear. Somewhere down the road, Emilio could conceivably do his time and get out of jail. The California penal system was so full of prisoners, even murderers got out early on good behavior these days.

Adding a shot of hot sauce to his rice, Cooper took a bite, knowing that he would tear Emilio limb from limb if he ever so much as looked at Celina.

She exhaled and took a drink of her margarita. "I had to give a deposition for them to use in Emilio's trial. I'd been here in Des Moines about three weeks when Dominic Quarters got a call from Director Dupé. Emilio wanted to see me. His lawyer had contacted the FBI office and told them Emilio was willing to give up information about some of his contacts in South America, but the only person he would talk to was me. I had to give my deposition anyway, so I went."

Cooper stopped eating. Tried to sound entirely normal as his steak suddenly felt like a lead brick in his stomach. "You visited Emilio in prison?"

She stared at her plate. "I wasn't given a choice."

Cooper put down his fork, not sure who he was going to tear limb from limb first, Quarters or Emilio. "Did he threaten you?"

She shook her head slowly. After a glance at the dancing couple, she said, "He told me he loved me."

Cooper tried to snort in disbelief, but found himself unable to force anything from between his clenched teeth.

Celina's gaze met his briefly before she glanced away again. "I had taken several photos of him a few days before the arrest was made. Just a couple of black and white shots of him at his desk and one shot of him with some of the kids in his old neighborhood. He paid a guy to drive an ice cream truck through the streets and he paid for all the ice cream the local kids could eat. He was their hero." Her voice drifted off, her eyes not seeing the couple on the dance floor. "That day at North Platte Correctional Facility, I looked at Emilio and saw a different man. His empire was gone. The business, the estate, all the people and things he cared about. He wanted copies of those photos to hang up in his jail cell. Reminders, I suppose, of all he'd lost."

"And you sent them to him?"

"I had a set on me. To give to Dupé if he wanted them."

The snort of disgust cleared Cooper's lips. He wanted to slam his fist on the table at her naivety. "So you bought Emilio's spiel and gave him the pictures."

"No," she said. "I traded them for information."

That shut him up for a minute and turned his irritation into confusion. "Information on what?"

Celina shook her head. "I traded the photos for information on Enrique's whereabouts."

Hel-*lo*. Celina had just surprised him again. "You got the info on Mexico City." Coming out of his mouth, it still seemed too good to be true. His rookie Fed was the mysterious informant that had helped him find Enrique's hiding place. Why hadn't Lana told him?

Unfortunately, Enrique had been dead by the time Cooper arrived. Toasted to a crisp in his house. Cooper guessed Petero Valquis had personally poured the accelerant on him before tossing the lighted match in his lap.

Celina smiled, the pink lip gloss gone. "It was too little too late, I'm afraid."

Cooper waved her off. They ate in silence for several seconds. "So what's the second thing you're scared of?"

Celina's hand stopped midway to her mouth. "That Valquis will hunt me down."

"Val was killed in the skirmish outside Mexico City by two *federales*. He can't hurt you, Celina. He's dead, too."

She twirled the liquid in her margarita glass. "Not in my nightmares," she murmured. "In those, he's still very much alive."

Memories flashed through Cooper's mind. A family of four whose father was a mule for the Londano operation brutalized and murdered. Dyer's limp body. Enrique's crispy remains. "Mine, too," Cooper told her. "Mine, too."

CHAPTER SEVEN

Celina never imagined that morning when she left her apartment that she'd be returning that night with Cooper Harris in tow. After her really sucky day, this was an unbelievably *good* thing.

Too good to be true, in fact.

It was past midnight; she and Cooper had discussed the San Diego operation during most of dinner. Over a shared fried ice cream, Cooper had entertained her with stories of some of his daring take-downs that she had no doubt he'd embellished, but that pleased her. He didn't need to impress her—she was putty in his hands and he knew it—and yet he had tried to anyway. And then, when their waitress had politely asked them to leave since it was past closing time, Cooper had offered, without any goading, to see her home.

As she parked the Civic at the snow-packed curb half a block from the entrance to her apartment building, she did a mental scan of her one-room efficiency apartment. Bed: unmade. Couch: cluttered with *Elle* and *Vogue* and her camera. Kitchen sink: full of bowls and silverware. Refrigerator: one Diet Dew and a half-eaten yogurt. Bathroom: fairly clean except for the pile of clothes on the floor.

In her fantasies where Cooper came home with her, it was a warm Southern California night. Her place, two blocks from the ocean, was spotless and smelled like homemade chocolate chip cookies. The refrigerator held Cooper's favorite beverage—

Corona—and plenty of fresh limes. A modest display of her best photographs were hung and spotlighted on various walls. The drawer of her bedside table contained a healthy stack of condoms.

She was dressed in a sexy, cleavage-enhancing black silk dress with a coordinating black lace bra and underwear. Cooper, so entranced with her beauty and wit, couldn't keep his hands off her as she fumbled with her keys to unlock the door...

A knock on the car window jolted Celina back to the present. Cooper stood beside the car, snowflakes falling on his hair. The streetlight at the end of the block threw shadows on him but Celina could see one of his brows lifted in question. She yanked the parking brake and grabbed the keys out of the ignition.

"You okay?" Cooper asked as she emerged from the car.

"Fine." Boy, if that wasn't a total understatement. Every last one of her cells vibrated with anticipation. She was finally, *finally* going to have Cooper Harris all to herself, and she refused to worry about the state of her apartment or her mismatched underwear and bra. She'd missed him so much it hurt, and he was going back to California tomorrow. Today, actually. She had a few more hours with him. That would have to be enough for now.

He fell into step beside her on the sidewalk. Pushing the front door open to the entryway, Celina looked back over her shoulder at Cooper as she headed for the stairs. "Hope you're up for a hike. I'm on the top floor and there's no eleva—"

The word died on her tongue. Cooper wasn't following her. He'd stopped in the doorway.

"It was good seeing you again, Celina." His eyes took a slow tour of her body. "Real good. But I'm not coming up. It's late and we both have a long day ahead of us, so I'll say goodnight here. When you get back to California, come see me."

Celina's heart fell an inch in her chest. *No, no, no.* "But you...but I..." She couldn't find the right words to make him stay. "You're kidding me. Even after tonight, you're going to walk away?"

"What? I'm not sure I follow."

The talking. The bragging. The flirting. All through dinner she'd known Cooper wanted her. She'd seen the way his eyes lingered on her mouth. Felt that incredible heat across the table. Every time he listened to her talk, even when she was talking about something as mundane as her new addiction to Whitey's ice cream, his eyes undressed her. He seemed especially entranced when she mentioned picking the miniature peanut butter cups out of her Moose Tracks ice cream and eating those first.

"You know *what*," Celina said, exasperated. "This is the part where you walk me up to my apartment and I invite you inside. You ignore the unmade bed and the dishes in the sink and the fact that I'm wearing a white bra that doesn't match my tiger-striped bikinis. And then you miss your flight back to California in the morning because you're still here. Upstairs. In my apartment. With me."

"Celina," he started, but she cut him off.

"Don't." Her heart couldn't take his gentle rejection. Not again. Not after this crushing day of bullshit. "I don't want to hear The Speech."

"I'm not the guy—"

"Stop." She shook her head, pinched her eyes closed for a moment. "I know this part by heart. 'I'm thirty-eight. You're twenty-four. I'm DEA. You're a Fed. You're part of my team. I can't and won't sleep with a subordinate. I won't break the rules.'" Celina opened her eyes. "But, wait, I'm not your subordinate anymore, Cooper. Remember? You kicked me off your team. You won't be breaking any laws, moral or otherwise, if you come upstairs."

Cooper's eyes had gone dark and Celina could see he was working hard not to sound pissed when he answered her. Since pissed was his normal MO, there was a definite strain in his voice. "I didn't personally kick you off the taskforce. That decision was made by Dupé immediately following the *Time* magazine cover and I concurred with his opinion that you were then ineffective as an undercover agent for my group."

He paused, ran a hand over his face. "And even though I'm no longer your boss, I still feel responsible for your career."

"God!" Celina slapped the handrail with her gloved hand. "You are so full of crap. You're not worried about *my* career— heck, I don't even have a job at the moment. You care about *your* career. You're afraid having any kind of relationship with a rookie agent like me will scandalize your precious reputation as the SCVC's agent-in-charge."

"It's a school-girl crush, Celina, and it would be wrong of me to take advantage of that."

"School-girl *crush*?" The accusation slammed her in the stomach. "You think I'm infatuated with you because I'm too young to know what I want?"

Cooper stepped inside the doorway, the door shutting with a jerk on squeaky hinges behind him. His voice came out low, controlled. "I've spent the last ten years with the DEA working my ass off to get where I am, Celina. I deserve the commendations in my personnel file and the respect of my team as well as my superiors. Your career is just getting started and you're already on thin ice after the media coverage you received on the Londano bust. Now you've quit Quarters' team. The last thing you need is a relationship with me."

Celina hung her head and looked at her wet boots. "The last thing you need is me," she countered. She lifted her head and met his gaze again. "So you flirt with me, lead me on all night, and then when you have the chance to make your move, you chicken out. You are so freakin' unbelievable, Cooper Harris."

She blinked away the hurt she was feeling. If she could just get him upstairs, she could make him forget his damn logic. She could make him smile and laugh and look at her the way he had over his steak. "Who's going to know if you come upstairs? You're two thousand miles from home. No one will know this night happened except you and me."

"Celina? Is that you?" a voice said from the hallway.

Recognizing the woman's voice, Celina sighed and leaned over the stair rail to greet her landlady. "Hi, Linda. Did we wake you?"

The forty-something woman rubbed her eyes before cinching her robe tighter and stepping down the hall. Her permed brown hair was flattened on one side, sticking out on the other. "Is everything all right?"

"Everything's fine," Celina lied. "I'm sorry we woke you. We didn't wake Jacob, did we?"

Linda shook her head, looked at Cooper. Ran a hand through her hair before holding it out to him. "Linda Findley."

Cooper shook Linda's hand as Celina finished introductions. "How is Jacob?"

"He has to be in Iowa City for his pre-surgical blood work at eight a.m. We should leave here by six, but if this snow doesn't quit soon, I won't be able to get the car out." She shook her head and ran a hand through her hair again. "I knew I should have taken him out today and stayed in that hotel near the hospital, but I didn't want to spend the money. A night in a hotel costs as much as a month's worth of his anti-seizure medication. But, now…" her voice trailed off. "If I have to postpone that surgery, it will be weeks before he can get his hip fixed."

Breathing out a sigh, Linda explained the situation to Cooper. "My son has cerebral palsy. His muscles and bones don't grow at the same rate. He's had two surgeries already, but his right hip bone keeps dislocating."

"The snow plows are out but the roads are slippery," Cooper said. "Do you have anyone who can go with you? Help you out if you have trouble?"

Linda shook her head. "Jacob's dad left me shortly after Jacob was born. It's just me and him."

"If you need help," Celina told her, "or a ride, call me. I know the local sheriff and can pull some strings. We'll get Jacob to his appointment."

Linda laid her hand on top of Celina's gloved one, smiled up at her. "Thank you, Celina. I appreciate all you've done for Jacob already." She leaned in closer, spoke in a sotto voce voice. "I believe you might be busy come six o'clock." With a wink, she left Celina and Cooper alone.

They stared at each other in silence. Cooper had shut down. He stood expressionless, just staring at her.

"I have to go," he said too abruptly. "Take care of yourself."

Celina watched him walk out the door into the snowy night. Sliding down to sit on the step, she closed her eyes and buried her face in her mittens. Unbelievable.

Cooper sat in the Durango, defroster on high, windshield wipers scraping across the ice frozen on his windshield. He'd brushed some of the snow off with the arm of his jacket, but his fingers froze in under thirty seconds in the blowing wind and he'd hopped inside the SUV for shelter. He was completely underdressed for a Midwestern snowstorm. Completely unprepared for Mother Nature's raw pillage of the world around him.

Completely unprepared for the assault on his senses Celina caused.

Unprepared was not in his vocabulary. Angry with himself, he dropped his fingers from the vent covers and sat back. It was going to be a few minutes before the Durango was clear enough for him to drive safely. He should check his cell phone. He'd shut it off before arriving at the Mexican place for dinner. No doubt, Thomas had already called to find out where he was, what he was doing since he hadn't made it back to the hotel. He also needed to program the vehicle's GPS to guide him from Celina's street to the hotel since he didn't know the area and couldn't get his bearings at night in the middle of a blizzard.

It all seemed like too much work. Telling himself it had been a long day and he was tired, Cooper watched a snowplow's running lights inch down the street toward him in his rearview. No way did his reluctance to join the real world have anything to do with Celina. No way was his refusal to play with fire making him feel less honorable instead of more.

Cooper stared at the entry door to Celina's building. He'd done exactly what Celina accused him of...flirting, bragging, charming her pants off. For a few hours, he'd relaxed. Enjoyed his dinner. Laughed a couple times. Desperate not to end the night, he'd offered to see her home, but on the drive to her apartment, all the reasons he'd used before to stay away from her surfaced. He'd tamped them down, ignored them, but they wouldn't go away. When the time came to actually take her pants off, he'd chickened out.

The snowplow drove by, an inch of snow arcing over the Durango. Cooper swore under his breath as the wipers made another pass and failed to clear the glass. His wheels were now sitting in several inches of snow. If he didn't leave now, he'd be stuck there until morning.

Stuck in bed with Celina. The thought hit him with the force of a body slam, just like the waves he often rode on his surfboard.

He could, right now, touch Celina, make love to her, wipe the hurt off The New Face of the FBI, and replace it with happiness. What the hell was wrong with him that he would pass that up? When had he lost his ability to throw caution to the wind and actually *live* his life? He'd been dancing with the devil for too long. It was making him old and...careful. Too careful. There were no guarantees. Tomorrow he could be in a wheelchair like Dyer. Or worse. He might die having passed up the best night of his life.

The snow was coming down harder and Celina's opinion that no one would know where or how he spent the night echoed in his head. "Okay, Mother Nature," he said aloud to the snow falling outside. "You win."

Inside the entryway, Celina was sitting on the second step, head down, face covered with her mittens. Cooper's breath caught in his throat. She was crying.

Over him.

Another slam of emotions hit him. All this time, he'd kept his distance from her through sheer will power. Seeing her slumped on the stairs, crying because he'd hurt her, did him in. He tried to speak her name, found his throat closed tight.

The door hinge squeaked behind him as he let it shut, and slowly, ever so slowly, Celina raised her face out of her mittens and looked at him.

Tears clung to her eyelashes and her cheeks were moist. But her eyes—damn. Hurt, sadness, confusion mixing in as second by second quietly ticked by.

Cooper found his legs moving forward, his body crouching in front of her. He raised one of his frozen fingers to her cheek and wiped at the tear running down it. Her skin was smooth and soft and oh, so warm under his fingertip.

She turned her head into his hand and his finger fell next to her lips. Still speechless, Cooper let his finger touch the outside corner of her frown. Her lips parted on an intake of breath and he slid his finger across her full bottom lip.

He found his voice, but it was ragged. "God, I want you."

And then she was kissing him, her lips fire against his. He kissed her back, pushing his body against hers to counterbalance her weight as she threw her arms around his neck. He grabbed the solid wooden spindle of the stair ballast with one hand, the back of her head with the other. His fingers slipped under the knit cap to tangle in her hair.

She drew him against her as she leaned back on the stairs, and he cupped her head to keep it from banging on the edge of the wooden stair behind her. Her tongue was shooting fire inside his mouth, and *sweet Jesus*, she tasted like spicy salsa and salty limes. Why had he waited so long to do this?

Because he was a stupid, stupid man.

Celina, still kissing the hell out of him, opened his coat. Her mittens were off and her cool fingertips brushed his neck, sending electric sensations shooting right to his groin. He pulled back from her lips and choked out her name, "Celina."

Her eyes opened to his, and she seemingly read his mind. "Right," she said, her breath soft on his face. "Not here. Upstairs."

He nodded, and rising, guided her to her feet. She picked up her hat and gloves, danced up the stairs toward the next landing. His cock was harder than granite and he tried unsuccessfully to rearrange it inside his pants as he watched her heart-shaped ass disappear around the corner.

He ran seven miles a day, surfed when he could, and put in three to six hours a week on the mat in hand-to-hand combat training. But three flights of stairs with a hard-on made him seriously question his stamina.

Until he made it to the top and Celina turned from inserting the key in her apartment door's lock, giving him that wicked smile of hers, all sex and heat and, *Jesus*—

He was on her before she could turn the knob.

Pressing her against the door, he kissed her, unzipping her leather coat and shoving his hands inside, past the lining, warm from her body heat, past her shoulder holster and straight to her waist. Fingers working on their own accord tickled her ribs and cupped her breasts. She moaned as his thumbs brushed over her hard nipples.

The door opened, and in they went, sliding off of it. Celina closing it. Cooper pinning her to the inside.

The apartment was dark, but a large west-facing picture window let in enough light for Cooper to see that the wicked smile was still on Celina's face. She wound a leg around him as her hands unzipped his coat the rest of the way. He let it fall to the floor.

Her coat followed. Then her shoulder holster with a dull thud as it hit the ground. His echoed it.

Thirty seconds later, her jeans were next to the jacket. Together they pushed her turtleneck up and off her head and Cooper ran his fingers over the lacy white bra filled to capacity with soft skin. She unzipped his pants as he groped her breasts, and Cooper absorbed her moan as she rose up on tippy-toes, straining to take him in.

One logical neuron was still firing in his brain. Heady from the intensity, it was all he could do to pull a condom from his wallet and cover himself. It took two tries to open the damn package, mostly because Celina removed her bra and Cooper's knees went weak from the sight of those plump breasts and dark nipples. As he yanked the condom on, she dropped her bikinis to the floor. Cooper palmed each side of Celina's bottom as she opened herself to him, her sock-clad feet wrapping around his hips.

Just like in his fantasies, Cooper took her hard, the fire inside him rushing to climax, almost violent in its animalistic need.

Celina took everything he gave and wanted more. She bucked and pushed and grabbed and met every thrust with equal enthusiasm.

Her release came swiftly. She cried his name into the dark apartment, burying her fingernails into his shoulders as she arched against him. Three strokes later, Cooper's own release hit him like a tsunami, knocking his equilibrium into a tailspin, his breath from his chest. He held her against the door for long moments, legs shaking from the exertion.

In the aftermath, they left the lights off and their clothes on the floor, climbing into Celina's bed. She snuggled against him, her smile now one of contentment.

Cooper fell asleep, only to awake a short while later to Celina's lips on his chest working their way downward. As she slid a trail of kisses down his stomach and, *ahh, God*, made contact under the covers, Cooper buried his hands in her hair and watched the snow falling soundlessly outside the window.

CHAPTER EIGHT

Celina felt like she'd just closed her eyes when her cell phone on the nightstand rang. Her body, deeply satiated and tired, was rolling onto its side and reaching for it before her brain caught up. The apartment was still dark; her eyes automatically scanned the red numbers of her alarm clock; 5:35.

This can't be good.

She interrupted the phone's second ring, rubbing her eyes, and dropping her head back on the pillow. "Hello?" she said, only then realizing Cooper wasn't beside her.

Where was he? Her fingers felt the pillow, still indented from his head. It was cold. Her eyes went to the bathroom, noted the door was open and there was no light on. The voice in her ear spoke in a low, quiet tone. "Sleeping well?"

Celina blinked and raised herself up on one elbow, goose bumps rising on her arms. Her brain absently noted Cooper's clothes were gone from the floor. Gun, jacket. Everything.

The voice came again. "Do you ever dream about me, Celina?"

Her brain engaged, her breath stopping in her chest. She sat straight up, any residue of sleep gone with the thudding of her heart. She knew the voice on the phone as well as her own.

"Why are you calling me?" A whisper that gave away her surprise. Her eyes flew to the red numbers again, double-checking the time. What prisoner had phone privileges at that time in the morning? "How did you get my number?"

"Did you think you were safe from me in Iowa? Did you think I wouldn't find you if you ran?"

Swinging her legs over the edge of the bed, Celina was up and moving—no direction at first, but moving all the same thanks to a sudden rush of adrenaline. She cradled the phone between her ear and shoulder and reached for her yoga pants. The clothes she'd worn the previous night were lying neatly folded on the couch. Her gun rested on top of the pile.

She slipped a T-shirt over her head, wanting to hang up—to sever the hold Emilio suddenly had on her through the phone line—but stopped herself. She grabbed the gun out of its holster and paced to the picture window to look out. The snow had stopped and the traffic lights below blinked their colors over empty streets packed white. Several cars parked along the street curbs were running, exhaust floating in the icy air in clouds as their owners brushed snow and scraped ice.

Taking a quiet breath, Celina forced herself to stay calm. Emilio Londano was not outside. He was four hundred miles away in a maximum security penitentiary. And apparently, he'd bribed a guard for a ten minute call.

But where was Cooper?

"I don't dream about you, Emilio." Her voice sounded strong. *He has no hold on me.*

Moving around her small apartment, she double checked locks and looked for the note she was sure Cooper—the lousy rat—had left her. "And I didn't run from California," she added, knowing that Emilio loved to play intimidation games. He wanted to scare her, but she knew he couldn't hurt her.

Cooper, on the other hand ... Celina shut down the sudden pain in her chest. "The Bureau transferred me to Des Moines. A job transfer, that's all. It had nothing, *nothing*," she emphasized the word again, "to do with you."

Emilio chuckled. "Ah, Celina. The consummate liar. You're very good at it. Do they teach you that in the FBI?"

Her reply was curt. "Among other things."

There was a sound on Emilio's end, like a match striking. She heard him inhale, wondering where this conversation was going, wondering when he took up smoking cigarettes. For him it had always been cigars, Cuban. Cigarettes were another hazard of prison life, she supposed.

"So they teach you how to carry an alias and lie," he said on the exhale. "How to hold a gun to a man's heart after you've fucked him over. But what do they teach you about fear?"

She leaned her back against the wall, a path of sweat icing her spine. This time she gave him the truth. "They teach you to face it. Overcome it. Use it."

"Is that what you're doing right now?" Another inhale. "Pacing around your apartment, checking locks. Are you facing your fear of me, Celina?"

Her breath stopped in her chest as her brain fired a clear warning to her body. *How would he know I'm pacing and checking locks?* Pushing off the wall, she took the safety off her gun. "Where are you?"

Emilio made a noise in his throat, a guarded laugh. "Does the FBI teach you about revenge?" His voice was soft again but no less dangerous. "Do they teach you how to avoid falling into the hands of the criminal you sent to prison? The man who is now so close he can smell you?"

Every cell in Celina's body froze. This had to be a game. "What do you want?"

Emilio's next words caught her off balance, almost sent her to her knees. "Your boyfriend is outside shoveling snow. I'm going to slice his throat and then," the low laugh again. "I'm coming for you. You, I'll take more time with."

Forcing her knees to hold her up, Celina raised her gun and pointed it at the door, already moving to open it. "Goddamn it, Emilio, where are you?"

The only answer she got as she opened the door was the faint smell of cigarette smoke as the line went dead.

Tripping down the stairs, Celina hit the front door at full

speed, gun raised. The sun was clearing the horizon, clouds dimming its light. It was cold, damn cold, but Celina only felt the cold inside her, fingers of dread closing around her heart. Cooper's black SUV was still parked halfway down the block where he'd left it last night behind her Civic.

"Cooper!" she screamed as her bare feet sunk in six inches of white fluff. She turned in circles scanning the sidewalk, the street, the rooftops of the buildings, the gun following her gaze. "Cooper!"

A motor was running a few yards away. Linda was vigorously scraping ice off the windshield, but stopped when she saw Celina running toward her. "What are you doing out here in your pj's?"

"Linda, get in the building. Now."

Snow sailed through the air into the street and then Cooper's head appeared on the other side of Linda's car. His eyes took in her face and her drawn weapon. "What's wrong?"

There was a man walking down the sidewalk, covered from head to toe in Carhartt coveralls, a red knit cap, and a scarf wound around his face. The only thing Celina could see were his eyes, slit against the cold and watching her intently. He slowed his pace and eyed her gun. His hands were buried in his pockets.

"Stop," Celina commanded, training the gun on him.

He jumped back, hands going up in the air. "What the hell?"

Cooper pushed Linda in front of him toward the apartment. His gun replaced the shovel in his hand as he moved next to Celina. "Tell me what's going on."

"Emilio." But the man in front of her was taller than Cooper. Even in the coveralls, she could tell he was heavier too. She leaned in and looked at his eyes.

His eyes weren't Emilio's. Celina slid her gun off to the side. "Sorry," she said, waving him on.

He took off at a jog, looking back over his shoulder at her as he ran away.

There was not even a hint of sunlight to reflect on metal today. No sign of anyone in the windows across the street. Celina turned in circles. "He's here, watching you."

Cooper followed her motions, tracked what she tracked. "Emilio's in prison."

She didn't take her eyes off her surroundings. "No. He's here. He just called me." She chanced a glance at Cooper. "He knew you were out shoveling snow."

Cooper's eyes narrowed for a heartbeat, and then his hand was on her elbow, propelling her toward the apartment building's entrance. "Get inside," he demanded. "Now."

CHAPTER NINE

Celina was shaking so hard that, even after he'd bundled her in layer upon layer of her clothes, Cooper wished they were alone so he could peel those clothes back off, throw her naked into the shower and warm her up.

But they weren't alone. Far from it.

And he was never, *ever*, going to see her naked again.

"So you spent the night here with Special Agent Davenport?" Chief Forester looked up from the notebook he was writing things down in. "That right, Agent Harris?"

Who would know? Celina's words echoed again in Cooper's head and he thought of his father's favorite saying that no good deed went unpunished. He was sure every agent in the land knew at this moment that he'd slept with The New Face of the FBI. Who would know? Huh.

Mitch, one of Cooper's men on the Jagger bust, shot him a *way to go, boss* grin. Thomas looked up from his laptop and gave him the geek-squad version of the same.

Dominic Quarters stared Cooper down.

No biggie, there.

The world of federal law enforcement was territorial, but close-knit all the same. A threat to one of their members tightened the threads. Five minutes after Cooper called in the report to the locals, Dyer, pulling his usual all-nighter in his San Diego condo by the beach, had called Cooper's cell phone. He'd beaten Cooper's unit chief and Director Dupé in getting the scoop. Thomas, Mitch, and the third man of Cooper's squad, Nelson Cruz, had showed up ten minutes later. The news was spreading like a fire out of control even though no one could believe it.

Emilio Paloma-Londano had escaped prison.

And he was coming after the agent who put him there.

He was going to have to go through Cooper first. If, that was, Cooper could survive the grilling Forester was handing out.

"He's already answered that question," Celina said through gritted teeth. Cooper couldn't tell if she was gritting them out of impatience with Forester or to stop them from chattering. "Move off the dime. That has nothing to do with Londano."

Every light in the apartment was on, even though the sun was pouring through the picture window facing the street. The apartment was one large room and Cooper now took a moment to really look at it. A smattering of furniture, the big bed in one corner with the covers still messed up, sitting like the pink elephant in the room.

What they'd done in that bed, Jesus. Even in the midst of the fan-hitting shit flying around the room, he could barely look at that bed without getting a woody.

A desk with a computer and the usual peripheries sat nearby. The bathroom was off to the left. Another table was scattered with cameras and piles of photos. More photos on the floor. Celina's hobby was paying off.

Back to him, she stood at the picture window looking out over the street. Feet planted, arms crossed over her chest made larger from the extra layers of clothes. Her backside very plainly sported her gun today. Not the agency-issued Glock, but a sleek Beretta.

Her partner, the other female agent in Forester's group, Ronni, was standing next to her. At the breakfast bar sat Forester, much too happy to turn the screw he had Cooper pinned with between swigs of his coffee. "Davenport, Punto, get away from the goddamned window. I'm not going to waste manpower if you're going to make yourselves sitting targets."

Celina's voice came out clear, no hint of fear, just continued irritation. "He's not going to shoot me, Chief. He likes things more personal."

Cooper exchanged a look with Thomas. Forester shook his head, threw up his hands, and swiveled on the barstool. Out in the hall, Nelson was accompanying several uniforms who were knocking on doors and asking if anyone had seen anything. Cooper knew it was a lost cause. He and Linda had been right outside the apartment's front entrance digging her van out of the snow, and had seen nothing. The owner of the cigarette came through a back door, but still no one had seen anything. The rest of the building's tenants had been sleeping or, if awake, watching the early morning news reports to find out about the weather conditions. The security camera over the back door had been ripped off its holder.

Forester set his coffee on the bar. Quarters continued to shoot bullets from his eyes. "You know what I hate about the DEA, Harris?"

Cooper knew what was coming, but forced a polite response. "No, sir."

Celina and Ronni turned from the window in unison. The frown between Celina's eyebrows grew deeper, but Cooper sent her a small shake of his head, signaling her to stay quiet.

"You believe your own hype." Quarters slapped one hand on the bar, challenge radiating from him. "You guys run around acting like *Miami Vice* and all the time it's guys like mine, FBI operatives, who keep this nation safe."

Cooper met the man's challenge with his own. "Yeah, Robert Hanssen. There's a role model."

Celina uncrossed her arms. "Stop it," she said, hands going to her hips.

Quarters ignored her, started to ream Cooper again, but before he could say anything, Ronni walked into the kitchen

77

area and grabbed a pot of coffee off the Krups coffee maker. "Let's heat that coffee up, Chief Forester." Her cheerful tone was a little too forced. She winked at Cooper as she topped off his cup too. "It's Cuban, from Celina's grandmother. Great stuff. Blows your head right off."

Cooper was ten hours short on sleep and a quart low on caffeine, and was about to go another round with Forester and Quarters. "Thanks, Ronni."

"I do the Dew," Thomas said from the other end of the bar. "Got any of that?"

Ronni pointed at the refrigerator. "Check the fridge, sweetie. Might get lucky in there. Celina's a Dew fan herself." Thomas gave Cooper a sideways look, but Cooper ignored him. He had enough on his hands right now without trying to figure out Ronni Punto.

Forester decided to give up on Cooper and faced Celina. "You sure it was him?"

She nodded and Forester made her recite her conversation with Londano again. Thomas sidled up next to Cooper with his soda and listened carefully.

Cooper could see Thomas and Forester thought it was a slim to nothing chance that Emilio had been outside the apartment door smoking a cigarette. "But you didn't see him or anyone else?" Quarters drilled Celina again.

No longer shaking, but still gritting her teeth, Celina glared at him. "No. I didn't see him. That doesn't mean he wasn't there."

Thomas screwed off the lid of the Dew and put into words what Cooper had been thinking from the start. "Londano probably just paid someone to freak you."

Celina's body stiffened. "It was him."

Forester eyed Cooper. "Security cameras?"

"The one we need was disabled."

"Linda barely makes enough on rent to keep this apartment building in decent shape," Celina said. "Jacob's medical bills are bankrupting her. She can't afford to fix everything."

Cooper's cell phone rang. It was Victor Dupé, a Bureau man who'd headed up the Southern California Violent Crimes division. A man Cooper had worked with for years. A man he respected. "Emilio is at breakfast with the rest of the inmates in Block B." As always, Dupé's tone was steady, no-nonsense. "The warden checked on him and confirmed it. Londano's last logged phone call was six days ago when he called his lawyer."

"Thanks, sir," Cooper said. He moved the phone from his mouth and repeated the information to Celina.

She shook her head in disbelief. "He called me. He was here."

Dupé spoke, calling Cooper's attention back to him. "When is your return flight?"

"Flights are delayed because of the snow and ice." He snapped his fingers at Mitch who was pretending to read news off the internet. "What are they saying about departing flights?"

"Two-hour delay," Mitch said without moving a muscle, "so figure at least four."

Resuming his conversation with Dupé, Cooper paced, all the while conscious of Celina's accusatory eyes following him. He wasn't sure what she was accusing him of. Did she really believe their world would stop? That he wouldn't go back to California today?

As Cooper disconnected the call, Forester waved a beefy hand through the air to dismiss Celina as he headed for the door. "No way was it this Londano, but since I don't know who it was or why the hell he'd harass you, I'll leave a man here for the day, in case your caller tries anything else." He stopped in the doorway and gestured at Ronni. "Keep her too."

"I'm not sitting in this apartment all day," Celina said, her tone of voice signaling her battle stance was ready.

"Then I'll escort you to headquarters," Quarters said, staring her down. "Your choice."

"We'll stay here." Ronni smiled at the two men. "I'll check in with you throughout the day."

Forester grunted, turned, and gave Cooper another glare. "Delay or no delay, don't miss your plane ride home, Harris."

Up yours, Cooper thought, but he raised the cup of strong brew in his hand as if in acknowledgment. Quarters gave him one more glare before he, too, walked out.

When the door closed, Celina's eyes searched his in appeal. "Emilio *was* outside that door, Cooper. He knew I was pacing the floor and checking the locks."

A natural assumption, Cooper thought, for anyone harassing her. Thomas had commandeered his laptop from Mitch. Cooper leaned over his shoulder. "Anything buzzing in the underground?"

Thomas clicked off the news site he was scanning. "I checked message boards and chat rooms. Nada on Emilio or any prison breaks."

Celina lowered her voice. "He was here. I could *feel* him."

Cooper had seen the way she looked when she came outside screaming his name. He believed that *she* believed Emilio had threatened both his life and hers, but her feelings didn't mesh with logic. "Then who's sitting in North Platte having breakfast right now with Londano's prisoner number on his back?"

They stared at each other for a moment, and Cooper saw something change in Celina's expression that made the hairs on the back of his neck tighten. She crossed her arms and rubbed them with her hands as if she were cold again. The name came out of her lips like a curse, "Enrique."

The tick of the clock on the wall seemed too loud for a second as everyone, including Thomas and Mitch, looked at him. He rubbed the skin on the back of his neck and said the only thing he could think of. "Shit."

"But he's dead," Thomas said.

But what if he's not?

———

Enrique is dead, Celina told herself and then realized she'd spoken it out loud. Either that or Cooper was able to read her mind. He nodded. "They ID'd his body after the fire," he said, setting down his cup of coffee.

Mitch was forming a circle with her and Cooper and Ronni. "You confirm the ID, Coop? Mexican officials are easily bribed."

Cooper shook his head and rubbed the back of his neck again. "Shit," he repeated. "I couldn't do a visual ID. There was nothing left of him but some bones and ash."

He paced away from Celina, came back, and started to say something, but stopped, paced back to the picture window. The wheels were turning in his head and Celina was glad to see the disbelief gone from his eyes. He knew, just like her, that while improbable, it was not impossible. The Londano's had pulled off tougher schemes.

Celina wished she and Cooper were still in bed, enjoying another round of lovemaking. Or maybe in the shower together. They hadn't even had a chance to talk about last night, much less repeat it.

Instead, she was handing him a nightmare on the Cooper scale of epic proportions. His reputation of honorable actions was now tainted, at least in his own mind, since he'd insisted on calling in Forester and alerting the rest of the FBI world, as well as his own agency, that Emilio had escaped prison and threatened them both. Then he'd had to explain why he was shoveling Celina's landlord out of the snow at 5:30 in the morning. He hadn't lied, hadn't even skirted the truth with Forester and Quarters. His internal turmoil had to be the size of the Battle of Troy to admit he'd slept with her.

Although, technically, the sleeping part was almost nonexistent.

Her eyes strayed to the door. She still couldn't believe she'd come that fast, up against the door no less. Obviously she'd been on the No Sex Diet far too long, supplemented only by the Cooper Fantasy pill she'd been feeding herself since the day she met him.

Shifting her attention back to Cooper, she saw him staring at her, and, there it was. The door episode. He was remembering it as well. The intensity of his gaze made her pulse throb.

But then he cleared his throat and looked away and Celina's heart did a little dive. He hadn't touched her since he'd rubbed her icy feet to warm them up. She'd been so shaken by Emilio's threat, she'd been unable to speak while Cooper massaged her feet and pushed her favorite fuzzy cotton socks on them. Adrenaline and fear had collided full speed inside her. While she'd looked down on the top of Cooper's head as he tugged her socks on, she'd clearly seen him lying outside in the snow, his blood turning the white crimson.

That was her nightmare. Combined with the fact that no one really believed Emilio had called her, had been outside her door. His voice suddenly hummed in her ears. It mixed with the idea of Enrique still being alive. A cramp hit her in her belly, and she nearly doubled over. Ronni's hand touched her back.

Using the fear, like she'd been taught, she turned it into anger. Leaving Ronni's hand, she tugged an overnight bag buried under piles of shoes out of her closet and threw it on the bed.

"What are you doing?" Ronni asked.

"Going to North Platte," she answered, tugging a jacket off a hanger and putting it in the suitcase. Next went in jeans, a couple T-shirts. She walked to her dresser and started pulling out underwear. "I've got to know."

Cooper watched. "Whoa, Celina. Slow down." He looked out the window, took a deep breath before looking back at her. "Odds are Warden Oxford's right and Emilio is in his prison. Even if Enrique's *not* dead, how would they pull off an exchange at a maximum security penitentiary? And, most importantly, why would Enrique, if he *is* alive, go along with such a scheme?"

Celina didn't know the answers to his questions and her brain didn't want to focus on them. She couldn't sit tight and wait for Emilio or whoever had called her that morning to make another appearance. She couldn't let Cooper walk out of her apartment as if last night didn't mean anything. She needed to take control of the situation or she'd go crazy. Needed to see Emilio in North Platte with her own eyes. Grabbing her camera case, she set it on the bed next to the suitcase.

"Why don't you ask Oxford to fingerprint him?" Mitch said.

Celina stopped, looked at Cooper. Cooper grunted "huh". Opening his cell phone, he speed dialed. When it connected, he explained to Director Dupé about his suspicions concerning Enrique and suggested they needed confirmation with a fingerprint or DNA swab. He listened for a moment, urged the point smoothly, nodded, and thanked Dupé.

"Dupé's doubtful but is going to place a call or two and get a fingerprint match," he told her. "We should know for sure in a couple of hours who's in North Platte."

Celina thought for a moment. "What if it is Enrique?"

"Then we hunt down Emilio."

He said it so casually, Celina almost forgot how freaked out she was about the idea.

A knock sounded on her door and Nelson Cruz entered. He nodded at her but spoke to Cooper. "Nothing. No one saw, or smelled, anything out of the ordinary." He glanced back at Celina. "Sorry, Celina."

The nightmare continued. "It's like a ghost."

Cooper made a motion to Thomas to pack up his laptop. "We need to get to the airport. Dupé's already made a call to get us on the first departing flight."

Celina felt her world screech, like fingernails on a blackboard, to a halt. "You're leaving?"

Thomas shut his laptop, started to gather his papers. Mitch and Nelson suddenly seemed to think he needed help. Ronni started gathering coffee mugs.

Cooper grabbed his jacket off her coat tree. "Yes, Celina. I'm leaving."

"What about last night? Aren't you even going to acknowledge what happened between us?"

Ronni dropped a cup in the sink, turned to the three men at Celina's table. "Any of you guys good with plumbing?" She grabbed arms and started hustling the confused men across the room. "I noticed Celina's shower is dripping. Maybe you could take a look."

Shoving them ahead of her, all four entered the bathroom and Ronni shut the door. As small as the bathroom was, Celina knew they were squished in there like sardines.

Cooper's jaw was set, a nerve jumping in it. His Terminator expression was back in play. "I've been acknowledging what happened all morning."

It figured he'd argue the point on a technicality. Figured he'd refuse to admit he was feeling anything except responsibility toward her. "I know this sucks for you. You're not one to air your laundry in public." She left out 'dirty' because what they'd shared last night was to her in no way dirty. Dirty in the Christina Aguilera sense maybe, but not dirty in the laundry sense.

"You understand that last night was just..." he paused and Celina braced herself for what she knew was coming. "For fun."

"For fun," she repeated, nodding her head as if she actually agreed. Nodded as if her heart wasn't breaking. "There's no Starbucks in our future."

The Terminator frowned. Celina shook her head at him. "This is the 'last night was fun, but we're just friends' speech, right?" She watched his frown deepen. "But wait, we're not really friends, either, are we Cooper? A friend would have called to check on me after I left California. A friend would have told me that Bobby was living in a wheelchair."

Drawing in a steadying breath, she plunged forward. "So what we shared last night was just sex—ungodly hot, fuck-me-against-the-door sex—but just sex for you. A one night stand."

"No," Cooper interrupted. "It wasn't just sex, but..." He

84

shook his head, tried again. "It was…" His eyes were no longer emotionless and Celina could see that he wished she could read his mind as easily as he seemed to read hers. "Last night with the storm and everything, it was like a different time, a different place."

"Not real," Celina offered, suddenly able to read his mind quite clearly. "You were stranded in Iowa during a blizzard and I offered to keep you warm. I told you no one would know and that would have been the case if Emilio hadn't called. You would have gone back to California this morning and last night would have just been a fantasy episode of *Lost.*"

"That's not what I meant."

But it *was* what he meant and she knew it. She'd helped him buy into the fantasy. And now he was leaving to go back to California, still believing there was no Starbucks in their future. There was no future for them, period. God, didn't that rank in the nightmare department right under Cooper bleeding out in the snow.

The bathroom door opened and Mitch came stumbling out. "Shower head needs a new washer…"

"Mitch." Ronni was in the bathroom doorway. "Not yet."

"Oh," he looked sheepishly between Cooper and Celina. "Sorry."

Cooper raised a hand to stop him from backing up. "Dupé will call you as soon as the results come back," he said to Celina. His hand made a rolling motion to Mitch, and he and the other men filed out of the bathroom, Ronni trailing behind and sending Celina an *I tried* look. "We need to get to the airport."

Celina searched his face. "What if Emilio is out there, Cooper? What if he comes after you?"

"Don't worry about me." He ushered his men, one by one, through the door. "If Emilio is out, you're the likely target. Keep your doors locked and your gun on you." He met her gaze, went still. "It was good to see you, Celina."

Then he was gone without a goodbye.

Ronni looked at her, looked at the door, back at her. "At least he didn't say, 'I'll call you'."

"No." Celina stared at the closed door, anger swirling through her like the previous night's blizzard. "He's too damned honorable to lie to me."

And too damned scared not to lie to himself about his feelings.

Ronni took out a bottle of soda from the fridge and handed it to Celina. Grabbed another and opened it, taking a long drink. "Sex against the door, huh?"

"You heard that?"

Ronni nodded. Celina unscrewed the lid on her bottle, took a drink. "Yeah. No-holds barred sex against the door."

"Damn," Ronni said. "That gunpowder and Wheaties diet must be something. Gotta get me a man on that."

Celina laughed unexpectedly. Whether it was from the lack of sleep or the emotional rollercoaster ride she'd been on that morning, she couldn't help herself. "To gunpowder and Wheaties," she said, raising her bottle in the air.

Ronni copied her and the two women touched the bottles together, laughing.

"Our plane doesn't leave for another two hours," Thomas said.

They were in the stairwell and out of earshot of the guard outside Celina's door. "I won't believe Emilio's in prison unless I see him with my own eyes," Cooper told him. "Enrique either. That fucker's supposed to be dead. I'm flying home. You're staying here to watch Celina. Once I get to North Platte and verify who's in there, I'll call you and we'll go from there. Forester, Quarters, and the locals can help you with backup if necessary."

"I thought Dupé was going to get the warden to fingerprint him."

They turned the corner and started down the next flight of stairs. "Money can buy a lot of things."

Nelson fell into step behind Cooper. "False fingerprints?"

"Whole new identities."

A sound of disbelief emanated from the young man's throat, but he nodded. "Even in prison."

Nelson was a first year agent. A little green yet but street smart. "In prison, in the real world, it makes no difference. Money and power rule. The San Diego Mafia is a family business that's been around for thirty years in this country alone. In South America and Mexico, probably a hundred years. They have all the money and connections you can imagine, and even in a maximum correctional facility, money talks, things happen."

Mitch was behind Nelson. "Dude, you think Emilio Londano got out of North Platte by forcing his twin brother, who's supposed to be dead, to impersonate him?"

"I don't believe much," Cooper said as they all hit the sidewalk. "But I do believe in the industriousness of criminals."

And his own ability to fuck up. Celina's face had said it all. There was no saving the day now. He had to find out what was going on with Emilio Londano and he had to stay away from Celina.

Thomas stopped to say a few words to the Fed at the building entrance. The guy was bored and ready to chat. Wanted to look important. Cooper stood there, hands on hips, scanning the street, the buildings, the rooflines, looking for Londano. Daring the mafia leader to take a shot at him. If he was really out there.

Nothing. Whoever was out there wanted Celina, not him.

Thomas shook the agent's hand and gave him his card. The schmoozing over, they headed to the Durango.

"You really think she's in danger?" Nelson asked as they brushed snow off the cab.

Cooper handed Nelson the keys to start the engine. Celina in danger? His stomach tightened. Unable to answer for a moment, he busied himself with a scraper Thomas handed him. "Worst-case scenario," he said, "Londano's out; then, yes, her life's in danger. Even if he's not, he could have hired someone to work her over."

Thomas used his booted foot to move snow from around the front tire. "But you're leaving her alone."

"No, I'm leaving you here to guard her. Don't screw up."

"Or you'll kill me."

"Yes."

Thomas glanced at the apartment building. "Dupé okayed this?"

"In a roundabout way."

Thomas scanned the street. "She leaves the building, I'll lose her. I can't keep her under surveillance by myself."

"She leaves the building, she better be sitting in this SUV with you."

"She'd be safer if she went to California with you."

All activity stopped as Nelson, Thomas, and Mitch looked at him. Deep in his gut, Cooper knew Thomas was right, and damn, if he didn't want to take Celina with him, but he couldn't. The gossip was going to be hard enough to handle without showing up at the office with Celina in tow. She'd be safe here, especially with Thomas on surveillance, and as soon as Cooper figured out what was up with Londano, he'd try to straighten things out with Celina.

CHAPTER TEN

You should have told me, Celina IM'd Dyer.

A moment later, Dyer's reply came back. *Why? So you could feel sorry for me?*

Celina shook her head. *Because I'm your friend, blockhead.*

Untwist your undies. You have more important things to worry about right now.

Slouching back in her chair, Celina stared at the laptop screen. All she'd done was worry for the past ten hours. Emilio was playing a game and she didn't know where she was on the game board.

She sure as hell didn't like waiting for him to make the next move, but there was nothing she could do to preempt whatever he was contemplating. Cooper was embarrassed that everyone knew he'd slept with her. He'd very publicly deserted her. Nothing to preempt there.

But every time she got mad at him, she thought about Emilio's threat and saw Cooper's imagined blood on the snow, and then she felt guilty for being mad. Her brain spun in constant circles.

Ronni had gone grocery shopping at the corner convenience store and had entertained herself watching Rachel Ray and concocting imitation recipes, which she'd then offered to Celina. Wanting to please her friend, Celina tried a few things. Food was the last thing she wanted.

She queried Dyer. *Why hasn't anyone called me with the fingerprint results?*

Takes time. Prisoner rights and shit. Lawyer has to be present. Be patient.

She wanted to ask, *why hasn't Cooper called?* but stopped her fingers before they typed. Instead, she wrote. *What are you working on?*

Officially?

Celina grinned at the screen. Un-.

Meth.

Labs?

Crackdown here has generated a lot of lab startups in Mexico. Londano was one of the first to take advantage of that. His cartel is still active south of the border. Mules are lying low but still working. Using radio waves through cell towers to warn each other of trouble. I track them, I find him. Simple network analysis.

You think L's out, don't you?

Too risky not to believe.

Too risky was right. *He threatened Cooper's life.*

C can take care of himself. He's not a blockhead like me. Except when it comes to you.

Celina sat up again. *What do you mean?*

He didn't fly all the way to Des Moines to arrest Jagger. Mann and Cruz could have handled that alone.

Her heart picking up its tempo, her fingers skipped on the keys. *He came to see me?*

No, John Deere tractors, blockhead.

Celina let go of a small laugh, but her humor faded quickly when she thought of her last conversation with Cooper. She'd fulfilled his fantasy during the night and then he'd left her. *He feels responsible for me because I was part of the team and I'm sure he enjoyed last night,* she wrote, her fingers shaking as she typed the next words, *but he made it clear there is nothing between us.*

There was a long pause and then Dyer ended the conversation. *Girlfriend's here for some afternoon delight. Gotta run. Or roll as the case may be.*

Celina rolled her eyes. Dyer always called his wife, Eliza, his girlfriend. To keep things fresh, he always said. After ten years of marriage, it must have worked. The two still acted like newlyweds. *Does Eliza know about her?*

Shhh. Don't tell. Celina could see Dyer's thick eyebrows doing his Groucho Marx impression. *Stay safe.*

She drummed her fingers on the table. Her suitcase sat on the bed, packed and ready to go, and she considered for the fortieth time that day whether to fly to California. There was no logical reason to do it. She didn't have a position there and her apartment was sublet for the rest of the winter. She was stuck here in Des Moines whether she liked it or not.

All was quiet. Dawn McBroom was on duty outside her door and Mike Sugars was downstairs in the foyer. Thomas Mann had been across the street all day. Cooper hadn't stayed but he'd left his teammate to guard her. She didn't know whether to feel irritated or relieved.

No phone calls from Emilio. None from Dupé or Cooper. For several hours, she'd paced the floor, mad that she was so out of the loop. She'd tried calling Dupé. Her call was intercepted by the notorious Lana, who knew nothing about the fingerprint match nor did she seem to care about Celina's situation.

Standing to stretch, Celina walked to the picture window, staring out at the low-hanging gray clouds. It was early evening, but streetlights buzzed to life and shadows hung over the street below. "This sucks."

Ronni flipped off the TV, wandered over to the piles of photographs on the table. "I could drive you to HQ and let Forester baby-sit you."

Celina gave her a *don't even think about it face.*

"Why don't you show me your pictures?"

For the next hour, the two friends sat on Celina's couch and went through her collection of photographs. Cityscapes were mingled with portraits. A group photograph of the SCVC taskforce, glasses raised in a happy salute, fell out of a handful into Ronni's lap.

She clucked her tongue. "That Thomas kid is a cutie. He do that Wheaties thing too?"

Celina stared at the picture, seeing only Cooper, his glass raised but no smile lit his face like the rest of the group. "I took this the day after I arrested Londano. Dyer's missing."

"The guy you were messaging? Who is he?"

Celina told her the story about Cooper, Dyer, and Valquis. At the end, a sadness hung over her like the gray clouds outside. As soon as the Londano thing was cleared up, she would go see Dyer. She'd bring him a bottle of his favorite whiskey and sit with him. Talk and drink a shot. Laugh a little. Take his picture.

Ronni yawned and started gathering up the photos. "I think I'll make some popcorn and see if Mike wants any company."

"I'm going to take a shower," Celina said. "After I get out, I'll make up a bed on the sofa for you."

Ronni nodded, yawned again. "Deal."

Celina dug out clean clothes from her closet and headed for the bathroom.

Setting the water as hot as she could stand, she washed herself several times with her favorite body gel. She scrubbed until her skin was rosy and her fingers were wrinkled. She washed her hair for good measure and then stood in the stream of water and tried to unwind. Her brain was as tired as her body and the thoughts and images had finally started to slow down a bit after bombarding her all day. She needed sleep, which meant turning them off. All of them. Even the sexy Cooper ones.

Hell with that. He might have left her high and dry, but there was no turning off those. She wanted to remember the way he looked at her over dinner the night before. The way he'd held her while they slept. Her anger at him had faded throughout the day and been replaced with the sadness she felt every time she thought about the chain of events that had led her to this moment. There were so many things she wished had turned out differently. Dyer. Emilio. Cooper.

Dragging herself out of the shower, she dried off and smeared her skin with creamy lotion. The TV was back on in the living room and Celina could smell Ronni's microwave popcorn. Suddenly her stomach growled. Wrapping her hair in a towel, she pulled on clean sweatpants and a T-shirt. Then decided to blow dry her hair. If she didn't, it would be a funky disaster come morning. She had enough to face without bedhead added to the list.

After five minutes, her hair was still more wet than dry and her stomach was starting to hurt it was so empty. She gave her head one more all-over blast, straightened, and pushed the hair dryer switch to off.

She was running a pick through her hair when, *BAM*, something heavy thudded against the bathroom door. Startled, she dropped the pick in the basin. A rush of nerves tightened her stomach muscles.

"Ronni?" Instinct made her grab her gun. "That you?"

At first, all she could make out was the muffled sound of applause on the television set. Staring at the door handle, Celina pointed her gun at it. "Ronni!"

What sounded like the brush of an open palm on the wood filtered through. A hint of shadow danced along the crack at the bottom. She called Ronni's name again and then yelled for Mike. Nothing.

Taking the safety off her gun, the trained FBI agent in her took over and squashed down the fear pulsing through her body. At Quantico, she'd favored obstacle courses over hand-to-hand combat, but at that moment, the cold, sleek metal in her hand felt as right as it ever had.

Slipping the lock off the door, she moved to the side and turned the handle. Slowly, inch by inch, she let the door creak open a crack…then another inch…

Ronni's hand fell through the opening and Celina gasped. "Ronni."

She threw the door open. For a second, Ronni stood

suspended, the door no longer propping her up. Her eyes were wide, mouth opened slightly. She looked at Celina with her surprised face as Celina automatically scanned her body, looking for blood, a wound, anything that would tell her what was going on. "Ronni, what's the matter?"

Her lips moved slightly. "Help me," she whispered. The words bubbled out of her mouth on a faltering breath.

And then she fell into Celina's arms. Her weight caused Celina to lose her balance, tumbling backwards and sitting down hard on her butt with Ronni in her lap. Celina's back hit the side of the tub.

A knife handle stuck out between Ronni's shoulder blades.

Celina's hand flew to her mouth to stifle a scream. She scanned the room behind Ronni's splayed feet, the gun following her line of sight. Popcorn lay in a trail from the bag where Ronni'd dropped it next to the bathroom door, through the living room, and out of Celina's view.

The front door wasn't visible. A good chunk of the apartment was hidden as well. But she knew without looking what had happened to McBroom, Sugars and Cooper's partner, Thomas. What should have happened to her.

Frozen for a minute, her gaze slowly returned to the hilt of the knife. Carved from the antler of an elk, it was inlaid with ebony and silver. A collector's bowie knife whose blade was now jammed up to the hilt in her friend's back.

Celina checked for a pulse. Her fingers trembled so hard, she could barely find the slow, faint throb under them. Hugging Ronni to her, Celina rocked her for a second. Then she gently laid her on her stomach and rushed for her cell phone. Gun still sweeping the area, she dialed 911. Her voice sounded flat and calm as she reeled off the information to the operator, and stalked toward the door.

In the hallway, McBroom was out cold, but breathing. No blood or wound she could see. She rushed back to Ronni, ending the call with the 911 operator so she could hold her partner until the ambulance arrived.

"Celina?"

The man's voice startled her and Celina jerked up her Beretta and aimed it at his face before recognition dawned. It wasn't Emilio. It was a man who should be dead…Thomas Mann.

His gun was out and he was crouching, shifting his eyes from Celina and Ronni on the bathroom floor to the room behind him. His gaze swept over Celina again, holding for a long second on her shaking, gun-wielding hand. "Are you hurt?"

Relieved to see Thomas was alive, a sigh of relief escaped her mouth. She lowered her gun, looked at Ronni lying in her lap. *Don't die.* "I called 911," she said, but her voice sounded too soft, too calm. "McBroom is hurt too."

Thomas leaned over, checked Ronni's neck for a pulse. He disappeared into the living room. A few seconds later, he was back with the comforter off Celina's bed. Celina and Ronni were suddenly covered with mandarin orange, marigold yellow and peacock blue daisies.

On autopilot, Celina helped Thomas tuck the edges around her, around Ronni, and around the handle of the knife. She knew they dared not move her or remove the knife. *Don't die.* "What about Sugars?" she asked Thomas.

He ignored her question, scanning her face, checking her pupils like a doctor. "I need to know if you're hurt."

There was excruciating pain cramping her stomach, and like Ronni's blood seeping slowly through the layers of her cotton comforter, it spread, lancing her heart and bubbling into her throat. *Yes, I'm hurt. I feel like I've just been drawn and quartered.*

Swallowing hard, she forced her shallow breathing to deepen. Her trembling fingers threaded softly through Ronni's apricot colored hair. Another crazy daisy in bloom.

"Did you see him?" Thomas asked. "Was it Emilio Londano?"

It was a ghost. A psychotic ghost from my past.

Over the next two hours, Celina would be asked about Londano ad infinitum by everyone from the lowliest rookies all the way up the chain of command to the head directors of the FBI and DEA. The only person who didn't ask her if Emilio Londano had killed Sugars and left McBroom and Punto in critical condition that day in his second attempt to terrify her was Cooper.

When The Beast finally called her and confirmed what she already knew—that Emilio had escaped by using his twin brother as a decoy—he didn't ask questions, only said the words she'd hoped to hear from him for a different reason. "I'm coming to get you."

CHAPTER ELEVEN

FBI Headquarters, Los Angeles, California

"Agent Punto is still in surgery." Thomas's voice was calm and clear over the speaker phone. Cooper was the only one in the conference room that knew he was shitting bricks. "The knife punctured a lung, may have nicked her spinal cord. We'll know more in a few hours. Agent McBroom was hit on the head and received a concussion. Could be severe. Again, it will be awhile before we know the extent of his injury."

There were twelve of them in the room at FBI headquarters in Los Angeles; eight were part of Cooper's taskforce. Twenty-four hours before, the Londano brothers hadn't been a blip on their radar screen. Now, after one had risen from the dead and traded places with his twin, they had a dead agent and two fighting for their lives. Suddenly the Londanos were the *only* thing on their radar.

"Bring me up to speed, Agent Mann. How was the other agent killed?" Lana Custov asked. Cooper's previous unit chief had gone to the dark side. She was now a section chief for the FBI. She'd made it a point when she walked into the conference room to shake everyone's hand but Cooper's.

"Agent Sugars apparently put up a fight and was stabbed with the same knife Agent Punto was stabbed with." Thomas answered.

"And where were you, Agent Mann?" Lana looked directly at Cooper.

Cooper fought the urge to answer for Thomas, to save the kid the lashing he was about to get. He'd already prepped him for the meeting, prepped him so he wouldn't come across sounding like a rookie even though he'd been in the SCVC for five years.

"I was posted outside the apartment complex," he answered. Nothing more. *Good man.* He was following Cooper's instructions.

"And you saw nothing?" Lana said.

"No one entered or left the building from the front entrance."

Her eyes were still on Cooper. "What made you decide to investigate the situation if you saw nothing suspicious?"

Thomas's deep breath was barely perceptible. "Agent Sugars left his post at 0100 hours. I figured he was taking a leak. After five minutes, he did not return and I became suspicious and entered the building."

It was somewhat of a lie, Cooper knew, since he had the full story. When Thomas saw Sugars leave the entryway, he'd assumed the man was taking a piss because he, himself, was about to burst, and his Dew bottle was already full. Peeing on the neighbor's tree seemed like a poor choice and since he'd been placed as a lookout by Cooper and not asked officially to cover the apartment building, he hesitated to hit Celina up for the use of her bathroom. He'd left his post, scooted between the buildings and peed in the alley. Rookie move, but every agent had been there at some point, and technically Thomas should not in any way be held responsible for what was, in Cooper's opinion, the FBI's screw up.

Lana shifted her eyes to her boss, and the SCVC's director, Victor Dupé. The aging leader sat at the head of the long table and met Lana's cool gaze with one of his own. The director sat forward and spoke into the phone. "Agent Mann, run through the entire scenario for us from that point forward."

Thomas was silent for a second and Cooper knew he was

remembering what he'd told him. *Keep it simple, keep it neat, keep it short. The less said, the less skin your superiors can skin from your body.*

"I entered the building and found Agent Sugars dead by the stairwell. His throat had been slit from side to side in a fatal arc. I called it in and ascended the stairs to the third floor. In the doorway of Agent Celina Davenport's apartment, I found Agent McBroom. She was unconscious. There was a trail of popcorn from her body to the bathroom where I found Davenport cradling Agent Ronni Punto on the bathroom floor. Agent Punto had the blade of a six-inch knife buried in her upper back area, next to her right shoulder blade. The blade had been inserted horizontally to her spine. She was unconscious and her breathing erratic. Agent Davenport was unhurt and had already dialed 9-1-1."

"Agent Davenport saw nothing?"

"No, sir. She reports she took a shower and was blow-drying her hair when the situation occurred. She heard Punta fall against the bathroom door, which prompted her to open it. She did not see the perp."

"And where is Agent Davenport now?" Lana asked.

"She is at a local FBI safe house."

"Thank you, Agent Mann," Director Dupé said. "Stay put and keep us informed. I'll check back with you in an hour with further instructions."

"Yes, sir. One other thing I think you should be aware of, sir."

"What's that?"

"The media's all over this. The *Des Moines Register* has it on the front page of this morning's issue."

Dupé's jaw clenched and Cooper felt his own tighten. "How did they get hold of it so fast?"

"Agent Davenport told me she believes Emilio did it. She says it's payback for what she, the taskforce, and in particular, the FBI did to him. He wants to show the world we're all incompetent."

"Thank you, Agent Mann." Dupé disconnected the phone and looked at Cooper. "You agree with Celina's assessment?"

Keep it simple, keep it neat, keep it short. "Emilio would love to see us sweat over this. Plus, it buys him leverage. While the locals expend time and energy handling the media, he can continue hunting Celina." It made his gut crawl just to think about it. "He's looking for revenge, pure and simple."

Dupé sat in silence, everyone else in the room following his lead, as he turned the situation over in his mind. Cooper hated sitting. It was a useless waste of time. He wanted to fly back to Des Moines, find Londano, and hang him by his balls. Grab Celina and hold her tight.

But Lana was watching him. She loved knowing he'd screwed up and slept with his young former taskforce member. She was wondering how much of a relationship he actually had with Celina. She was waiting for him to jump up, pace, and ping off the walls. Then she could drop subtle hints about his questionable actions. His character. His leadership abilities. It would be her greatest joy to kick him off the case this time around. Have him removed from his position as agent-in-charge of the SCVC taskforce.

So he sat still, keeping his hands in his lap and his face blank.

Lana threw out some questions. The others tossed ideas back and forth. How did Emilio successfully substitute Enrique for himself? Were people at the prison paid off? What does the State of California now do with Enrique? Are the warrants for his arrest still good after he was declared legally dead? How can we be sure it's Emilio stalking Celina? And how do we stop him?

The questions and answers went around the table, but Cooper purposely tuned most of it out and waited for Dupé to come up with a plan of action.

"You're quiet, Agent Harris." Dupé sank back into his chair. "You must have thoughts about this. I'd like to hear them. What should we do to capture Emilio Londano?"

Payoff for being patient. "We can play this game his way, or we can play it ours. First, we have to lure him back to California so he's in our jurisdiction. Then we control the game board." Several heads on both sides of the table nodded.

"Lure him back?" Lana tapped manicured nails on the table. "Easier said than done."

Cooper tuned her out. "Once he's in our jurisdiction, we set a trap and use what he wants as bait."

Lana raised a narrow eyebrow. "He wants revenge on the FBI, Harris. You going to use all of us as bait?"

Cooper took his gaze off Dupé and looked her straight in the eye. She was always dead on with the details, but she could never grasp the big picture. Maybe she needed to spend time with Dominic Quarters and Chief Forester. "Don't flatter yourself, Lana. He doesn't want you." Her fingers stilled. "He wants Celina Davenport."

She leaned forward. "Then why didn't he kill her last night?"

"And end the game?" Cooper shook his head. "He wants to see the FBI and the DEA sweat. He likes knowing that we're sitting here racking our brains trying to figure this out. That we're running in circles playing catch up to him. He's three steps ahead of us already, but the thing he's living for right now, the ultimate power he wants is to terrorize the agent who brought him down."

There were more head nods around the table. Cooper redirected to Dupé. "If I were you, sir, I'd bring Celina Davenport back to Carlsbad."

Dupé's pager went off. He stood without missing a beat or glancing at the readout and picked up his coffee cup. "All right, Agent Harris, bring her back. Safely. Chief Custov, call the airport and get one of our Cessna's ready to fly Cooper to Des Moines. Have a safe house set up for Agent Davenport when they return." He held out his hand to Cooper, and Cooper stood to shake it. "I'll be waiting for your report when you and Agent Mann get back."

In other words, let the game begin. "Yes, sir," Cooper said and gave Lana a satisfied smile. She glared back as she rose, pushed in her chair, and swept her Daytimer off the table.

Cooper followed Dupé out with the rest of the group. Lana snuck up behind him. "Does Agent Mann know you sacrificed the last man you called partner for Celina Davenport? He's lucky he didn't end up in a wheelchair because of her as well." She snickered under her breath as she pushed past him.

It was all Cooper could do not to clock her.

Instead he snatched his cell phone from his jacket pocket and dialed Celina's. "I'm coming to get you," he said when she answered.

He tucked the sigh of relief he heard in her voice deep into his chest and went to work.

CHAPTER TWELVE

West Des Moines

The safe house was ensconced in a posh, but somehow benign neighborhood. Unlike the homes around it, it had wires on every door and window, bugs in every room and on every phone, fax, and cable line. Video cameras were tucked into the smoke detectors and ceiling fans. Everything that happened here would be recorded, analyzed, and used to not only keep her safe, but to document Emilio's guilt if he showed up.

"He'll find me here." Celina stared at her reflection in the car's window, expression closed, just like the FBI had taught her to keep it.

Forester, seated next to her, held himself responsible for the death of his agent and the injuries of the other two. Ronni was out of surgery, but still in serious condition. Forester had let Celina go to the hospital and sit with her for several hours. She hoped Ronni had heard her apologies through the drugs keeping her sedated.

So far, Forester hadn't laid any blame at her feet and that surprised Celina. All hell had broken loose at HQ, the perfect time and circumstances to use her for the fall guy. Now, though, he was stepping up and taking the responsibility on his own shoulders. And he wasn't letting her out of his sight.

Miracle of miracles, he seemed to be listening when Celina told him things. He even seemed to believe her.

That didn't stop him from questioning her, however. "We've changed cars three times and done a heat run all over Des Moines proper. Our escort keeping tabs on us swears we're not being followed. How's Londano going to find you?"

When Celina didn't respond, he sighed. "How long until he shows up?"

She shrugged. "A day at most."

Forester grunted. "Goddamn SOB." His hands formed a circle in the air. "Gonna get my hands around his little neck and squeeze it until his eyes pop out."

Looking at Forester's giant mitts, Celina found the energy to smile. He'd never get his hands on Emilio, but the image made her feel better. "Save me a seat so I can watch."

He nodded. "Damn straight. If you don't kill this piece of shit, I will."

We're bonding over killing a man. Weirdville, here we come. She held out her hand to him and felt rewarded when he grasped it across the seat between them. "Deal," she said, and they shook.

"So, how we gonna do this?"

Celina released his hand. "I have a plan, sir. I've already initiated it."

He froze, gave her an exasperated huff. "Just don't leave your gun in the car this time, okay?"

Celina laughed softly and gave him the only answer she could. "Yes, sir."

The house was small by the neighborhood's standards, but contemporary by Des Moines, Iowa's, standards. The woman that opened the front door for Celina and Forester was older than Celina by a few years, taller than her by a few inches, and could give Jillian Michaels a run for her money, even though her bulky, powder blue sweats tried to hide it. She had her hair in a ponytail and a gun hidden in the waistband of her sweatpants.

Ex-Secret Service. Had to be.

She smiled and welcomed Celina in like they were old friends. Celina wondered if she'd been told what happened to the last female agent guarding her.

Forester introduced her as Mary—no last name—a specialist the FBI hired on occasion for her services. They discussed Celina's case briefly and then Mary gave her a tour of the house. As they stepped into the bedroom Celina would be using until Cooper arrived, Mary gave her the house rules like a camp counselor. *No opening windows. No going outside without permission and an escort. No smoking.* Celina dropped her overnight bag on the floor, tested the mattress, and agreed.

Once the door closed behind Mary, Celina flopped over on her stomach and stared at the stitches in the Amish quilt draping the bed. They were meticulous, perfect in proportion, flowing one into the next with a precision she admired.

Tracing a line of them with her finger, she thought of the coming days and what would happen, but it was too exhausting to consider all the possible scenarios in her already drained state. She found instead a memory floating up of her brother Luke.

He'd put a lizard in her bed when they were kids. Living in Miami in a little white house four blocks from the Kmart store, they often found green anoles in their bathroom, on palm trees outside, and even in their pantry. That night, a light ocean breeze and a ceiling fan cooled Celina's room. It was late, and she was tired from a day spent selling her mother's flowers at the street corner. She'd been upset because one of the neighborhood bullies had taken her leftover gladiolas and stomped them into spots on the sidewalk.

She'd walked all the way back home without crying, sat through dinner with her parents and her brothers without telling anyone what had happened. But as she'd buried her face deep into the pillows on her bed later that night, she let the tears flow. Before her crying jag was over, she felt something cool and sticky crawl across her back. It wasn't the first time one of her four older brothers had stuck something alive in her bed, but that night, a dragon unfurled his tail in her stomach and breathed heat into her until all she felt was red-hot anger.

Luke, a year older, saw the look on her face when she entered the living room and started to run. She tackled him amidst her mother's shouts before he made the back door, and they both went skidding into the sandy yard. Celina hit and kicked him before her father pulled her off, and even though she got as much as she gave, including a black eye, she felt better afterward. Vindicated.

Celina and her brother both learned an important lesson. Blood relation or complete stranger, bullies would not be tolerated in her corner of Miami.

As sleep teased at her, Celina closed her eyes and let her hand stay on the tiny marching threads. Let her mind stay in the little white house in Miami. Sleep was exactly what she needed, not just to forget the awful day, but to prepare for the coming ones.

CHAPTER THIRTEEN

The sun was already setting. Cooper glanced at his watch and took into account the time difference between California and Iowa. "Just in time for the six-o'clock news and a full-blown story at ten," he said to Thomas, pulling into the driveway of the safe house. "By tomorrow morning, the major networks will have picked it up and it will go national. Everyone will know The New Face of the FBI is back in Carlsbad."

"You're taking Celina back to California and you want it on the news?" Thomas's face showed utter confusion and dislike of Cooper's plan. "Dupé's going to shit monkeys."

Cooper didn't know who was more tired, him or Thomas. They were both strung out. Cooper had caught some zzz's on Dupé's Cessna—nice of him to share the FBI's wealth since commercial flights were murder—but he was still aware of the lead weight hanging on him. Whether from sleep deprivation or the grim reality of Emilio's plan, Cooper wasn't sure.

"Celina's idea, actually. Dupé's okay with it since the media's already been tipped off. Along with the story about her, the FBI's putting out the national manhunt story on Emilio. He wanted publicity, he's got it. We're not running from this. The more publicity we generate about him, the more likely we are to catch him."

The neighborhood was relatively quiet, but a few stay-at-homes and work-at-homes were filtering out to see what was going on. A couple local uniforms had barricaded the cul-du-sac with their cars. As Cooper scanned the area, he saw the first white van drive up with a satellite dish on its roof. According to Celina, there would be at least three more to follow. So far, her plan was working.

Thomas glanced up at the house's second-story windows. "Forester's going to kill you for exposing the safe house."

Cooper watched another van arrive. The first reporters harassed the cops to let them in closer. "Lana's called Dominic Quarters and informed him what's going down. Once we get Celina in the car, Quarters, Forester, or whoever, will hold a press conference on the front steps and read the info Lana gave them. Everything else will fall into place. Dupé will deal with Forester if he's gotta problem with it. Our job is Celina."

The last words caused Thomas to turn to him, his tired eyes narrowing slightly. "When Forester kills you, am I in charge of taking Celina back?"

"Worst-case scenario—Forester kills me—then, yes, the responsibility falls to you. But come on, Forester kill me? Never happen."

Thomas looked at him as if he thought Cooper's confidence was misplaced. Cooper shrugged. "If he kills me, shoot him. In the balls. Twice."

"You got it, boss." Thomas's fist came up and Cooper banged his own in agreement.

Cooper shut off the SUV and climbed out, watching as two more local news agencies pulled up short at the barricades. He tugged his hat down on his head and adjusted his sunglasses. Thomas came around the front of the car and Cooper motioned at his jacket. "Show time, Agent Mann. Get your badge out where the cameras can see it, but keep your head turned away from them."

Thomas fished through various pockets and hung his DEA badge on his belt. "Forget Forester, Celina's going to kill you for the way you left her yesterday."

He'd be so glad to see her alive and unharmed, he'd probably make a fool out of himself and throw his arms around her. He'd been an idiot to doubt her, to leave her on her own. "She's a professional. She'll save it until we get her back to California." *I hope.*

They took the sidewalk to the front door, treading carefully over patches of ice that hadn't been cleared. Thomas rubbed his hands together, blew on them. "I'll lay odds she gets in at least one good blow before you get her out the door."

Cooper considered this as he took the front steps. "You're on."

He raised his hand to use the doorknocker, prepared for the blow Thomas was sure he was going to take and found himself face to face with Eugene Forester. "What the hell are you doing, Harris?"

Celina sat at the dining room table, halfway through a plate full of scrambled eggs and toast, and watched as Chief Forester blocked Cooper's entry. She listened to Cooper's voice, smooth and low but demanding, and felt her pulse quicken.

I'm safe now.

So glad to hear his voice, to know he was there, she wanted to run to him and throw her arms around him.

That wouldn't do, of course. But what *was* the right thing to do? Pretend she wasn't happy to see him? Act like their night together was already forgotten? Give him the cold shoulder? Setting down her fork, she pushed back the plate and rose to get her bags from the bedroom. She had more important things to worry about than how to greet him.

Cooper and Thomas pushed inside just as she was going down the hallway. "Hi, Celina," Thomas greeted her.

"Hey," she replied, her gaze on Cooper. He was hours past needing a shave, the stubble on his face giving him a slightly sinister look. Combined with his mirrored sunglasses and the frown on his face, his appearance was the Terminator Revisited.

Celina tried to tap down the relief at seeing him. Tried to call up her professional, unemotional FBI face. "Thanks for coming to escort me back."

Lame. So lame.

Cooper gave her a tight nod. "Get your things." No *hello*. No, *I'm sorry about Ronni and the others*. "We need to get moving."

Business as usual. Okay, she could do that.

"Somebody going to tell me what exactly's going on here?" Forester said, standing between Cooper and Celina.

"Part of my plan." Celina turned away, repeating in her head: *Stay professional*. She left them to get her bag and camera from the bedroom.

When she came back, Forester was on his cell phone yelling at someone—sounded like Dominic Quarters—and waving a piece of paper in the air. Mary was on hers speaking in undertones. Cooper and Thomas stood sentry by the door, hands centered in front of them, quietly waiting for her.

Thomas took her bags. Cooper handed over her coat. "Media's outside. Be sure they get a clear shot of your face."

Celina drew in a breath, braced herself. "I want to give the announcement about the manhunt."

"That's Forester's job. We want Emilio to see you, but I'm not letting you stand there in front of God and country and give Emilio a clear target."

Celina looked up into Cooper's eyes and the mirrored sunglasses showed her nothing but her own image. Tired and anxious. "You know he won't do it that way. He wants his revenge to be slow and painful. He's a psychological bully and he won't use a gun on me. Too easy. Too quick."

A nerve in Cooper's jaw jumped. He took her elbow but didn't say anything as he steered her toward the entrance.

"Don't you walk out of here," Forester yelled from the living room, cell phone stilled glued to his ear.

"Go." Cooper guided Celina through the door. As they hit the bottom step and started toward the driveway, they were met with a barrage of questions and camera flashes—the reporters had broken through the cop barrier and were flowing toward them en masse. Forester, two steps behind Cooper, drew a sharp breath as he saw the crowd advancing like a wave. "You SOB," he said to Cooper's back.

But Cooper wasn't listening. He moved Celina from the steps to the driveway, shoving her into the back of a black Durango, the same SUV he'd driven before. Thomas threw himself into the backseat next to Celina as Cooper started the SUV's engine. As the reporters closed the distance around the lawn, they continued to yell questions at them.

Cooper shifted the vehicle into gear and Celina braced. Just as he stepped on the gas, the passenger door flew open and Forester jumped in. He was breathing hard, but Celina wasn't sure if it was from trying to catch up with them or from anger.

"Director Dupé will explain everything," Cooper told him. "Now please get out and make the manhunt announcement as planned."

Celina was proud of his sincere, respectful tone. He had to be as exhausted as she was and Forester's constant goading and yelling was enough to make anyone lose their cool. But not Cooper.

"The hell I'll get out." Forester faced Celina in the back seat. "She's my agent and I am now her personal bodyguard. Where she goes, I go."

Reporters pressed around the Durango. "She's going to L.A." Cooper said, gripping the steering wheel tight, Celina knew, so he didn't do something stupid, like shove Forester out on his butt. "And I'm her new bodyguard."

Forester motioned at the street. "Then let's go to L.A. I've never been there. Heard it's full of assholes like you."

Someone banged a fist on the SUV's backend. Another leaned across the windshield with a microphone. Clamping his jaw, Cooper glanced at Celina in the rearview mirror.

She shrugged. Forester was nothing less than a bulldog. If she'd learned anything in the past six months, it was the pointlessness of fighting with him once he sunk his teeth into something.

Cooper took a deep breath, and shoved his foot down on the gas pedal. Everyone's head inside snapped back and the crowd jumped out of the way. He maneuvered around an on-looker. "Did you give them your face?" he said to Celina.

As they cleared the entrance to the neighborhood, she met his eyes in the mirror. "Did my best *Vogue* impression in the whole micro-second you let me woo the cameras."

"Score." Thomas snickered. "You owe me."

Celina lifted a questioning eyebrow.

"I don't owe you squat." Cooper took off his hat and ran a hand through his hair. "You said *before* I got her out the door."

"I don't even want to know what you two bet on." She slid down in the seat. "The first part of the trap is set. Now we see if Emilio takes the bait."

Forester switched his gaze back and forth between Cooper and Celina. "You really think Londano is watching this charade?"

They both answered in unison. "Yes."

CHAPTER FOURTEEN

The man watched the black Durango drive out of the gated community property before shifting his eyes to a male FBI agent on the front steps reading from a piece of paper. As the Fed started another sentence, the man scanned the crowd gathering around the speaker, closed his cell phone and walked around to the back of the house.

Anger brewed deep in his gut. He'd seen her this time, the face he knew as well as his own. The face America knew. The face he was soon going to cut into tiny pieces.

The house was rigged with alarms and cameras that had been installed because of men like him. He lowered his ball cap a notch and entered on cat feet.

The female agent inside looked like a normal American woman in her baggy sweatshirt and pants. She was standing in the living room, her back to him as she looked out the window next to the stone fireplace at the group gathered by the front door. She was talking on a cell phone, her ponytail bobbing with impatience as she shook her head and rubbed a hand behind her neck.

He listened for a minute, scratching the carefully shaved stubble on his chin as he heard her succinctly describe the scene that had just taken place inside the safe house. As she hung up, he moved in behind her, keenly aware of her size and strength and also of the hundreds of eyes just outside the window.

Blue Sweats tried to yell, but his forearm cut off her air

before she could make more than a squeak. Strong legs resisted his weight and she tried to jackknife her body to flip him. They tussled for a second, his extra fifty pounds of muscle, and the fact she couldn't draw air, aiding him.

Pushing her forward, he slammed her against the fireplace, knocking her head into one of the stones hard enough to daze her but not render her unconscious. Her cell phone clattered to the hearth. She struck out, landing a blow to his throat, and a kick to his shin.

For a moment, he toyed with the idea of raping her, not because she aroused him, but the idea of taking her, or any female agent, in striking distance of other enforcement officials did. But today, this moment, wasn't about him. He sparred with her for another minute, gained the upper hand, and put his face next to hers. "Where are they taking her?"

She inventoried his coffee-colored eyes, flat nose, and umber skin, and struggled to draw his likeness from her memory. She should have been able to recognize him, but she couldn't bring his name, his person, to full identity. Like so many of her counterparts, he was simply another one of *them.*

He repeated the question. She brought her knee up and fought at him, but a constant diet of kicks and punches since childhood had him parrying her attempts with ease. Again, he banged her head against the fireplace and her knees bent and bounced back. He flipped her around to face the stones, one of his hands able now to hold both her wrists. He threaded the fingers of his other hand into her hair across the back of her head and pushed her face into the rough surface. She winced but did not cry out. She would tell him something now.

"I don't know," she slurred, the stone pulling her lips out of shape.

The man glanced to his right out the window. The FBI agent on the front steps was waving off questions; his time was nearly up. He pressed harder into Blue's head and felt the intake of her breath. He shoved his body into her, jamming her breasts, her stomach, her thighs into the fireplace. Then he twisted her head to the left and raked her cheek across the stone. Her eyes squeezed shut and she whimpered as blood seeped down her skin and into the neck of her sweatshirt.

"I've already killed one agent and put two in the hospital. I will kill you if you do not tell me where she is going."

Silence, an internal struggle. He pressed harder.

"California," she whispered. "L.A."

With panther-like speed and grace, he grabbed her ponytail, snapped her head back, and slammed it as hard as his well-muscled arm allowed into the stone that had just cut her cheek. Her body slumped to the floor, covering her cell phone.

As the man passed the flat screen mounted on the wall, he blew a kiss to the computer camera it was equipped with. The Federal Bureau of Investigation was no match for him.

CHAPTER FIFTEEN

On the flight to California, riding in a nicely furnished Cessna that Celina knew was Dupé's private jet, she tried to maintain her distance from Cooper both physically and emotionally.

First, she used the plane's high-tech communication system to phone her parents and her brothers to warn them all she would once again be on their local news. She was worried about their safety and told them to be alert for anything or anyone out of the ordinary. Her mother threw a fit, begging Celina to come home. Celina explained that returning home would only endanger her family. She did her best to reassure her mother that she was going to be safe in the house the FBI had set up for her, but her mother dissolved into tears. Celina spent another half hour trying to reason with her. When she ended the call, she was almost in tears herself.

Immediately calling her youngest brother John, she told him the situation and asked him to drive over to their parents' house and console their mother. Reluctantly, he agreed.

Sinking down in the padded airplane seat, Celina closed her eyes and rubbed them.

"My mom would be freaking, too."

Cracking one eye open, Celina saw Thomas sliding into the ivory leather bucket seat across from her. He handed her a blanket. Forester was across the aisle, but appeared to be asleep.

"It's hard for her, me being an agent," Celina said, unfolding the blanket and laying it over her lap. "She strokes out just thinking about me carrying a gun."

Thomas smiled, white teeth perfect for a toothpaste commercial. "When my mom asks what I'm working on, I tell her it's top secret. National security and all that. Sometimes after a bust goes down and it's all over, I call her and tell her to watch CNN for the story. But I don't ever tell her ahead of time. She'd end up in the cardiac unit."

Thomas was incredibly cute and incredibly nice. His hair was perpetually overdue for a cut, bleached blond by the sun, and curling on the ends over his ears and around his neck. With his lean body and sun-induced freckles, he looked one hundred percent like a Southern California surfer boy. Celina had always had a thing for surfer boys. Their deep tans with the smell of the salty ocean on their skin. Their balance and love of the ride. But try as she might, she couldn't work up any attraction to Thomas. Oh, she liked him; who wouldn't? She just didn't *like* him.

She hadn't felt that kind of *like* for anyone since the first day she met Cooper. For a week after she'd been assigned to his taskforce, she could never raise him on the phone or catch him in his office. Bobbie Dyer, amused at her frustration, took pity on her and finally gave her a heads up: Cooper ran every morning on the beach around six. So the next morning, a Sunday, she'd camped out and waited for him.

Dyer's description of the SCVC agent-in-charge—"big guy with a buzz cut and a cannon hidden in his shorts"—lacked a few important details. Cooper Harris wasn't a surfer boy. Cooper Harris was all out sin on a surfboard. So perfectly packed from head to toe, the ex-Marine, ex-cop, DEA operative sported a healthy six-pack, glistening with sweat, a Dues Paid tattoo on his left arm and a mad dog tattoo on his right arm that bulged with every pump. A classic jaw line that still held the night's worth of stubble growth.

As he'd approached her, she felt his eyes—hidden as always

behind shades—rake over her in a salacious *hel*-lo, but he didn't so much as check his stride when she fell into step beside him and introduced herself. For the next three miles, he picked up his pace, his long strides making her double hers as she tried valiantly to keep up with him while still answering his questions about her background, training and experience (*none, but eager to learn, sir*).

The next two miles passed in a silent test. Would she give up? Would she have a heart attack and pass out? She wasn't in as good of shape as he was, but she had boatloads of determination. After mile eleven, Cooper stopped, looked her sad self over with just a trace of a grin on his face, and told her to meet him the next morning for another run. He'd decide on her assignment then. Barely able to stand up straight, let alone breathe, Celina had thanked him and agreed to meet him the next morning in the same spot, knowing she was dead meat if he kept up that crazy pace.

But her FBI training gave her a boost, and the next morning she endured the run again. At the Academy, they'd regularly run seven to ten miles a day. By the end of the week with Cooper, she was running a twelve-mile stretch like a marathoner and had completed her first assignment for Cooper without a hitch.

Two short weeks later, her morning runs with the agent-in-charge came to an abrupt halt as Londano entered the picture. Instead of Cooper handing her an assignment, an assignment—and a wanted criminal—had picked her.

She now stared at Thomas. "What's it like being Cooper's partner?"

He dropped his head back against the seat, flipped his hands up off the armrests in an open gesture. "Big opportunity. Big shoes to fill. Could make or break my career with the DEA."

Not exactly what she wanted to know, but Celina nodded. "Why'd he pick you to take Dyer's place?"

"The gods smiled on me?" He shrugged and gave her a wink.

"Who can understand the mind of The Beast?"

Cooper's voice came from the front of the cabin. "Watch it, Mann."

So he *was* listening. Celina sighed. It was just the four of them in the plane. Would it have been so hard for him to be the one to bring her a blanket? To sit and talk? Give her some support?

"We went waterfall tramping one weekend," Thomas said. "Guess I made an impression on him."

"Waterfall what?"

"Adrenaline cocktail. Hiking, rappelling, whitewater swimming and cliff jumping. Like a special ops obstacle course. One of the gals in our group got tangled up in a dangerous current. Sucked her under and slammed her up against the cliff below us. I jumped in and saved her."

One of the gals? Celina started to ask, but stopped herself. Cooper's past *gals* were none of her business. And she'd be damned if she'd ask one single thing about them and suggest to the eavesdropper that she might be jealous.

"So," Thomas said, "what's it like being hunted by Emilio Londano?"

Forester cracked open one eye and glared at Thomas.

"Jesus!" Cooper yelled. "Mann, get the hell away from her and let her have some peace."

"Sorry," Thomas said, exaggerating his frown to Celina. "I guess that was insensitive, huh?"

"It's okay," Celina said loudly so Cooper could hear her. "At least he cares enough to ask."

Thomas smiled at her. "Score," he said softly and held out his closed fist.

Celina smiled back, leaned forward, and banged his fist with her own. "I put Londano away once, I can do it again."

Forester harrumphed and went back to sleep. Thomas grinned. "Wonder what *Time* will do with your mug then."

"My mother framed that issue and hung it beside Jesus in

119

her living room. She doesn't understand why it embarrasses me, why it ruined my career before it even got off the ground. In my neighborhood, I'm ranked right up there with Shakira and JLo now."

"And Jesus."

They shared a laugh. Celina rearranged her blanket. "My brothers are all jealous. The four of them were named after saints while I was named after my grandmother who came from a greedy money family in Cuba. I think they assumed they were all higher in my mother's esteem simply because of that. Now," Celina held up her hands in a *what can you do* gesture. "I'm the golden child."

"Ever figure out who gave the editors all that information about you?"

"An anonymous source inside the Justice Department was all they would tell Quarters, but I think it came directly from someone inside the FBI—someone trying to undermine me. The editors couldn't believe the Bureau was upset about the article. I was Cuban American, female and top of my class at Quantico. Hell, I overcome a learning disability during my school years so they could check that box, too. The New Face of the FBI is a poster child for life, liberty, and the pursuit of happiness. In their words, 'it was too good of a story to pass up'."

She could site quotes directly from the article. *In the decade after 9/11, the men in black are giving way to the women of color.* Which wasn't true. White male special agents outnumbered Hispanic female agents forty to one. But *Time* magazine wasn't above sensationalizing a story, regardless of the facts.

"It was an inspiring article." Thomas grinned. "If I didn't know the real you, I'd be asking for your autograph. Or setting your picture beside my one of Jesus."

Celina smacked him on the arm.

Two hours later, the Cessna was over the Grand Canyon when Cooper replaced Thomas in the seat across from a sleeping Celina. Her iPod sat cradled in one hand in her blanketed lap, her head on a soft felt pillow. Celina's chest rose and fell in small puffs.

She's alive. Contentment filled him as he watched her breathe. He wished he could stop time, for another hour or two, so he could keep her in the air, away from Emilio, where he knew he could keep her safe. Emilio had gotten close, too close, and Cooper knew he would be even bolder the next time.

Only this time, he'll have to go through me.

CHAPTER SIXTEEN

Los Angeles

It was raining. Hard. Pounding the Escalade like a drum and setting Celina's teeth on edge. Cooper had the wipers on full speed and still the windshield was a blurry mess. A strong gust of wind hit the Escalade as he spun it into the parking garage of the L.A. FBI building and Celina grabbed her door's armrest. A sudden quiet descended on them and Celina unclenched her teeth.

Inside the building, past the guarded entrance, Cooper pulled her aside, giving Forester and Thomas a hand stop sign to keep them from following. His hat and jacket were gone; the sunglasses left in the Escalade. "First thing." He pointed a finger at her. "Dupé, Lana, and probably a dozen other Feds are upstairs waiting for you. My taskforce is too, along with my DEA section chief, Kipfer. They're going to want to hear every detail about what's happened so far. Keep it simple. Keep it short, and don't give more information or explanations than necessary. Choose your words carefully. Understand?"

Don't mention sex against the door. "Got it."

"Second thing," he continued, glancing around the entryway, "don't let Lana rile you. Keep the emotion off your face and out of your voice. Dupé likes you, but you're still a rookie in his eyes. Your quote to *Time* tooting your own horn was a rookie move. Quitting Quarters' unit, same thing. You need to make a good impression here, Celina, if you have any hopes of coming back to work for him in Southern California. Lana is now Dupé's right hand man and she'll be trying to trip you up. She doesn't like you. Doesn't like anyone. You'll have to stand your ground with her, but the best way to do that is to ignore her insults and snide comments and remain professional. You show emotion, get upset, she'll crucify you in front of everyone."

Lovely. "Can I make a voodoo doll of her when this is over and stick her with pins?"

The hint of a smile tweaked the right corner of his mouth. "Whatever gets you through the next hour in one piece, kid."

Kid. Even after everything she'd been through, she was still kid in his book. Well, they'd see about that.

Dupé was waiting for them on the twentieth floor with a squad of agents. A woman, a red-headed version of Dolly Parton, was standing next to him in a gorgeous Mediterranean-blue suit. Forester and Thomas were on Celina's sides, Cooper behind her.

Like their male counterparts, women were creatures of evolution. They instinctively sized up each other without giving it a second thought. Celina looked at the woman again and thought, *efficient, calculating, manipulative.*

Lana? No way. Lana was a black belt who benched two hundred pounds. The woman standing next to Dupé looked like she'd tip forward on her air-bag breasts if she lifted so much as a coffee cup.

Yet, when their eyes met, her expression was hard, eyes cold.

Lana's assessment of Celina took all of a second. She took in her kinky hair, her wrinkled clothes, and the boots on her feet, and Celina saw a mocking shadow cross her features. She shifted one petite, stilettoed-foot forward like a model posing.

Cocky, Celina added to her list.

"Celina." Victor Dupé stepped forward and reached for her hand. Celina dropped her overnight bag to the floor and accepted his handshake. There was more salt than pepper in his hair, more worry than laugh lines around his eyes. He was broad-shouldered and medium height, and when she shook his hand, he used his free one to squeeze her elbow. Very Bill Clinton, not quite regulation, but not solicitous either. He was a good man—energetic for his age and this top position—and one who cared about his agents. Celina let out the breath she was holding and gave him a small smile. She was glad to be back under his umbrella.

Dupé turned her toward the woman and introduced her. Lana Custov, ex-DEA, and now his section chief, but instead of shaking Celina's hand, Lana put her hands on her hips, a deliberate move that both snubbed Celina and opened her jacket to reveal her badge.

And her cleavage.

She had good reason to be cocky. *But I've been in Iowa where they grow them just as big and all natural.*

As Celina went to introduce Chief Forester, however, she realized the effect Lana's chest had. Forester was a deer frozen in headlights. Celina ignored Lana's look of conquest as she introduced the Chief to Dupé.

Then she asked for an update on Ronni.

"She's out of surgery," Lana said.

"I know that," Celina said. "Has her condition been upgraded?"

Lana breathed impatience. "She's in serious condition, but she'll survive." She turned to Dupé. "Everyone's in the conference room waiting."

Dupé nodded. "We have a lot to cover." He motioned them toward the bank of offices down the hall to their left. Forester fell into step beside Lana. Thomas lagged behind, exchanging a funky handshake with one of the Feds passing by.

Cooper and Celina hung back. "She's a machine," he murmured under his breath, picking up Celina's bag. "Doesn't care about anyone."

"She's a pixie in a power suit."

They stood there together for a moment staring at Lana.

Just as the woman reached the door to the conference room, Forester pulling it open for her, she turned and glanced back at them. It was a subtle, over the shoulder look, her left eyebrow rising ever so slightly at the sight of them standing together, Celina's bag in Cooper's hands. Celina saw the mocking shadow pass over her face again and a second later Lana was on her way back.

Cooper stiffened beside her.

"From here on out, the DEA has ceded authority on this case to the FBI." Lana smiled at Cooper. "Your presence here is not necessary..." She paused for effect. "Nor wanted."

Cooper opened his mouth to respond, but stopped and forcefully closed it.

Celina admired his control. She, however, was more than up for Lana's challenge. Engaging her expressionless perfunctory smile, Celina stepped toward her. "I had an instructor at Quantico who always said, 'an effective leader uses all the tools in his toolbox, and uses them wisely', meaning don't use a hammer when you need a screwdriver."

Lana took the challenge. "Your point?"

Engage warmer smile. Manipulate the manipulator. "Like you, Agent Harris has years of experience with Emilio Londano and his organization. Like you, he's looking for a successful outcome here. You may be the hammer that drives this mission forward, but when it comes time to put the screws to Emilio, you'll need the screwdriver to get the job done."

After a second, Lana mirrored her smile with absolutely no warmth. "How metaphorical of you, Agent Davenport, but from my experience Agent Harris has never been a team player. He's undisciplined, unprincipled, and"—she did that pause thing again as she glanced at Cooper—"unmanageable."

How un-*tidy*, Celina thought, keeping her smile in place. Cooper was none of those things. The complete polar opposite of those things in fact. Kind of like Lana seeming to be the exact opposite of how Cooper described her. What was with these two? "Director Dupé has already given Agents Harris and the SCVC taskforce clearance to help with this mission." Celina dropped her smile and did her best innocent look. "I'm surprised he didn't mention that to you."

Lana's lips tightened. *Bingo.* Lana knew...she just didn't know *Celina* knew.

Lana tapped her foot on the floor, passing her gaze between Celina and Cooper. Down the hall, Forester was still holding the door, gaze locked on Lana. Dupé stuck out his head. "Chief Custov?"

"Coming," she said, giving him a true smile.

Wants to snag the boss, Celina added to her list, and then something clicked in her brain that made her look at Cooper. He was a statue, looking down the hall but seeing nothing. Saying nothing. Had Lana been one of *the gals?*

Lana turned back. "Let me give you a piece of advice, rookie." She was completely cool, completely ignoring Cooper, completely emphasizing the annoying term. "You weren't the first and you won't be the last in Agent Harris's bed, but if you're ever going to be a part of *my* team, you better chose your fuck buddies with more discretion."

O-*kay.* Celina closed the distance between them, put her nose to Lana's. "How dare you tell me what—" Cooper's hand touched her arm and she stopped in mid-sentence, remembering his instructions. Taking a deep breath, she stepped back. Forced her gaze to mimic Cooper's.

Lana smiled. She marched to the door, heels clacking confidently as Forester ushered her into the conference room.

Studying Cooper's face, Celina forced herself to keep breathing. "So you and Lana..." she let her voice trail off.

"Hate each other, yes," Cooper said. "Thank God she's one of you now and I rarely have to deal with her." He gave Celina a wink and ushered her forward. "Your metaphor was off. I'm a power tool. Y'know, like a Dewalt drill driver, 12volt, XR pack kind of guy."

Cooper never joked. He was trying to take her mind off of Lana, distract her so she'd calm down.

"You lied," she said under her breath to him as they approached the conference room. "That woman has never bench-pressed a weight in her life."

"It took her less than thirty seconds to make you lose your cool," he said, matching her voice. "Never underestimate what she can do."

CHAPTER SEVENTEEN

Throughout her teenage years, Celina had a reoccurring nightmare. She stood in front of a group of people wearing nothing but a rosary. Cooper's estimate of how many people were waiting for her in the sleek, modern, high-tech conference room of L.A.'s FBI headquarters was conservative. At least twenty-four pairs of eyes focused on her as she entered the room and Celina froze in mid-stride. She double-checked to make sure she was still wearing clothes.

Most of the SCVC taskforce was present and an FBI profiler. There was also a female fugitive apprehension agent who looked like she could pass for Celina's sister.

"Sara Rios," the woman said, shaking Celina's hand. "How are you doing, Agent Davenport?"

"I've had better days." *I'd rather face Emilio than speak in front of all these people.*

Celina shook hands with the rest of them and took a seat reserved for her next to Dupé. Lana sat directly across from her, her face a blank. Cooper was also on the other side of the table, but farther down next to Thomas.

Dupé updated the group on the current situation, including the manhunt. Celina noted Emilio's picture had been added to the FBI's Top 10, hanging poster-size, on the walls. One drug cartel leader in among terrorists and serial killers. In Celina's mind, Emilio fit perfectly with the others.

Dupé directed his next comment to her. "After you left the

safe house in Des Moines, the agent in charge had a visitor."
Pushing a button on the remote in front of him, a black and
white image of the safe house's living room appeared on a
monitor in front of each person. Mary had her back to the
camera. She was talking on a cell phone and looking out the
front window next to the fireplace.

Her voice was too soft for the audio to capture, but Celina
strained to catch what she was saying. A man emerged behind
her, his back also to the camera. Not tall—about the same
height as Mary—but well-muscled. While a ball cap covered
much of his head, Celina could see his hair was dark and cut
close to his skull. He hesitated for a moment, head cocked to
listen to the agent. Mary closed the phone and he moved
toward her with grace like a cat, and something clicked in
Celina's brain.

Cooper sat expressionless, but the rigidity of his back
confirmed what Celina's mind was saying.

Emilio was that close.

The next few minutes of video unfolded in silence except for
the voices of the agent and Emilio. At the end, he left her on the
floor and blew a kiss at the camera as he passed. The ball cap
was pulled low enough to shadow his features and his hand
helped conceal even more, but something about the gesture
rang false to Celina. Before she could put her finger on it, Dupé
stopped the recording and everyone's eyes swung to her.

"What I want to know," Lana said, picking up a pen and
rolling it between her fingers, "is why Londano killed a male
agent, but only injured the female ones. Why stab the first one
in the shoulder and not in the kidney? Why interrogate this
agent and then leave her with only a head concussion like he did
McBroom?"

Celina shrugged. "Emilio has never murdered a woman that
I know of."

"Why not?"

Cooper spoke. "His MO does not include direct involvement

in murdering anyone, male or female. In the past, he's always directed Valquis or one of his other lieutenants to do his dirty work. Killing Sugars—"

"My question still stands," Lana interrupted. Her eyes continued boring into Celina. "Why didn't he kill the female agents?"

"They have names," Celina said. "Ronni, Dawn, and Mary."

Lana stopped rolling her pen and Celina felt mental ice daggers shooting across the table at her.

The profiler sat forward in his seat. A middle-aged guy with thick-rimmed glasses and a facial tic that made him smile at the end of every sentence, every pause. "Emilio and Enrique were raised by their mother." *Smile.*

"That's right," Celina jumped in, glancing around the table and settling her gaze on Dupé. "In Mexico City. Their father, Ernesto, and their uncles who ran the original drug cartel supported a local politician, Muendez, who was active in their organization. He helped them stay out of prison and they funded his rise up the political ladder. But a deal between Emilio's uncles and Muendez went bad and all the parties chose to blame Ernesto. Muendez sent some of his men to the house to find Ernesto and exact some revenge, but he wasn't there. Emilio's mother was beaten in front of the two boys but she refused to tell Muendez's men where Ernesto was hiding; maybe she honestly didn't know and eventually they killed her. Ernesto never returned to the family and Emilio and Enrique went to live with their uncle Jose Prisco. That's where they learned the business."

Lana tapped her pen three times in succession. "Was there an answer to my question in that story, Agent Davenport?"

Celina glanced at the profiler. He nodded, and answered. "Emilio is opposed to killing women because of what happened to his mother." *Smile.*

"But that fact will hardly help us capture him," Celina said, her eyes now locked on Lana's. "So really it's a moot point."

Lana's pen stopped in mid-swing.

"May I?" Celina asked Dupé, pointing at the remote. He handed it to her. "The real question is why is Emilio doing this? What's his motivation?" She rewound the last thirty seconds of the video feed and let it play again. Emilio dropped the agent and blew a kiss at the camera.

Thomas cleared his throat behind her. "You said it was revenge. He wants to make the FBI look incompetent."

Celina rewound the feed again, and the scene unfolded once more. "Too simple," she said, still distracted by the tight feeling in her stomach. "I had a lot of time on the plane ride back here to think about it and I believe revenge is too simplistic of a motive for Emilio. He's never been driven by emotion. Enrique, yes, but not Emilio. Emilio's cerebral. Goal-oriented. He's a business man, motivated by deal-making and long term strategy to further his bottom line. Revenge seems..." Her voice trailed off for a moment as Emilio blew a kiss at the camera, at her. "Trivial."

Sitting across from Cooper, the DEA section chief, Hart Kipfer, drummed his fingers on the tabletop. He was forty and balding in all the wrong places but, like Dupé, he was highly respected by all the operatives in the room. "A smart man would head for the border. Self-preservation first, payback later, when he felt safer."

"Exactly," Celina said.

The profiler agreed. "It doesn't fit with his personality to take these kinds of chances." *Smile.*

"It's like he's flaunting himself at us." Celina stared at the frozen man on the screen again. "Risking everything, when he could disappear to Mexico or South America and lay low until the worst is over. He has a complete, multi-layered business in place down there even though the Mexican *federales* took out a bunch of his connections in conjunction with our arrest. He still has contacts and people willing to risk their life for his. Why break out of prison and then not run?"

"Prison changes a man," Cooper interjected. "Especially the intelligent ones like Londano. They lose their future and start taking things one day at a time. Risk doesn't matter. Revenge does."

Dupé checked his watch. "Understanding Emilio Londano's motivation is important to figuring out his next step, but not necessarily critical. Celina?" She broke her stare at the monitor and Dupé continued. "Will Emilio follow you back here?"

"He tracked me to Des Moines. And then to the safe house. Whatever else is on his agenda, it does appear he's after me. He'll come to California."

The profiler nodded agreement; several others around the table did as well.

"If he was truly after you," Lana said, "why didn't he get you at your apartment?"

This was another thing Celina had had more time to consider. "Thomas interrupted him, I think. He probably wanted me to find Ronni and the others before he kidnapped me or tortured me, or whatever he was going to do. Thomas showed up and threw his plans off track. Self-preservation won out that time."

"How lucky for you." Lana's voice held the slightest trace of sarcasm.

Was she imagining it? Not likely since most of the men in the room dropped their eyes to the table. Everyone except Dupé and the DEA chief.

Agent Rios, the fugitive apprehension agent sitting off to the side, gave Celina a supportive smile.

Dupé steepled his fingers under his chin, considering. "I don't believe he's stupid enough to come after you now with a nationwide manhunt and a five million dollar reward on his head. Too risky."

"He seems to like risk." Forester spoke for the first time. "And a challenge. Hell, he got himself out of prison without so much as a burp."

"So how do we catch him?" Kipfer asked, but the question was directed at Cooper.

"That would be my job," Rios interjected, standing up. "While the manhunt continues, I'll coordinate follow-up on the calls made to the tip hotline. I'll also be looking at alternative ways to catch Londano in case none of those pans out."

"Has anyone called yet?" Celina asked.

Sara gave her a quirky smile. "About two hundred last I checked."

Celina heard Cooper whistle softly under his breath.

"Two hundred?" she repeated.

"He murdered an FBI agent and severely injured three others in order to get at the New Face of the FBI. He's got a lot of people's attention."

"Any credible leads?" Cooper asked.

Rios shook her head. "So far, no. Few calls have come from people here, in California, or from Iowa. Fewer still match our exact description or timeline. At this point we have three to five sightings that seem viable."

Three to five? How pathetic. Celina held back a sigh. "What can I do to help?"

"For now," Dupé told her, "I'm sending you to a safe house with guards posted around the clock."

"But," Celina started, and Dupé held up a hand to stop her. She ignored it. "But this is my case," she continued. Seeing Dupé's eyes darken, she added, "Sir."

Lana doodled on a page in her Day-Timer. "There are no safe houses available. I checked a few hours ago and they're all full."

Dupé showed disbelief. "Seven safe houses between San Diego and L.A. and they're all full?"

"L.A. has sent us three witnesses in protection for the Buffico trial. Northern CA sent us two families displaced by mudslides, and West Coast ATF is using the last two for temporary housing for some of their special units in training at Camp Pendleton. We're booked."

Frowning, Dupé shook his head. "Do you still have your apartment here in Carlsbad?" he asked Celina.

"I sublet it before I left."

Dupé rubbed his chin with his fingers. "Get a hotel room and bill it to me." He shot Forester a look. "You're staying?"

Forester gave him a brief nod. "I'll bunk with her."

Celina's smile fell off her face. Lana stopped doodling and chuckled under her breath.

Cooper cleared his throat, and Celina refused to look at him, knowing he was enjoying the image of her and Forester sharing a hotel room.

"My group can help with hotline tips," he offered.

Dupé stood up, pushing back his chair. "Good." He gathered papers and his PDA. "I have a Homeland Security meeting in Washington tomorrow at oh-eight-hundred hours. I'll be back by fourteen hundred tomorrow and we'll meet here at that time to reevaluate our position."

He pointed at Celina. "Stay in the hotel room and lay low. Agent Kipfer will set up a security detail for you. Lana will see to it you have everything else you need."

Lana sighed, and Celina recovered from her shock. "Yes, sir," she said, sending Lana a merciless smile. "Thank you, sir."

"I'll see you when I get back." His eyes lit on Celina's face for a second too long and Lana briskly closed her Day-Timer and stood. Following Dupé out of the room, she cast one long scathing look over her shoulder at Celina.

Celina glanced at Cooper. As Lana disappeared from sight, the two of them shared a smile.

"Let's find the restroom," Sara said, grabbing Celina's hand and hauling her toward the door.

"Why?" Celina grabbed her overnight bag from the floor as they passed.

"You'll see."

A minute later, Celina was in the twentieth floor women's restroom, shedding her clothes and watching Sara shed hers.

"You really think Emilio's back in California already and watching this building?"

"It's a possibility, isn't it?" She handed Celina her shirt, grabbed the one Celina handed her in exchange. "From a distance, few people would be able to tell us apart. If he's out there and decides to follow me instead of you, I'll catch him."

She dropped her eyes, kicked her left foot into the heel of the right boot, and slipped it off.

Celina put on the pink shirt and started buttoning. When Sara had pulled the other boot off, she scooted them across the concrete floor to her. "Anything I should know about your relationship with him?"

"He's both charming and vindictive." Celina took the jeans Sara handed her and tugged them on. They were tight and a little long. She zipped them up anyway. "When he's ready to kill me, he'll want to do it himself, slowly and privately."

Sara thought for a moment, sliding into Celina's jeans. "So he'll try to get close to me."

Celina sat down and drew on one of Sara's boots. It was a perfect size seven and a half. "Be cautious. He's very resourceful."

Their clothing exchange completed, Sara motioned for Celina to turn around. She wrapped Celina's hair in a low bun that she clipped at the base of Celina's neck. Celina then helped Sara muss her hair up so it looked more like hers.

"We're good," Sara said, placing an arm around Celina and turning her to face the mirror.

"Are you Cuban?" Celina asked.

"No, I'm a mishmash of a bunch of things." She pulled an FBI cap out of a backpack and stuck it on Celina's head, snugging it down low over her eyes. "Stay with your security detail at all times."

Celina shook Sara's hand. "Watch your back." She took a deep breath. "Emilio will not be happy if he figures out we've tricked him."

"If you catch him before I do," Sara said softly, "put a bullet in him and be done with it. He doesn't deserve to live."

Celina opened the door for her and thought again about Ronni and the others. Emilio deserved more than one bullet.

CHAPTER EIGHTEEN

In Celina's top ten nightmares, she never imagined anything as horrifying as spending the night in a hotel with Chief Eugene Forester. Still dressed in Sara's clothes, she sat on the single king-size bed and wondered if things could get much worse.

Celina had insisted on staying in Carlsbad. Forester had insisted on driving her to the hotel. All through L.A., he'd swerved and sworn and Celina had held on to the Jesus handle in the Taurus rental as if her life depended on it. She wondered how her security tail managed to keep up with them. To make matters worse, Forester wouldn't let her sit in the car while he picked up the key cards at the front desk for the room reserved for them. He'd insisted Celina never be out of his sight, even though her security guards were sitting directly beside them in the hotel parking lot.

She tried unsuccessfully to convince the chief to get two separate rooms, but he wouldn't cooperate. It wouldn't have mattered; the hotel was booked with the exception of one room—a single, king-size bed with not even a pullout couch. Celina sat on the bed now debating the merits of sleeping in the straight back desk chair or the bathtub.

Sleeping outside with the security guys held more appeal.

What she really wanted was to sleep with Cooper. He was outside the hotel somewhere; she could feel it. He'd told her he was going to the Carlsbad satellite office to catch up on paperwork and assign the team members he could spare to follow up on the hotline calls, but that wasn't all he was up to. Like he'd told Forester, he was assuming the position of bodyguard. He might have been out of sight, but he was keeping close tabs on her as he lay in wait for Emilio.

While the security detail and a couple of local cops formed a circle around the hotel, Cooper watched their circle. He worked like that, thought in layers. A single security layer was easy to breach. Every layer added to the circle made it harder for the perp to break through without getting caught. Emilio had become quite adept at slipping by trained law enforcement officers, killing those who stood in his way. It wasn't his style, his MO, but then like Cooper had told the group in the conference room, prison changed a man.

The Cooper on duty outside didn't fit the Cooper she'd witnessed today with Lana. The woman was competitive and mean-spirited, but Cooper's version of her was ridiculously exaggerated. Celina couldn't believe he was so immature as to make up outlandish stories. There was something more between them, she'd bet her pink polka-dot underwear on it.

Underwear. She went to her carry-on bag and rummaged through the clothing. As soon as Forester was out of the bathroom, she was going to run a big tub of hot water and take a soothing bath. Get out of Sara's clothes and relax. She'd been on such a whirlwind for the past twenty-four hours, she needed a few minutes without distractions to think about Emilio and figure out what he was really up to.

Her hand stilled in the clothes as her mind circled a mix of images. There was something about that video from the safe house in Des Moines that kept popping to the surface. Something about the way he looked or moved that was wrong. It was him, but it wasn't. Why couldn't she place it?

Just like his new smoking habit, something in his mannerisms had changed.

Making a mental note to discuss her intuition with Cooper, she went through her clothes again. Normally, she slept in as little as possible. Under the current circumstances, that was obviously out of the question.

Settling on yoga pants and a T-shirt, she went to the patio doors where she pushed the curtains aside. The room was on the top floor, facing the courtyard below. No patio, just a railing nailed across the outside of the glass to keep guests from using the patio doors and taking a big fall into the part-tropical, part-desert garden below. Mixed in with the palm trees and gardenia bushes were succulents the size of a car and cactus plants that sported spines as long as her thigh.

The hotel curved in a U-shape so that most of the rooms had an ocean view. An ocean view that, Celina decided, craning her neck to look around the leaves of a palm tree waving in front of her window, could only be seen with binoculars even on a clear day. Outside the courtyard was the front drive. Beyond that, the coastal highway, then the boardwalk, and beyond that, in the distance, the Pacific Ocean. Since it was dark, the most she could see were the flashing stoplights on the highway.

Flipping the lock on the patio door, she slid it open and took a deep breath of cool air. She could almost smell the ocean. She strained her ears, listening, and in between cars on the highway, she heard the waves. Closing her eyes, she imagined standing in the waves when this was over, and felt some of the tension drain from her shoulders.

She was stuck in a hotel room that featured a patio door without a patio, her oversized, gruff-as-a-linebacker ex-boss, and no clean underwear. But being on Emilio's list was the real nightmare, one she had to bring to an end soon, before anyone else got hurt.

"Davenport," Forester barked behind her. He was finally out of the bathroom. "Get your fanny away from that window."

Drawing in another deep breath, Celina stepped back, shut the door and closed the curtains.

Turning, she froze, staring at her boss in total disbelief.

Her boss, *sans* shirt.

"Don't you have any sense?" Forester asked her.

"Don't you have any sense of decency?"

His hands went to his hips. "What? You've never seen a man bare-chested before?"

Oh my god, Celina thought, and went and locked herself in the bathroom.

———

Long, hot soaks in the tub weren't normally her thing. She was always running late and preferred showers. But every once in a while, when her mind was in full ADD-mode, a hot bath slowed her blood pressure and reduced her mental pressure to a manageable spin.

Forester was on his cell phone when she emerged from the bathroom. He was also flipping channels on the TV back and forth between CNN, MSNBC, and Fox News and eating a slice of pizza. Celina was relieved to see he'd put a shirt on.

His gaze flicked to her, sized her up in her yoga-wear, and returned to the television. He grunted something into the phone, snapped it shut, and motioned with his head at the plate of pizza on the desk. "I ordered room service. And your friend dropped off some soda for you, but I'm guessing he mostly wanted to check on you. Wouldn't let me interrupt your bath, though."

He said 'friend' in a way that meant Cooper. The smell of sausage and mushrooms fired up her stomach. She was starving. "He's a good agent."

"Punto's improving. The lung the surgeon fixed is hanging in there and the prognosis is good. She'll need some time to recoup and maybe some physical therapy, but she said to tell you hi."

"She's awake?"

Forester nodded. "Her family's there. I talked to the sister. She said Ronni doesn't remember what happened yet. Doc claims it'll come back to her once they ease her off the sedatives and pain medication. Be a few days."

Celina nodded, glad for the update as she sat in the chair and ate pizza. It was still hot, and tasted delicious.

"You've been on all the news channels." Forester pushed a button on the remote. "Lead story."

"That was the plan," Celina said, licking grease off a finger.

"Dupé seems less than happy about your plan."

"He'll be happy when we catch Emilio."

Forester grunted and changed the channel.

There in full color was Cooper leading her away from the house in Des Moines. Celina scooted the chair forward and scanned the crowd as the camera panned the property. She was looking for anyone wearing a red ball cap. She saw no one.

"You're lucky Dupé likes you," Forester said, scanning the crowd like she was. "You seem like trouble to me. I'd have fired your ass after that *Time* thing."

The clip ended and the news anchor appeared with a head shot of Emilio hanging in the air to her right. It was a copy of a picture Celina had taken. He looked intelligent and confident. The news anchor dispatched the nationwide manhunt information.

"You're letter of the law," Celina said, eyeing the chief. "I'm more essence of the law."

Forester made an exasperated noise in the back of his throat, rose from the edge of the bed, and grabbed another slice of pizza. "The law is the law, Davenport. Don't hide behind some mumbo jumbo 'essence' crap."

Celina chuckled. "So I'm a little unconventional. I get the job done. That's why they stuck me on the SCVC taskforce."

"Huh."

They sat in silence, chewing. Another minute and the pizza was gone.

"How do you multitask so well when you're driving?" Celina asked him.

Forester raised an eyebrow.

"You know," she said, "that thing you did the first day I arrived in Des Moines. I had to ride with you to the bank robbery for my initiation. You used your knees on the steering wheel while you were loading your shotgun. Talking on the radio while you took a corner doing ninety. Cooper does that too."

Forester almost cracked a smile. He grabbed a glass from the mini-bar and opened one of the Cokes room service had delivered with the pizza. "Practice."

He offered Celina the other soda, but she grabbed a Dew instead. "That's what I told Ronni. I just need more practice."

Forester drank some soda, picked up a chocolate candy mint with the hotel's logo on the wrapper and broke it in half. He handed one tiny piece to her.

Celina accepted the mint and studied the chief. Anyone who shared a piece of chocolate wasn't all bad. She raised her quarter inch of the mint to him. "Here's to the successful capture of Emilio Londano."

Forester raised his glass, having already inhaled his portion of the mint, and took a big drink. "You sleep with him?"

She choked. The mint stuck in her throat. "Of course not!"

Forester gave her a nod. "Good. Let's get some sleep. I'll take the floor."

Cooper was six seconds from falling asleep when Thomas said, "I can handle this, Coop, if you want to catch some zzz's."

The partners were situated five hundred yards southeast of the hotel on an overpass that eventually hooked northbound traffic up to the Pacific highway. Construction work had closed the outside northbound lane, but the construction workers were long gone and Cooper had moved a few barricades and squeezed his Tacoma into the perfect vantage point. He and Thomas were protected from any late-night traffic flowing up the overpass, and could watch the back of the hotel.

It was only midnight, but they were still sleep-deprived, jet lagged, and hungry. They'd analyzed everything about Londano that had been discussed during the meeting at FBI headquarters: his means of transportation, whether or not he had a fake ID and was therefore able to fly, how soon he'd reenter California by plane, train, or automobile. They also went over a few things that hadn't been discussed in the meeting. Like what he might do to Celina if he kidnapped her.

That last discussion still grabbed Cooper by the gut.

Taking the night-vision binoculars away from his eyes, he rubbed a hand down his face. He fed his gut check with an image of Londano getting near Celina. It kept him awake better than the six cups of coffee he'd downed in the past two hours. "I want this bastard. I personally want the satisfaction of nailing him when he shows up."

The younger agent stretched out on the passenger side, stifling a yawn. "You haven't slept in days. You're a walking zombie."

"You haven't had much yourself."

"Yeah, but I'm young. Doesn't bother me."

Cooper took his focus off the hotel for a second. "You see that railing, Mann?" He gestured with his chin at the concrete and metal outside Thomas's door.

"What about it?"

"You keep it up with the disrespect and you'll be dangling by your toes from it."

Thomas chuckled. "I have no doubt you'd throw me over the

side without an ounce of remorse, *sir*." After a minute, he glanced at Cooper. "You know, you scared the shit out of me when I was assigned to the taskforce."

Cooper returned the binoculars to his eyes. "Obviously that's changed."

"That first month, I really believed you had some kind of super human powers. Celina kept throwing herself at you, but you ignored her, shut her down. The rest of us were all like, how does he do that? *Why* does he do that? Then that whole takedown with Londano and the arrests. The Dyer thing. Man, you were like a machine." He yawned, sat forward, and drummed his hands on the dashboard in a quick rhythm. "Des Moines changed that though."

Des Moines changed everything. Cooper ground his teeth together.

Thomas rolled his head around on his shoulders. "You became human just like the rest of us poor pathetic schmucks, Coop."

Cooper grunted.

"Oh, don't worry, we still know we're not worthy to kiss the boots of The Beast, but now, you know, we don't feel like such losers."

Cooper tried to work up annoyance over the comment, found he felt a touch of relief instead. "Shut up, Mann, and quit squirming." He gave the agent a hard, disdainful glare that even in the dim light from the street, Thomas should feel to his bones. "We've got a job to do here and a woman's life depends on it."

"Forester got the good job. Being Celina's personal bodyguard, getting to sleep in a nice hotel room, order room service. Tell me again why we didn't volunteer for that assignment?"

Thomas was right. Forester had suddenly become a leech. A leech that got to sleep in the same room with Celina. Cooper drew a breath, prepared to swear, but his cell phone chirped, interrupting him.

Caller ID told him it was fugitive recovery agent Sara Rios. "We received a call," she said, bypassing the normal hello. "Our man's in your neck of the woods. The Palomino Apartments in Carlsbad, fourth floor. Landlord there saw the man's face on the ten o'clock news. Says the guy's home. You know the place?"

Cooper threw the binoculars on the seat and started the SUV. The Palomino Apartments...why did that sound familiar? "We're less than a mile from it."

"SWAT team's on their way. Thought you might want to be in on the takedown."

Cooper moved the phone from his mouth and instructed Thomas to alert the agents in the inner circle to stay alert, they were following a lead. Then he slammed the vehicle into gear and shot out of the barricaded lane. "Damn straight," he said to Sara. "We'll be there."

CHAPTER NINETEEN

A sharp, rhythmic buzzing woke Celina from a deep sleep. Heart thudding, she slapped at the alarm clock on the nightstand. It didn't stop, and it was so loud, it echoed in the room. The previous night's occupant had forgotten to turn off the alarm setting, or housekeeping had accidentally knocked the switch on. She sat up, fumbled with the buttons on the clock, sure the neighbors next to her were cussing her out.

The room was dark and Celina searched for the light switch on the lamp next to the bed. The digital read out on the clock read 4:14 a.m. as she turned the switch.

No light.

"Chief," she said, over the blaring noise. She turned the alarm clock over, kept trying buttons. "I can't get this thing to shut off."

No answer.

Celina ripped the cord from the wall. Still the buzzing continued. *Battery-backup,* she thought and fumbled for the battery case. It was empty.

Celina looked around, her brain finally registering the sound.

Not an alarm clock. Fire alarm.

"Chief," she called again, all her instincts on high alert. She didn't smell smoke, but she was on the third floor. The fire could be on another floor. Her eyes adjusted somewhat to the dark room and she wondered why the auxiliary lighting hadn't come on. Did the hotel have a generator? Had it malfunctioned? Had someone tampered with it?

She felt around the nightstand for her cell phone. It wasn't there. She'd fallen asleep with it in bed. Running her hands over the tangled blankets, she still couldn't locate it.

The warning bell in her head matched the clanging of the fire alarm. She grabbed her gun from the nightstand and took a deep breath, readying herself. Where was Forester? Why didn't he answer her?

Inching her way around the end of the bed, she strained her vision, checking everything she could see. The door was closed although she couldn't tell if it was still locked. The curtains were drawn. Skirting the bed, she saw the white sheets and tan blanket piled on the floor where Forester had bedded down.

The chief was gone. She swept her gun in controlled arcs around the room, looking for any out-of-place shadow or sudden movement.

Her back to the wall, she slid around the armoire that held the television. Then the desk, making it to the curtains. As she yanked one side back from the other, soft light slipped in. Keeping herself hidden, she peeked out. All looked normal except for the people gathering below. No fire trucks. Celina scanned the windows and doors of the hotel within her view and saw no smoke.

Her heart in overdrive, she drew back from the crack in the curtains and considered her options. That's when she felt it.

Someone else was in the room.

All her senses screamed at her to get out. Without hesitation, she flipped the lock on the patio door and pushed it open, but before she could catapult herself over the iron railing, a hand grabbed her by the hair and jerked her backwards. Her chin pointing at the ceiling, she stumbled against the intruder. Definitely a man.

She jerked her right elbow back, aiming for his stomach. It caught him in the side. He barely flinched as he wrapped one arm around her waist and tugged her farther away from the window. Releasing her hair, he tried to knock the gun from her hand, but she stretched it out and firing, sent three rounds through the glass of the patio door. Glass shattered and fell to the ground and Celina hoped it was a clear enough call for help.

Over the buzzing of the alarm, the man—Emilio?—grunted with anger. He shoved her against the wall beside the desk, moving with quick efficiency to slam her wrist with the gun against the edge of the desk.

A bone snapped. Celina clamped her lips together, refusing to cry out at the pain. But her hand opened and the gun fell to the floor.

Emilio pushed her against the wall with full body contact, his face in hers, his breath warm on her cheeks as he spit angry words at her. She couldn't understand them against the backdrop of the fire alarm, but their meaning wasn't lost in the noise. Struggling, she pushed at him, but drew in a sharp breath when her right hand registered pain at the force. She tried to bring her knee up, but he'd spread her legs outside of his when he'd pushed her and the knee could do no damage.

Emilio grabbed her face with both hands and slammed her head into the wall twice with such force his dark image swam in front of her. She closed her eyes and forced her knees not to buckle. At the same time, she swung her good arm and landed a fisted blow to his stomach. She stomped on the top of his foot with hers.

The punch seemed to do little, the heel stomp even less, since she was barefoot and he wore thick leather boots. In the next second, the cold metal of a knife bit her at the base of her throat.

Although she was already pinned against the wall, she instinctively flattened herself farther, trying to become one with the paint. The tip of the knife slid down and opened a cut across her collarbone.

The fire alarm stopped. In the sudden silence, its echo

vibrated in her ears along with her breathing. Emilio was a bulky presence against her, the knife a cutting one. Her head throbbed and her vision blurred as she took another swing at him. This one he blocked, catching her wrist with his free hand and chuckling low in his throat. "You are paying for what you did. One by one, they will continue to fall, until you have no one and nothing left to live for. Then I will slit your throat."

In the hallway, men yelled. Feet pounded outside the door. "Try it. I'll put a bullet in your head."

She head-butted him, but Emilio didn't seem to care. He smacked her upside the head. "Live in fear," he murmured in her ear. And then he licked her collarbone where his knife had drawn blood.

Celina slapped his face, her pain morphing into rage.

The door opened with a swift bang. Emilio let go of her, running for the patio door.

"Halt!" a man yelled.

He didn't stop. As he grabbed the railing, the security agent fired, but Emilio was over the railing in a heartbeat, the shot sailing over his head.

Celina's security agents rushed the room to the patio doors, guns ready. Pushing herself off the wall, she hobbled past the desk and followed them. Emilio had survived the fall and was running across the courtyard, but the security team pulled up without firing a shot. The courtyard was full of people.

A moment later Emilio disappeared behind an incoming fire truck.

CHAPTER TWENTY

Red and blue lights cut through the night as Cooper shot past fire engines and drove into the hotel parking lot. A police officer stopped him, but a flash of the badge hanging around his neck got him through the barricade. He swerved around people and vehicles into a No Parking zone and parked.

The SWAT team and the taskforce had descended on The Palomino Apartment building en masse and came up empty-handed. While they'd been at the apartment Emilio Londano had rented, Emilio was at the hotel terrorizing Celina.

Cooper was so mad he was ready to spit nails.

Too late. Too goddamn late again.

Thomas, next to him, kept flashing his badge until they found a Carlsbad PD lieutenant that recognized the tight expression on Cooper's face and understood it. "Agent Davenport took a bit of a beating," Sam Pressfield told him as he led both men toward an ambulance with its doors open wide. Sam and Cooper went back to Cooper's days on the beat. "But she'll be okay."

Cooper heard the words but didn't believe them. Wouldn't believe them until he saw Celina in person. Did his own evaluation. "How'd he get to her?" he ground out between clenched teeth.

"No forced entry. We think he scored a key card. Used that."

"What about Forester?" Thomas asked. "Was he injured?"

"Agent Davenport's security detail can't find him." Pressfield pointed toward two men flanking the sides of the ambulance. Agents Simmons and McCain nodded a dour greeting.

Cooper and Thomas exchanged a glance, knew what the other was thinking. Thomas shook hands with one of the agents and Cooper took a look inside the ambulance. Celina sat on the gurney with her head between her knees. An EMT was wrapping her gun hand with white tape. "How is she?" Cooper asked.

Celina looked up and Cooper's stomach heaved. Blood covered the front of her T-shirt under a very white gauze pad taped to her collarbone. He looked away, looked back. Forced himself not to go ape-shit.

The EMT glanced up, went back to wrapping. "Broken bone in her wrist. Possible mild concussion. Superficial knife wound that requires stitches. We'll be transporting her as soon as she cooperates."

Celina smiled weakly. "I'm fine and I wanted to talk to you. Matt Simmons told me you were on your way." Her voice sounded weary and tired. "I made them wait."

Climbing in, he sat on the gurney beside her and realized with the cramped quarters, his leg had nowhere to go except against hers. He stared at the faded denim of his jeans against the soft black stretch pants she was wearing and tried to ignore the metallic smell of her blood. "What happened, Celina?"

She told him the story, all of it; from her frustration with Forester and his shirtlessness right up to the false fire alarm and the sight of Emilio disappearing into the night. "It wasn't Emilio."

Cooper shifted on the gurney to look at her more carefully. One of Emilio's neighbors had told Thomas there were two men living in the apartment they'd raided. "Who was it?"

She shook her head. "The man who attacked me…" She stopped, started again. "He was familiar, but not like Emilio. About the same size and build, but…well—" She gave him a grim half smile… "You're not going to like this."

"Enrique's still in jail. It can't be him."

"Not Enrique. Petero Valquis."

"Val's dead." As soon as he said it, he slapped his hands on his thighs. "As dead as Enrique. Shit."

"Yeah," Celina said. "My thoughts exactly." She looked back down at the bucket. "I thought it was him when I saw the tape of the safe house, but I didn't say anything. It was too crazy, even for me to believe."

The Mexican officials had kept Valquis' body in Mexico. DNA results had verified his identity, but anyone could be bought off. Or blackmailed. Threaten a person with physical torture or the death of a loved one and they'd do and say whatever you wanted. "What about his voice?"

"Fire alarm was going off so most of what he said I couldn't make out." She winced as the EMT cut the end of the tape around the splint and gave a little tug. "When the alarm stopped, he said something like, 'you are paying for what you did. One by one they will all fall until you have nothing and no one left. Then I will slit your throat.'" She shuddered. "The last thing he said was, 'live in fear.'"

The EMT looked over his handiwork and released her hand. Celina dropped her head between her knees again and drew in a deep breath. "Every time I think about it, I want to throw up," she said, bringing her injured hand in close to her body.

"She should be lying down." The EMT gave her a look of reprimand and then shifted the look to Cooper. "She's lost blood and could be going into shock. She should be at the hospital with a heavy dose of pain killers in her system and a dozen stitches in that wound."

"I don't want to lie down," she said to the floor. "And I don't want any pain killers. As soon as the nausea passes, a Diet Mountain Dew, some M&M's, and a clean shirt will do the trick."

Cooper felt queasy himself every time he looked at the blood covering her shirt and thought about Valquis touching her. He was going to hunt the bastard down and pound his fist into his face and pull his balls out through his nose and—

"They'll put you in a gown when you get to the hospital," the EMT said, ripping open a bag that held an IV drip. "You don't need clothes."

"Have they found Chief Forester?" Celina's head was back up but she was dangerously pale.

Cooper shook his head, wondering just how much longer she could remain upright.

Her eyes went back to the floor. "Oh, god. He's probably dead, too." Her voice broke. "This is my fault."

He shushed her. "Thomas is getting an update. I'll let you know as soon as we find out anything. In the meantime," he patted her leg, his fingers lingering a moment on the soft fabric, "you need to get to the hospital, get your wrist x-rayed, and get stitched up. I can't have you bleeding out before I can get you back on the SCVC team."

Her head snapped up and he saw confusion, quickly replaced by a spark of hope, at the idea of rejoining the taskforce. She nodded, a tiny dip of her chin, but then the spark left and she looked away. She bit the inside of her bottom lip and he knew she didn't want to go. "I'm serious about the clean shirt." She pulled out some forced bravado from somewhere. "No way am I wearing a hospital gown. Think you could find my bag and bring it to me?"

It was her eyes that gave her away. She'd just been attacked by a psycho who'd licked her blood and broken her wrist. Her two hundred and fifty pound bulldog was missing. Cooper knew what she was really asking him for. "I'll get the bag and I'll meet you at the hospital."

The relief that flooded her eyes and the smile she gave him this time was more enthusiastic.

Standing, he bent at the waist, and gently drew her legs up and onto the gurney. "You lie down and let the EMT take care of you. I'll meet you at the hospital and I promise I won't let you out of my sight, okay?"

Celina leaned back and drew another deep breath, still smiling. She closed her eyes and sighed. "How about that Diet Dew?"

Cooper couldn't stop himself from patting her cheek. "I'll call ahead and make sure they've got a cold one waiting for you."

Before he could take his hand away, Celina grabbed it with her good hand. It felt small but firm on his. "Thanks, Cooper."

He gave her a nod as the EMT moved in and started prepping her arm for the IV needle. Jumping out of the ambulance, Cooper took his own deep breath and forced his mind to forget about the blood and her smile and the firm warmness of her hand and focus on what he needed to do.

The first man his attention fell on was Thomas. "Go to Celina's room and get her bag and bring it back down, fast. We're following the ambulance." Thomas took off at a run and Cooper motioned to the security agent Thomas had been talking to. "Simmons, ride up front," he instructed. "Anybody or anything tries to stop this ambulance, shoot them, got it?"

The man nodded agreement and went to get in the ambulance. Cooper turned to the other man and jerked a thumb at the still open door. "McCain, you ride in back, same instructions."

As Cooper waited for Thomas to return and the EMTs to close up the ambulance, he scanned the crowd. Catching Lieutenant Pressfield's eye, he waved the man over. "Anybody see anything?"

The detective flipped through a small tablet. "Perp came in the cook's entrance, pretended to be a new guy. Left for the bathroom according to one of the busboys and never came back. Probably lifted a key card from a cleaning cart, set off the alarm and went after her. We've taken the security camera tapes to confirm all that. Crime scene investigators are already in the room."

"No sign of the FBI chief?"

Pressfield shook his head. "I requested uniforms at the

airport and the train station and we've set up roadblocks
all over Carlsbad, but the perp's probably long gone and we
don't know if he's still on foot or has snagged a car. One of
your men said you thought you had this guy a few blocks from
here."

"Call to the hotline came in. Feds have their investigators
combing the apartment to see what we can get."

"You think it was Londano?"

Cooper gave him a nod.

"He working alone?"

Celina had been shocky and her perception of what had
happened in the room might have been colored by the intensity
of the attack, the noisy fire alarm, and the lack of light. But for
all Celina's inexperience, she was a trained agent with good
instincts. Even in the worst circumstances, she would know the
difference between Emilio Londano and Petero Valquis.

Even if the asshole perp was Valquis, how did an
approximately five-ten, one hundred and eighty pound man
move another man the size of Forester without help? It didn't
compute. Forester either left under a gun or Valquis had help.
"There may be a second perp."

Thomas arrived, out of breath, Celina's bag in his hand. "Got
it."

"Check the dumpsters," Cooper told Pressfield. "Trunks and
cars within a half mile radius of this hotel. We're going to the
hospital. You can get hold of me there. I want to know
everything you come up with, and in return, I'll share
everything the DEA has on this guy."

Pressfield shook his hand and walked back into the crowd.

"You think Forester's dead," Thomas said a minute later as
Cooper gunned the Tacoma out of the parking lot behind the
ambulance.

Cooper stuck his cop light on the top of the SUV and turned
on his siren. "You don't?"

"Londano couldn't have gone far with him. Chief's a big man.

What I can't figure out is how Londano got him in the first place."

"He might have had help."

Thomas shot Cooper a look. "The second guy the neighbor talked about?"

Cooper nodded, hand tight on the wheel. "Celina said the man who attacked her wasn't Emilio. Similar, but not him."

"Enrique?"

"Enrique's still in jail awaiting his arraignment."

"Are we sure about that?"

Cooper ran a red light behind the ambulance. Decided to see how far Thomas might go with his speculation. "That attack was pretty violent for a wimp like Enrique."

"True. Enrique's more into drinking and slutting around."

"Not a lot of motivation. No balls compared to his brother."

"Plus, he doesn't have the emotional investment in Celina that Emilio does. Enrique might want revenge on her for screwing up their business, but he'd be less personal with it."

Cooper cut his gaze to Thomas. "You're starting to sound like a profiler."

"I thought about joining them." He took out his cell phone. "FBI tried to recruit me, but when I found out the profilers rarely get to shoot anybody, I quit taking their calls."

Cooper reached out, patted him on the shoulder. "Good choice."

Thomas made a call and confirmed Enrique was still in jail. As Cooper drove into the hospital parking lot, he found a slot, shut off the light, and sat watching the EMT's unload Celina from the back of the ambulance and whisk her into the ER door. "Can you think of anyone else our second man might be? Anyone else that matches your profile?"

"What are you thinking, Coop?" Thomas was watching him.

Cooper was mostly thinking about Celina and how much he hated hospitals. Hated blood. Hated Emilio Londano and every other maggot like him and Valquis who lived and breathed

Southern California air. "Celina says it was Petero Valquis."

Thomas's reaction was understated. He thought about it a minute, nodded. "It fits. At least it would if he were alive."

"Enrique's alive."

Thomas drummed his fingers on his knee. "And maybe Val is too. Interesting. That makes it a whole new ballgame, doesn't it?"

"Give me her bag."

Thomas handed him the nylon bag and Cooper caught a whiff of Celina as he set it in his lap. He didn't know if it was perfume, shampoo or what, but it smelled good. Clean and healthy and impossibly young. He handed the car keys to Thomas. "Go home, get some sleep. I'll call you with any updates."

"I want to stay. I can make some calls and do stuff from here. Keep your coffee cup full."

Looking at his partner, Cooper saw a younger version of himself, understood Thomas's request. He'd made a few like it when he was starting out in law enforcement. Thomas was a good kid and smarter than he usually let on. One of the things Cooper liked about him.

He nodded. "All right. Let's go."

CHAPTER TWENTY-ONE

"What's that?" Celina asked the nurse. The woman was short and plump and holding a syringe filled with something the ER doctor had rattled off a few minutes ago in his orders. Celina figured it was the morphine she'd told him she didn't want. The doctor had ignored her refusal and now the nurse was doing the same.

"That broken wrist must be painful." Dark curls of hair framed the nurse's face. Her nurse's top was covered with cartoon cats. "On a scale from one to ten, ten being the most painful, give me a number for your pain level."

Ten, Celina thought. *Ten plus a few, actually.* Her wrist, her hand, her whole arm ached. The ER doctor had stripped the EMT's handiwork off, x-rayed her wrist, confirmed she had a fracture, and then rewrapped it. Since her job required her to shoot a gun accurately, any problem with her wrist was serious. A specialist had been called in to discuss surgery.

Celina's whole right side throbbed from the indelicate treatment. Her hand and wrist were propped on pillows. They'd moved her out of the ER and upstairs to the med/surg floor. Her stitches hurt too. The topical Novocain the doctor had swabbed her cut with before stitching the wound closed was wearing off. And, on top of all that, her head pounded. The man who attacked her had been strong. Emilio-strong. Still, she didn't believe it was him.

Valquis. The weasel. She'd had little time around Emilio's

lieutenant while undercover, but she'd bet her last Mountain Dew it was him.

Eyeing the syringe, Celina ignored the part of her brain begging for the contents. Pain medication would make her sleep. Sleep made her an easy target. As the nurse tore open a small square pouch and pulled out an antiseptic wipe to clean a port on Celina's IV, Celina shook her head. "I don't want it," she lied.

"Don't be silly, young lady," the nurse chastised. "This will help you sleep." She stuck the end of the syringe in between her teeth and used them to remove the cap, but before she could stick the needle in the port, Celina sat up.

"I said no." She jerked out the IV tubing and the syringe went flying to the floor.

"What's going on in here?"

Cooper stood inside the door, his face a block of granite, looking from Celina to the nurse. In his hand was a soda Celina had requested. She choked back an unbidden sob of relief. Just the sight of him bringing her Mountain Dew made her want to weep.

"She's refusing to take the pain medication the doctor ordered." The nurse, pissed now, retrieved the syringe from the floor and placed the cap back on the end. "And wasting it in the process."

"I'm sorry for making you drop it." Vertigo hit and the room swam in front of her. "But I don't want to sleep."

"The doctor ordered—"

Something inside her broke, snapped as cleanly as the bone in her wrist. Shock and rage and guilt boiled inside her. "I don't give a monkey's pink ass what the doctor ordered."

With her good hand, she grabbed the metal rail on the side of the bed to keep from swooning as the room continued to spin. "I don't want pain killers. I don't want to sleep. For three nights straight, a psychotic killer has terrorized me. He's stalked me, killed an agent guarding me, and stuck a knife in my partner's back." Angry tears bubbled up in her eyes and she blinked to keep them from falling. "Tonight he beat me up and God only knows what he did to my section chief." She used her shoulder to brush away a stray tear and lowered her voice. "If I don't want the fucking morphine, than I damn well have the right to say no."

Cooper must have moved in behind her and set down the soda, because she felt his hands on her upper arms. "It's all right, Celina."

He drew her back against the pillows and spoke to the nurse, who'd taken a step back and was looking at Celina as if she'd grown a second head. "Give us a minute," he told her and the nurse sighed and gave him a curt nod.

As she retreated from the room, Celina called after her, "And I'm not a young lady. I'm a full-grown woman. An FBI agent." The door shut and Celina glanced at Cooper who had one eyebrow raised at her. "What?"

"Jesus, give the poor woman a break. She's just doing her job. You don't have to take the morphine."

Celina settled her injured wrist on the pillow and covered her eyes with her left arm. Her hair was a mess and she had no makeup on. She had exchanged the bloody T-shirt for a clean one but she smelled like the hospital: antiseptically clean and medicinal. It turned her stomach. "Damn right, I don't have to."

Celina heard a soft *ssss* beside her. Cooper had opened her Dew. She peeked under her arm and he held it out to her. "But you do need sleep." He helped her sit up and take a drink. "It's going to be hard to sleep if you're in pain."

Celina let him take the bottle out of her hand. She wiped her lips, rubbed her eyes. It felt weird using her left hand for everything. "You ever see *Nightmare on Elm Street?*"

"I don't watch horror movies, but I know what it's about."

"This is like the Emilio version." Celina slid down in the bed. "I close my eyes, the slasher comes after me."

Cooper's next words hit her hard. "I won't let him get you, Celina."

He looked worried, tired, burned out. His stubble was filling in; he'd have a beard in another day. What would happen in that time? If he stayed with her, would he be the next one to disappear? To die?

She shook her head. "You're not responsible for me. You can't protect me."

He placed his hands on the bed rails and leaned over her. "I want you to take the medicine the doctor ordered." When she started to protest, he stopped her. "A half dose of what he ordered if that makes you feel more in control, but you need to sleep. You can't help me catch Emilio if you're sleep deprived. I need you well rested and ready to go. I'll be right in that chair," he motioned to the chair in the corner. "I won't let Emilio get you."

He stared at her and Celina felt that familiar heat flowing between them.

"I promise," he added.

Her heart beat a crazy little rhythm. Her left hand reached up and touched his face. The stubble tickled her palm. "You're unbelievable," she murmured, loving him for his courage and his strength. "But, if anything happens to me, you have to promise me you will not feel responsible."

She saw something shift in his eyes. Saw them soften. "I can't promise that."

"Then no deal." She dropped her hand, forced her voice, her demeanor to channel the Terminator. "No morphine, no drugs, no sleep. The next time you turn your back, I disappear, and I handle Emilio alone. I will not let you put your life in danger or make you responsible for mine."

Cooper shoved off the bed, crossed his arms over his chest. She knew he purposely towered over her in an effort to intimidate her. "You drive a hard bargain, kid."

Celina turned her head away, focused on the wall. She was too tired to fight with him over the moniker. She hoped he didn't call her bluff. Walking out of the hospital and going after

Emilio on her own was out of the question at the moment. She couldn't even sit up without getting dizzy.

"All right," Cooper said, his acquiescence a bit too easy, too tidy. Celina knew he was cutting her slack. "I promise. Now will you take your medicine?"

Celina turned her face back to him. "A half dose, like you suggested, but just this once."

Cooper smiled at her as he pushed the call button. The nurse returned and two minutes later, the morphine was spreading through her veins, the warmth it brought with it easing the aches and pains and forcing her to relax. Cooper pulled up the chair next to her bed, sat watching her.

"At least I got in a few good jabs."

"Mary did, too, at the safe house. Guy's got to be feeling a little pain tonight as well."

"Have they found anything out about Chief Forester?" she asked, stifling a yawn.

Cooper shook his head. "Crime scene techs will turn up something. Don't worry."

She moved her arm pillow to the left side, turned her body toward Cooper and scrunched up in a fetal position. Laying her injured wrist on the pillow, she used her left hand to tug the hospital blanket over her shoulder. "How did he get Forester out of the room?"

They both knew who 'he' was. "Did you look through your overnight bag to see if anything was missing?"

"My cell phone," she told him. "I had it next to me in bed when I went to sleep in case you called with news. It was gone when I woke up, but it's probably lost in the sheets." She suddenly straightened and pushed up on her elbow. "But what if he's got my cell phone? He's got my family and friends, all their phone numbers. He can find them, Cooper."

"I'll put Thomas on it." Cooper pushed her gently back down as he went to the door. Sticking his head out, he called for Thomas.

Celina mentally groaned at the thought of another of her SCVC teammates seeing her lying in a hospital bed looking the way she did, but her concern over her family's safety trumped her ego. She gave Thomas the names of everyone in her cell phone's address book and as many numbers as she could remember off the top of her head. Maybe it was the morphine, or maybe it was the fact that she had set up most of her family and her closest friends in speed dial, but she found she couldn't remember many. As Thomas left to go to work on notifying everyone, Celina closed her eyes. "I want protection for my parents."

"Dupé will agree, I'm sure," he said. He held her good hand, and as she drifted off to sleep, she heard him on his cell phone ordering security agents to be sent to guard each of her brothers and their families as well.

CHAPTER TWENTY-TWO

Sara Rios felt Cooper Harris's eyes on her. She was standing in the bathroom of Celina's hospital room giving him, Thomas Mann, Nelson Cruz, and Mitch Holton an update on her hunt for Emilio Londano.

All of their gazes rested heavily on her, but Cooper's eyes were especially intense. He was sizing her up from the tip of her head to the soles of her shoes. He was pissed and scared and it was pure, raw emotion keeping him standing. As much as his posture—head and shoulders thrown back, arms crossed—screamed top dog, leader of the pack, his eyes told her he was second-guessing himself. While it wasn't her job to reassure him, she wanted to anyway. She liked him. He reminded her of another alpha male she just happened to be married to.

"Emilio and his partner are traveling under false ID's," she told the mix of agents in a quiet voice. Celina was sleeping, hence the meeting in the bathroom. "They used a private jet, registered to Ernesto Gonzales to fly to a private airstrip outside of Des Moines, and a similar one here in California. Flight plans were filed. Records on the Cardinal show the pilot goes by Adelie Hemingway. That name is real, but the man we traced it to is a victim of identity theft. The real Adelie is a produce manager in Bangor, Maine, and has no experience as a pilot. He had no idea his name and social security number had been stolen."

"Emilio's used the Ernesto alias before," Mitch Holton said, "in Dallas, 2008."

The others nodded. Emilio's empire had stretched into Texas and as far as Miami, his aliases as well. Sara had seen the twenty-six page database Holton had developed in 2009, and added to since cross-referencing Emilio's extensive and artistic aliases with his business deals.

"He's been able to move as fast as you," Sara said to Cooper. "You broadcasted you were bringing Celina back to L.A., but how did he find her at the hotel so quickly? He didn't buy my impersonation, obviously, and found her within twenty-four hours of her touching down." She glanced at the men forming a loose half-moon in front of her. It was a good thing the bathroom accommodated wheelchairs or they would have been shoulder to shoulder. "My guess is Emilio's got a tracking unit on her."

"A tracking device?" Thomas looked frustrated. "Couldn't be. Emilio, or whoever that was in the hotel room, didn't have physical contact with her until four a.m. this morning."

"Her bag? Her bra?" Sara shrugged one shoulder. "I don't know, but there's something like six-hundred hotels and motels between L.A. and San Diego. There's no way Emilio or anyone else could have found her at the Quality Inn in Carlsbad in under a day of landing at a desert airstrip fifty miles away unless someone told him she was there, which means we've got a leak on our team, or he's got her bugged."

Cooper continued to stare at her with his intense gaze. The wheels in his head were laying thick rubber on the roadmap of his brain. A leak or a bug. No safe houses, Lana had said, hence the hotel. "No one on my taskforce is a snitch. For the rest of the FBI, I can't vouch." He motioned at Thomas. "Get Celina's camera bag."

Sara saw light bulbs click on over the other men's heads and they exchanged nods. "She never goes anywhere without her camera," Mitch told Sara.

Thomas scooted out of the room, and a second later, returned with a black backpack. Cooper unzipped the main compartment and began handing the camera body and lenses out to Thomas. He, in turn, began an assembly line, passing the equipment to Nelson. Nelson handed the camera body to Mitch, who began an intense scan of it, opening flaps, looking through the eyepiece.

Cooper handed Sara several cords, a set of batteries, a memory chip. Grabbing a clean white towel, Sara spread it on the floor and laid out her treasure. "I used to work for another government agency," she said, checking the ends of the cords and the battery charger's internal workings. "GPS and other bugs can be microscopic and created to look just like ordinary, everyday objects. It could be her hairbrush, her glasses, her ink pen."

Nelson handed her the two lenses in his hands. She gave them a cursory glance, laid them on the towel. Cooper was running his hands inside the backpack's pockets. He withdrew a set of pictures from the outside pocket and went still, looking at the top photo.

Sara couldn't read the expression that passed over his face, but she was willing to bet the photo tapped a distant memory. One he'd forgotten until that moment.

He shoved the photos into Thomas's hands without looking at the rest and went back to rummaging in the backpack.

"Still," Thomas said, flipping casually through the photos, "how could Emilio have tagged her camera? She's always got it with her." He handed the photos off to Nelson, and said to Cooper, "Did she have her camera at the office after the Jagger take-down?"

Cooper paused in his search, scanning his brain. "That was the day she quit. I was there when she stormed out. This backpack was on her, so yes, she had it at work that day."

He turned the bag over, ran his hands over the handle at the top, the padded straps. Found nothing. "Emilio could have tagged her while she was undercover. She took a lot of photos of him while they were together."

Sara scanned the bag, her eyes stopping on the small plastic feet on the bottom. "Check the feet."

Cooper flipped the bag over. The second foot held what looked like a miniature watch battery in its hollow belly. Cooper held it up to the bathroom light. "I'll be damned," he said.

Mitch took it, turned it over in his palm. "Low-tech, but reliable. Gives off a pulse, like an alarm to a base unit once the unit's within a thirty- to fifty-mile radius."

"But how—*when*—did he plant it?" Thomas demanded. Sara could see he liked puzzles as much as she did.

"He switched places with Enrique on Monday afternoon." Creating a timeline might be the thread to unravel the mystery. "He didn't make contact with Celina until Wednesday night."

"Technically, it was Thursday morning," Thomas interrupted her.

Normally, she was the one hung up on technicalities. In her previous life as a CIA operative and counterterrorism expert, technicalities had been her specialty. Sara smiled at him. "You're right, Thomas. Thursday morning at approximately..." She looked at Cooper. "Five? Six a.m.?"

He gave her a curt nod. "Around then, yes."

From the way he bristled, she was treading on dangerously thin ice, but it was important to get a few details about that morning from the one person who was there beside Celina. "Can you tell me what happened, *time-wise*," she emphasized, "from the point you went downstairs and outside until Celina ran out, claiming Emilio was at the apartment?"

Cooper's eyes hardened, but Sara saw the wheels turning again. The look he gave her would have made most men shrink, but Sara didn't cower. She'd spent quite a bit of time with strong-willed and overbearing men. Underneath the Brawny-tough exterior they projected sat the heart of a teddy bear.

Cooper took his time before answering. "Emilio had access to her apartment for at least three or four minutes from the time she ran out to warn me until I got her back upstairs. It's possible he tagged her then."

"This tracking unit"—Mitch held it up—"could have been planted before Celina even bagged Emilio. The battery is a simple watch battery. It could transmit for a year or more before running out of power. Most likely, he or Valquis inserted it while Celina played Londano's girlfriend. He would have wanted to keep tabs on her, and this was a way to supplement direct surveillance."

"Get her other stuff," Cooper said.

Thomas slipped out and returned with Celina's overnight bag. The assembly line took place once more; the contents of the bag removed, Cooper handing the more private items—bras and panties—to Sara to examine while maintaining his stiff, professional demeanor.

The other three men seemed less interested in appearing professional. They ogled openly at the sheer fabrics, the detailed lace, until Cooper cleared his throat. In the intense glare of his eyes, each man was sentenced and found guilty. Eyes dropped in shame as they held out their hands and shuffled Celina's clothes, toothbrush, toiletries bag, and hairbrush down the assembly line, ending in a pile at Nelson's feet on a second white bath towel. The bag itself was examined thoroughly, but this time they came up empty.

Sara grabbed her tote bag hanging by its strap on the hook on the door. "I brought you footage from the security cameras at the hotel." Turning on a tablet computer, she moved in between Thomas and Nelson so everyone could get a view of the screen. As Sara held the tablet with her left hand, she used the touchscreen with her right. An image of their man, his signature cap covering his head, appeared.

"This is our perp entering through a staff entrance." The next scene showed him exiting an elevator, cap still on, but also wearing a white apron. He was pushing a large rolling bin used for laundry.

"The hallway Celina and Forester's room was on was not straight. The angles of the hotel were created to maximize their ocean views so each hallway was architecturally built to accommodate the U-shape of the building. Three rooms on each floor in the curve jutted backwards toward the east, because of the shape, but also because of the increased depth of the interior walls for support. The cameras in these hallways show the elevator on one end and the stairs on the other, but parts of the hall itself go out of view."

On the computer screen, the man followed Sara's commentary like an actor taking directions. Off the elevator with the laundry bin. Disappearing off camera. Reappearing in the next shot. "We never see him at Celina's room, but my guess is her chief ended up in that laundry bin. He may have stepped out to grab something from the vending machines or to check in with the security personnel."

"Shit," Thomas said under his breath.

Cooper shook his head. "He wouldn't have left Celina alone."

Sara reached for anything pertinent. "Unless, maybe he heard something in the hallway and went to investigate?" Footage from the parking lot appeared on screen. "This is behind the hotel on the east side near the staff entrance. The camera's mounted on a light pole, twenty feet up to avoid tampering, so the view is wide-angle and doesn't help with IDing our man."

The perp pushed the bin out the door. Another man appeared, seemingly out of the shadows. His head was covered with a hooded sweatshirt. Baggy jeans added to the overall disguise. It was hard to tell whether he was fat or just layered.

"You'll find this interesting," Sara said, using a finger to point to the men. The hooded man looked in the bin, shook his head, brought a hand out of his sweatshirt's front pocket and motioned. "They seem to be arguing."

The man in the cap threw up his hands but then the two pushed the cart to an old car partially obscured by the building.

Only the hooded man was still on camera. The trunk lid went up and the hooded man bent over, strained to pull something out of the bin and set it in the trunk. The lid went down. Hooded man gestured with his hands again and cap man came back into view, pushing the cart quickly to the entrance. He swiped a key card across the lock and was in.

The scene switched back to the inside of the hotel. Cap man followed his previous pattern. Off the elevator but without a laundry bin this time. On the wall below the camera, he set off the fire alarm, then hurried down the hallway, disappearing from view.

"At this point, he let himself into Celina's room, accosted her, and left via the balcony. There are no cameras in the courtyard except one in the pool area. He never shows up on that one."

"Someone want to tell me what you're all doing in my bathroom?"

Celina stood in the doorway. She was cradling her right arm with her left as she noted the assortment of her belongings lying in piles on the bathroom floor. The half-moons under her eyes were dark, and her hair needed brushing. Her skin was slightly ashen and she seemed younger without her makeup.

And when Celina gave each of them a questioning eyebrow raise, Sara saw the haunted look she'd once seen in her own eyes. A look that came with age and extreme circumstances.

Handing her tablet to Mitch, Sara knelt down and scooped up Celina's jeans and folded them, putting them back into her overnight bag. She'd already repacked her personal items, thank goodness. "I apologize for the invasion of privacy. We found a tracking device in your computer bag." She glanced up at Celina as she re-rolled a shirt. "That's how Emilio found you so quickly here in Carlsbad."

"You should be in bed," Cooper said. Not a request, but not exactly a demand either. Sara admired his restraint. She could tell by his posture and the set of his jaw that he wanted to reach out and grab Celina. Steady her as she now leaned on the doorframe for balance. Sara wouldn't have been surprised if he'd scooped up Celina and deposited her back into bed like a child.

"Where's your IV?" Thomas asked.

"I don't need it." Celina raised her chin a notch. She knelt and picked up her toiletries bag from the floor with her left hand. "I'm feeling a lot better."

When she rose to stand, however, she lost her balance. Sara reached out to grab her, but Cooper was already there. He'd moved so fast, even Sara, right next to her, hadn't seen him actually cross the two steps to Celina's side. Sara grabbed Celina's other elbow.

"Back to bed. Now." Cooper put an arm around Celina's waist, avoiding her injured arm. Sara stepped over the bag and camera accessories as she helped Cooper turn the young woman around.

"No," Celina protested, pulling back. Before she could say anything else, Sara's cell phone rang. Celina stopped struggling and all eyes went to her. Sara didn't give up her hold on Celina as she pulled her phone off her belt. Checking the caller ID, she heard Cooper's cell phone ring, followed by Nelson's, Mitch's and Thomas's in order.

Something was wrong. "Rios," she answered.

"The Mexican *federales* found a body about twenty minutes ago west of Tijuana," her contact inside the CIA said. "They reached out to San Diego and L.A. Word is, it's your missing chief."

The man on the phone did not work for the FBI, but he was high in the Agency hierarchy and also Sara's husband. At times, he found out info before she did, and passed it along under what he called 'interagency cooperation'.

Once upon a time, they'd been spies together, partners in every sense of the word. Their jobs were different now, but they were still partners.

Cooper held onto Celina with one hand as he answered his

phone with the other. Nelson and Mitch simultaneously answered their phones. Then Thomas.

Sara saw the look on Cooper's face. He was receiving the same news. "Thanks for the head's up," she told her husband. "You know anything else?"

In the room, Cooper released Celina and covered his other ear with his hand. "Say again?"

Nelson, Mitch, and Thomas, still side by side, were doing the same as they all tried to talk and listen to the information coming in. Cooper's gaze cut to Celina and then away. "Ah, Jesus."

"Chief Forester was filleted," Sara's husband said. "From his hairline down to his toes. It would have made ID difficult and postponed it for a while if it hadn't been for the message the killer left behind."

"Message?" Sara echoed.

"'She's next' was cut into his chest."

Ah, Jesus, is right, Sara thought. She averted her eyes from Celina, afraid the other woman might read the depth of her disgust.

"I gotta go." She disconnected, wondered how Cooper would break the news to Celina.

"What's going on in here?"

It was a nurse, standing in the doorway, her plump hands on her non-existent waistline, sending each person in the room a scolding look. "You people can't be using cell phones in the hospital. Don't you know there's a rule against that?"

Cooper hung up, ignored the nurse, and took Celina by the hand. "They found Forester."

It seemed impossible, but her face paled even more. "He's dead, isn't he?"

Nelson, Mitch, and Thomas were closing their phones and shuffling their feet.

The nurse cleared her throat. "My patient needs to get back in her bed and the rest of you need to leave. This isn't good for her."

Sara turned on the nurse. "Could you excuse us for a minute?" Without waiting for a reply, she slammed the bathroom door in the astonished nurse's face.

"Tell me the truth." Celina stared at Cooper. "Forester's dead, isn't he?"

Cooper nodded once, failed to elaborate. Sara and the others took their cue from him and remained quiet.

"Where is he? What happened to him?"

"Thomas, Nelson, Mitch, take off. Get to the site and see what you can find."

The three men nodded at Cooper and exited the room. Sara heard the nurse start badgering them.

"Tell me," Celina demanded. "I want to know. All of it."

"Maybe you should sit down," Sara said quietly. "Let's get you back to bed."

Celina's voice hitched. "It's that bad?" She shook her head when Sara moved to her side. Firmed her stance. "Just tell me. I'm not a kid. I can handle it."

Sara saw Cooper assess Celina's strength. He paused, but only for a second. Ran a hand over his face. "Emilio and his partner took him over the border, strung him out, cut him up."

Celina's face blanched. "And the message?"

"'She's next.'"

Celina rocked on her feet. Sara had her hand ready to catch her. "That bastard," Celina whispered. "Why doesn't he just take me?"

"This is not your fault," Cooper said. Sara could see that he too was waiting for Celina to lose her balance, for her knees to buckle. "They've outwitted us at every turn. Injured and killed trained FBI agents. We all look like a bunch of rookies."

Celina flinched, and Cooper said, "I didn't mean it like that…"

She raised a hand to shush him, and her voice came out steady and firm. "I'm going to put on my shoes and brush my hair." Her face was void of emotion. "Then I want you to take me there, to where they found the chief. I want to see it. See him."

Cooper and Sara exchanged a brief glance. "That's not a good idea," Cooper told her. "You don't need to see it and you haven't been discharged yet. The nurse is right. You should be in bed. The surgeon still has to look at your wrist and decide if you need surgery."

Celina turned to Sara. "Help me brush my hair and get my shoes on, will you? I can shoot with my left hand, but I can't even brush my hair with it, and I certainly can't tie my shoes with my right hand immobilized like this." She held up her hand, the brace covering half of her forearm as well.

Determined. She was definitely determined. "I'd be glad to help. Then we'll talk about you staying in the hospital, okay?"

Cooper gave Sara a grateful nod and excused himself from the bathroom. Before the door shut behind him, Sara heard the nurse giving him hell.

Sara washed Celina's face, helped her open a bottle of face cream; apply mascara and a swipe of lip gloss. The two of them sat on the floor as Sara brushed Celina's hair and Celina slowly repacked her camera bag. "What about the bug?" Celina said.

"I have an idea." Sara stood, pulled Celina to her feet. "You go with Cooper, I'll stay here. The bag and the tracking device stay with me. I'll draw him here to the hospital and maybe capture his skinny ass."

Outside the bathroom, Sara and Celina found Cooper and the nurse in a silent standoff. The nurse opened her mouth when she saw Celina, but Celina held up her good hand to stop her just like she'd done with Cooper. "I need another minute. Please."

The nurse threw her hands up and left the room.

"Sara and the bug are staying here," Celina told him. "She's going to pretend she's me, just in case Emilio decides to come after me here. You and I are going to Tijuana."

"Like hell we are."

Sara laid a hand on Cooper's arm. "She should go. She needs to see what happened and the place where it happened. It may spark something that will help us catch Emilio and the other man."

"Absolutely not."

Celina picked up her camera bag, slung it over her left shoulder. "If you don't take me, I'll call a cab."

Cooper crossed his arms over his chest. Sara held her breath.

Five minutes later, Sara crawled into the hospital bed, pulled the sheet up to her face, and stuck her Glock under the pillow.

When the nurse came in, she got quite a surprise.

CHAPTER TWENTY-THREE

South of San Diego

For the first time since their night at her apartment, Celina and Cooper were alone. Really alone. No one standing guard outside the door, no nurse about to burst in on them. As Cooper drove the highway south to the border, Celina felt his physical proximity and his emotional distance in the pit of her stomach like a tangled ball of yarn.

What she had to decide was which string to pull.

About the other night...

Prepare me for what I'm about to see...

Thanks for watching over me while I slept...

About the other night...

"How's the wrist?" Cooper asked.

"Fine," Celina lied automatically. Her fingers were stiff and swollen. The light dose of pain killers at the hospital had worn off. She flexed her hand and smiled at Cooper through the pain. "I won't be winning any arm wrestling matches for a while, but I never won those anyway." She saw the flash of disbelief in his eyes. "I'm fine. Really."

He did that chin tilt nod of his and kept his eyes on the road. "This is gonna be ugly, Celina. You're going to have to distance yourself emotionally to keep your professionalism intact."

"Yeah, I know." But in a sense, she didn't know. "Chief Forester was a human being. A gruff, unforgiving SOB, but still a human being. He didn't deserve this." She shifted in the seat, held her injured arm with her good one. At least she and Cooper were talking, maybe not about their relationship, but she'd take what she could get at this point. "So why do I have to stay professional? Why can't I pitch a fit if I'm angry? Why can't I cry if I'm sad?"

Cooper's focus stayed on the road. "Because emotions get in the way of logic. They override it. If you want to understand the killer, want to figure what motivates him and how to catch him, you have to shut down your emotions and use your brain."

Celina sighed, laid her head on the back of the seat. "You sound like my Academy teachers. I can do that with fear, but the rest..." She shook her head.

"It takes practice," Cooper said. "You have to show up and do the job, just like showing up at the firing range and plugging paper men with holes. The more you do it, the better you get at it."

"Until you're as tough and hard and impenetrable as The Beast."

That got his attention off the road. For a second. "Yes. My job requires a certain level of hardness."

"Like, on the Mohs scale of hardness, you must be a hundred."

"The Mohs scale only goes to ten."

You break the scale, trust me.

About the other night...

"So what if I look at Forester's body and I toss my cookies?"

Cooper shrugged. "Worst-case scenario, you'll pass out stone cold, but more likely you'll vomit and move on. Everyone in this job *tosses their cookies* at least once. Real-life blood and body parts are a whole lot different, a whole lot worse, than horror movies."

"Do you always view life as a worst-case scenario?"

"Yes," Cooper said to her, absolute as always.

"Why?"

"If I expect the worst, I'm never surprised by it."

"And if something less than the worst happens, you're happy?"

Another shrug. "I don't do happy."

"I noticed."

He cut his gaze to her. "If something less than the worst happens, I'm pleasantly surprised. How's that?"

Celina smiled. "Better."

They drove in silence through the border checkpoint and into Mexico. Drawing closer to the site where a host of law enforcement officials, both American and Mexican, were waiting for them, Celina decided to pull the string that was tickling her stomach the most. "About the, um, other night…"

Dirt sprayed as Cooper drove off the road. "There are better times for this conversation."

"Humor me. I need the distraction."

Celina heard him draw a slow, deep breath as he flashed his badge at a local officer who motioned them through the barricade. "I set up a rule for myself a long time ago," he said quietly. "I don't sleep with women I work with. It's unprofessional and it could endanger both our jobs and our lives. It doesn't work."

A jumble of cars huddled a few yards away, their black and tan colors blending into the desert. Red and blue lights spun circles, drawing her nearer with each flash. "This rule is based on past experience? Like, say, with, oh, let's see…Lana?"

"What?" Cooper's face showed total disbelief. Then disgust. "God, no."

"You and Lana never showed each other your badges?"

Cooper's disgust turned to amusement. He actually laughed. Out loud. "Now that is a worst-case scenario. I can't even get my mind around that one."

"So you never had sex with a co-worker," Celina said, as they pulled up alongside an unmarked brown car.

"Not until you." Cooper shifted the Tacoma into park, turned in his seat to face her. "Truth is, I've never been attracted to anyone I worked with. Until you."

"Really?" Celina's heart did happy quite well. It was good to sit in the car with Cooper's solemn gaze on her. His eyes were soft and warm, like the other night in the restaurant. Comfortable. If she could sit there for just another minute or two... "So, women with guns are not your type."

"Right."

"What *is* your type?" This wasn't a stall tactic. She really wanted to know.

Cooper pulled his badge off his belt, hung it around his neck. "Intellectuals."

"Braniacs? Like..." Celina racked her brain. "Professors? Scientists?"

"Yes," Cooper said. "Teachers, doctors, lawyers. I like smart women. In skirts."

Celina punched him on the shoulder with her left hand. It packed about half the force her right would have.

"Really short skirts," he continued, smiling as he popped open the glove compartment and took out several latex gloves. "They hop up on their desk, shake their hair loose from the required tight bun at the back of their head, and slide their skirt up."

Now Celina laughed at his surprisingly graphic sexual description of what he liked. "Logical women," she said, ignoring his blatant distraction. "You like women who use logic in their jobs."

"And wear short skirts."

Celina breathed an exasperated sigh. "Short skirts, big brains. I get it."

"Yeah." His smile was warm enough to make butter slide off pancakes. "You've got the brains, and a pair of balls to go with the smarts, but you don't wear enough short skirts."

He wanted to kiss her; she could see the look in his eyes, but Celina could also see Thomas walking toward the Tacoma behind Cooper's head. "About the other night," she said again.

Thomas rapped his knuckles on Cooper's window. Cooper straightened, saw Thomas, rolled down the window.

"Oh, hi, Celina." Thomas, surprised and confused, leaned down to look at her. "I didn't know you were coming."

"Of course I came." She reached for the door handle and bumped her cast. "Ouch, shit."

"Here, let me get that." Thomas ran around the front of the Tacoma.

"Why don't you sit tight for a minute," Cooper said. "Let me check it out first so I can prep you."

Celina took a deep breath. She called on all her mental abilities to affect her professional, unemotional face. "I can handle it," she told him with more flippancy in her voice than she intended. Thomas opened her door and she gave Cooper the chin up nod that he was always giving her. "Let's go."

Cooper met her at the front of the Tacoma, stopped her with hand on her arm. "You know JFK's brother, Bobby?"

"Sure. Attorney general who fought organized crime in the labor unions before he went on to be a U.S. Senator and then a presidential candidate. He was assassinated like his brother."

Cooper nodded. "Robert Kennedy valued courage above all other human attributes."

"Courage," Celina repeated, the word filling her mouth.

"Yes." Cooper squeezed her arm and handed her a set of gloves. "Courage, Celina."

CHAPTER TWENTY-FOUR

Celina stood in the ring of men surrounding Chief Forester's body and felt her insides draw in tight. Her stomach, her heart, her entire circulatory system, seemed to recoil and shrink, as if each could run back to the Tacoma without the rest of her body. Her feet felt like they were stuck in cement as she stared at the sight in front of her. *Fidelity, bravery, integrity,* she chanted the mantra in her head. *Courage, courage, courage.*

Chief Forester's huge body was naked, spread-eagle on the dirt. His hands and feet had been chained to stakes driven into the ground. Deep gouges caused from his struggle against the chains ringed his wrists and ankles. Blood from the knife wounds on his body had dried and caked in places on his skin; flies buzzed around.

Chunks of skin had been ripped out. The ground next to his body was stained a dark brown from more blood. Words had been roughly carved into his chest, his stomach, his thighs.

FBI slut.

Next.

Fear.

Pain.

A bloody lump of a body part was bagged and sitting on the ground next to the body. A woman, a Mexican medical examiner, moved around the body, stepping over the bag, and directing a crime scene investigator, also Mexican, to change angles and shoot close-ups of the carved words. The men watching were a mix of American and Mexican law enforcement officials.

The area had been sectored off in a grid-by-grid search for clues to the perpetrator's identity and evidence to use against him. He'd left his calling card behind; a hunting knife was bagged and tagged and being passed around the circle to Cooper. Along with it, a Taser, no doubt used to subdue Forester in order to kidnap him. As the bloody knife landed in Cooper's hands, Celina clamped her jaw down, covered her mouth, and turned her head away. *Fidelity, bravery, integrity.*

Hands touched her shoulders. Glancing around, she saw Thomas behind her. He gave her shoulders a little squeeze.

"Do we have a time of death?" Cooper's voice sounded loud and far away. Celina's ears seemed to pull in and join the rest of her insides in trying to run back to the Tacoma.

The medical examiner maintained her crouched position, attention on the body. "I would place it around four to five hours ago, but we'll know for certain once I get his body back to the lab and do a thorough examination."

A man in cowboy boots and a navy blue jacket spoke. "As soon as the Mexicali's here release the body, he'll be transported back to Carlsbad for our coroner to perform his own examination. I'll fax the results to your office, Harris, as soon as I have anything substantial."

Cooper nodded and Celina tried to remember the man's name, found she couldn't. He was American, a detective that she'd met at the hotel after the man had attacked her, but her brain would not bring up his name. She concentrated hard on his face, trying to retrieve it, trying to avoid looking at the Chief.

"Cause of death obvious?" Cooper again.

The Mexican woman looked up, her gaze evaluating Cooper now. "Not obvious." She stood, giving Cooper the opportunity to return the evaluation.

Celina did her own eval. Short hair expertly combed to

frame her strong jaw line. Subtle lip liner to emphasis her full lips. A sweep of blush across her cheeks to highlight her dark eyes. Beautiful.

"But probably exposure," the woman finished.

Brainy. Intellectual.

Fidelity, bravery, integrity.

"Exposure?" Thomas was incredulous. He pointed to the bag on the ground next to the body. "He got his balls cut off. The birds picked him apart. He bled out."

Celina's eyes went to the bag on the ground next to the Chief's body, grim understanding mixing with horror. She felt the world tip slightly, felt her knees dip.

Thomas's hands tightened on her shoulders.

"He lost a generous amount of blood," the medical examiner said, still directing her comments to Cooper. Her English sounded smooth and mellifluous with her soft Spanish accent even though she was talking about murder. "But the cuts, with the exception of the castration,"—every man in the group flinched—"were superficial. In cases like this one, exposure is the ultimate cause of death."

"Our Mexican friends found him thanks to the crows." The American detective rubbed his fingers over his mustache. "It was like a Hitchcock movie. Just hope the Chief was dead before the birds started on him."

"That I won't know for sure until I do the autopsy," Miss Coroner said.

Celina stared at the horizon. The Chief had been tortured, carved with a knife, castrated, and left to die alone in the desert.

With birds eating his flesh.

Because of her.

Her stomach heaved and she broke free of the circle, half-running, half-staggering as she gave into her body's demand to exit stage left.

Thomas called her name. She heard Cooper tell him to leave her be.

She stumbled back to the Tacoma. Setting her hands on the hood, she ignored the pain in her right wrist and braced herself for her stomach's revival. Luckily, she hadn't eaten since the previous night.

No one needed an audience when they were puking. All sets of eyes, including Cooper's were on Forester's body. All except Thomas's.

Thomas, who had tried to impress Celina with the story about his waterfall-tramping rescue.

Thomas, who had wondered how and why Cooper had ignored Celina's flirting and open invitations to share her bed.

Thomas, who had wished out loud he had been sleeping in the same room with Celina.

Hell, even here at the site of Forester's murder, he'd tripped over himself to open Celina's car door.

And now, Cooper knew, his young partner wanted more than anything to rescue the damsel in distress over at the Tacoma.

Thomas had fallen for Celina. Hard.

Cooper took a deep breath, tried to concentrate on what the medical examiner, Roxanne Navarrette, was saying to him. Previously, she'd worked with a taskforce responsible for ports of entry along the California-Mexico border. From Mexicali to Tijuana and down to Ensenada, Navarrette had seen the results of drug trafficking, violence and bribery...hundreds of murders in Mexico that had spilled over into Southern California. She had on more than one occasion given Cooper and his SCVC group extensive access to her files of victims murdered by the Arrellano-Felix organization as well as the Londano mafia.

But what he really wanted to do was box Thomas upside the head.

"This cell phone," Navarrette held up another of her department's bags, "was stuffed in the victim's mouth."

"It's Agent Davenport's," Sam Pressfield told Cooper. "That's how we initially ID'd the body."

"Any fingerprints?" Cooper took the bag from Navarrette.

Rueben Guerrero, a Mexican police detective who'd worked with Cooper's group on the Londano case, spoke up, "Dusted and sent back to our lab. Because of the current events, the department has deemed this a priority one. Results should be coming in shortly."

"Appreciate it." Cooper removed the phone from the bag with a gloved hand, flipped it open.

"The only incoming calls were from you and Celina's mother," Pressfield said. "There was your message about the take-down at the Palomino Apartments, and another six messages from Mrs. Davenport."

Cooper stared at the screen. It was a picture of the ocean with a lone runner on the beach. A man, shirtless, stood silhouetted against the setting sun.

It was him. Even though he always ran in the morning, except when he'd been out all night on a stakeout. Then he ran in the evening.

The picture didn't show the details of his face or the tattoo in his right shoulder, but Cooper knew it was him anyway.

"Hey." Thomas was suddenly looking over Cooper's shoulder at the phone, "That's—"

"Celina's phone," Cooper interrupted. "Yes." He pushed a couple of buttons looking for the call log. "Any outgoing calls?"

Pressfield shook his head no.

And then the phone in Cooper's hand rang. Private caller. Cooper tapped the answer button, but said nothing, listening. Waiting for the caller to identify him- or herself.

The caller obliged. "Give Celina the phone," the man's voice was rough and accented.

Londano.

Cooper made eye contact around the circle, and two hand motions later, every agent and officer had his gun in hand and was scanning the area.

"Emilio, buddy. You have to talk to me instead."

"Give her the phone or Valquis will kill her where she stands."

Cooper grabbed Thomas by the sleeve and propelled him toward Celina. "If you wanted her dead, you would have done it already."

A shot rang out over the desert. Dust puffed into the air a foot to the left of Cooper's feet. He pulled up short and stared in the direction it had come from as the rest of the group started scrambling for cover. A cliff, little more than a hill, was southwest of him. Londano, or at least Valquis, was close enough to spit at.

Thomas had already grabbed Celina and pulled her to the ground, using the SUV as a shield. Cooper crossed the last few feet to her, his attention never leaving the hill. He crouched next to her and she looked at him, her eyes saucers in her face. *Emilio?* She mouthed and he nodded his head.

Her fingers trembled as she reached out to take the phone with her left hand.

Courage, Cooper mouthed back at her. He hit the speaker button.

She took a deep breath. "Stop shooting. I'm here."

"You belong to me," Emilio said. "And because of your betrayal, you must be punished."

Celina's eyes narrowed. Cooper looked her in the eye and mouthed, *ask him what he wants.*

But she looked away. "If you want to punish me," she countered, "than let's have a go at it. You and me. One on one."

Emilio laughed without humor. "That would be too easy, Celina."

Now she straightened her back and Cooper almost took the phone away before she could say something stupid, like...

"Scared of me, Emilio?"

...issue a challenge.

Emilio snorted, a partial laugh.

"That's it, isn't it?" Celina said. "You sent Valquis to nab Chief Forester, because you're afraid to come face-to-face with me yourself. You know I'll get you, just like I did that night on the beach."

"Your chief screamed your name before he died."

Celina stiffened, gripped the phone harder. "Except this time," she said, as if she hadn't heard, "I'll use *my* gun and I won't just *point* it at you."

She paused, eyes still narrowed, staring past Cooper, past Thomas, seeing something Cooper could only imagine. "This time, I'll shoot you. Not to kill, just to wound. You're a man in name only at this point, Emilio, because this time, when I show you up? When this FBI agent takes you out? You'll have a very large scar between your legs as a daily reminder of who you messed with."

Emilio did not laugh this time. "You will die, begging for your life just like the others, Celina. But not until I've tattooed your body like I did your chief's. Not until I've violated every inch of you."

The phone went dead.

Celina, still in her trance, handed it to Cooper. Then before he could say anything, she rose to a standing position...

And took two long strides out from behind the Tacoma into the scrub brush, raising her arms to the sky. Cooper reached for her leg, but she dodged him. "Here I am, you chicken shit, son of a bitch," she yelled, moving away from Cooper, away from his protection.

She ran another half dozen quick, forceful steps out into the open. "Make true on your promises. Come and get me. I'm right here. Take me out. Right now. Do it!"

Shit, Cooper thought. *This is not what I meant when I told her to have courage.*

Thomas was up and moving as fast as Cooper. The two were neck and neck, but Cooper reached Celina a split second sooner. Thomas raised his gun, ready to cover Cooper's back.

Cooper picked her up by the waist and twirled her around so his back was toward the sniper rifle.

All the other agents, including the coroner, were in guarded positions. Guns were drawn and covering Cooper as he ran Celina back to the truck, set her firmly down in the dirt, and crouched behind the vehicle, pulling her down with him. They were both breathing hard.

Celina stared at the ground.

"What the hell was that?" Thomas spit at Celina. He was back at the side of the truck, too, both hands on his gun pointed over the hood. His hands shook slightly.

Yep, his new partner was in love with Celina. Waterfall tramping like he'd never experienced before.

A small sound came from her lips and Cooper glanced at her. She was jerking in air, hyperventilating as she tried to get control of her emotions.

"No one...else....dies," she said, looking up at Cooper. Something had definitely changed in her eyes. They were hard, no longer as innocent as they had been minutes before.

He patted her leg. "Okay." He really didn't know what else to say. He wanted to comfort her somehow, but there was nothing he could do. She'd just challenged Emilio to a one-on-one confrontation.

She nodded her head. "Except Emilio." Her eyes, trance-like again, stared at the ground. "He's...mine."

Cooper patted her leg again and realized his own hands were shaking.

CHAPTER TWENTY-FIVE

Carlsbad

Cooper's house was vintage midcentury-modern Southern California. Nestled in the side of a steep granite cliff, the 1950's one-story looked over scrub brush and palm trees at the bottom. Its roofline blended with the texture of the cliff rising behind it. As the Tacoma wound its way up the inclined drive, the sun was setting in the West, orange and pink waves bathing the terracotta stones around the front French-style doors.

It had been hours since Celina had seen Chief Forester's body. After Emilio's phone call, the manhunt had kicked into high gear. A helicopter flew over the open ground and the nearby hills. ATV's and dune buggies covered the desert area, searching for any trail. Forensics teams covered every square foot radiating out from Forester's body in a grid-by-grid search.

Sara Rios arrived, taking Celina on foot to examine the site believed to be ground zero. They assumed Valquis had been the one to shoot at Cooper, but they weren't sure. Either way, both men had been present, so Sara and Celina searched on hands and knees with at least a dozen other agents until they uncovered a hole in the ground…an opening to a tunnel.

The Londano mafia as well as others had used tunnels under the U.S.-Mexican border for years. Structurally unsound and too small for shipments of drugs, the tunnels' main purpose was for escape. Emilio had planned well. He'd brought Chief

Forester to that specific area to kill him and lie in wait for the multi-agency gathering to take place before him. Celina's presence had been an unexpected but pleasant surprise and he'd used it to its full-court press advantage.

By the time Sara and Celina found the entrance to the tunnel, Emilio had an hour lead time on them. Not knowing where the tunnel ended, not knowing what was waiting for anyone brave enough to crawl inside, a tactical unit had been called in. Another hour wait.

The two men who'd entered on the Mexico side of the border lost radio contact with those above ground at least a dozen times. Every time their end went silent, Celina's stomach cramped. Every time radio contact was restored, she hugged herself. *No one else dies* became her new mantra.

The tunnel spanned north less than ten miles, ending abruptly at a cave-in. Consensus was that Emilio had intentionally caused the cave-in, but Celina held out hope he'd been crushed in it.

Back in Carlsbad now, Cooper drove into the carport, shut off the SUV. He'd brought her here, to his home, to stay the night. He hadn't asked her permission, hadn't so much as discussed it as an option. He'd simply loaded her into the massive black vehicle and driven back across the border.

Late afternoon traffic between San Diego and Carlsbad gridlocked sporadically, making the drive back to the surf town slow. Neither of them spoke, comfortable with the silence that enveloped them, but lost in their own thoughts of Emilio Londano's and his partner's whereabouts.

Celina sat looking at the house while Cooper grabbed her bags out of the back. He came to her side, opened her door, and gave her his hand to help her out. Bobby Dyer had told her once that Cooper never invited anyone to his house. It was his private space, his personal sanctuary where he balanced out the demands of his career. Bobby had been there, of course, but not the others on the taskforce. *He doesn't mix work and his personal life*, Bobby had once told her. *Just like he doesn't bring personal stuff to work.*

Celina sat still, ignoring Cooper's hand. "You shouldn't have brought me here."

"I passed the *shouldn't* line with you a few days ago."

"There's a line?"

"Between you and me, yes." His eyes were so tired, Celina felt sorry for him. "At least there was, until I crossed it in Des Moines."

"So you brought me home with you because you suddenly realized you're in love with me?" She tried to sound coy, like she was joking, even though she wasn't. "This is your knight-in-shining-armor mode? Like at the hospital?"

He simply stared at her.

"Okay, not so much. So why *did* you bring me here?"

"You need a safe place to stay. I need some sleep. So far, I've sucked at my bodyguard job, and I intend to step up my game."

Logical, of course. Celina sighed. "I'll be safer here than I was at the hotel?"

"Yes." Cooper grabbed her good arm and guided her off the seat. "But not if we continue to stand out here and yak."

Cooper led her through the side entrance off the carport, which brought them into an open kitchen and dining area. A modern glass and steel dining table sat in front of a floor-to-ceiling window. It looked out on fichus trees, palms, and ferns. A fifty-gallon fish tank held various brightly colored fish, some as big as Celina's hand.

Cooper set down her bags on the floor, pressed keys on a security alarm system pad. Moving to the kitchen, he flipped a light on over the sink, offered her a bottle of water. Celina took it and leaned on the counter while he grabbed a second bottle for himself. In silence again, they both drank.

"Thought that was you." Bobby Dyer zoomed into the kitchen in a motorized wheelchair.

"Bobby!" Celina threw her arms around him, bending down

to hug him as best she could with her water in one hand and the other immobilized.

"Hey, gorgeous," Bobby pulled her tight. "About time you came to see me."

Celina stood again, motioned at his face. "Nice beard. You look like Colin Farrell in *The New World.*"

He rubbed his chin with a hand. "Exactly what I've been telling Eliza. She says Ferrell's still hotter. Can you believe that?" He lowered his eyebrows and dropped his chin. "I've even got the tormented glare down pat. What do you think?"

Celina laughed, forgetting for a moment. "I think Colin better move over."

"Smart girl," he said to Cooper.

"So *not* a girl," Celina countered.

Cooper drank more water. "What's the latest?"

Bobby grew serious. "Emilio's in the wind, so is Val. Fingerprints from the hotel and the apartment confirm both men were there. The rifle he used to shoot at you, Coop, was stolen. Identification number filed off, but ATF believes it came from a shipment they confiscated over a year ago in El Paso. Same make and model as a dozen others. Our Mexican *compadres* are mining the tunnel to see where it leads, but that will take days. Meanwhile," he turned his wheelchair around and said over his shoulder, "I've got some new toys for you."

Down a hallway, Celina followed Cooper who was following Bobby. She glimpsed a stone fireplace in the living room, which was done in chocolates and blues. A bar and lounge area came next. The glass doors led outside to a pool. A master bedroom filled with guitars and surfboards made her gawk.

Cooper cleared his throat and she hurried to catch up. The room Bobby led them to was replete with high-tech gadgets. Windowless, it was part recording studio, part computer hub, and part security center. Dark paneling covered the walls. Hanging from the walls in a semi-circle were flat screen TV's showing camera shots from around the house and driveway.

Acoustic tiles overhead flattened Bobby's voice as he spoke. "Percocet." He lifted a small brown bottle off the table beside him and handed it to Celina. "For pain management. One pill every six to eight hours. You can supplement Motrin in between doses if you need it."

The afternoon had been full of the search for Emilio. Celina had used that as her pain management. It had made her feel better to be hunting Emilio, rather than waiting for him to show up.

On the endless ride back to Carlsbad, she'd felt the swelling and sharp pains in her wrist catch up with her, and had almost asked Cooper to stop at the drug store for aspirin.

"Thank you." She took the bottle and skipped the lecture about sharing prescriptions. "Have you heard how Ronni's doing?"

"Her condition's improved. Before you left the Tijuana site, Coop called me and asked me to check on her. You can call her any time now. Doctor said she could talk to you."

Bobby held up a cell phone, "And you can do it with this new phone, properly bugged and wired and encrypted so Emilio can't locate you when you use it, but if he does, I can trace a location he's calling from faster than with your old phone. I got most of your address book entered already." He smiled at her. "The only thing left to do is set up your speed-dial numbers."

Celina was touched. She slipped the flat black case into the back pocket of her jeans. "Thank you. Does Ronni remember what happened?"

Bobby shook his head. "It may be a few days or even longer before her short-term memories come back."

He pointed at a line of Motorola two-way radios docked in separate stations. "Next, we have these babies. One for each of us. I borrowed these from my friend in the Army. Each SC700R has a range of twelve miles even in backcountry where cell phones won't work. Rechargeable with battery backup. This call button," he pressed a red half-moon and the other radios emitted a high-pitched squeal, "gives an emergency alarm. Trouble finds you, hit the button. The others give a readout of your GPS coordinates."

Handing Celina and Cooper each one, Bobby stuck one on his belt buckle. The fourth, he pointed at. "I'll give this one to Thomas when he shows up."

"And why do we need these?" Celina asked.

"Easier and faster communication," Cooper told her. "Ever try dialing a phone with your left hand? Even 911 is a bitch with a broken wrist. Cell phone towers go down or you're out of their limited range, you're in trouble. If you get into a situation, you need either one of us, hit the button. We'll find you. Of course that is, if you're in range."

Celina looked back and forth between the two men in front of her. "You think Emilio and Valquis will track me here, to this house."

"They're getting bold," Bobby said. "You ditched the tracking device Em had on you but he still has a lot of resources, his biggest one being Valquis. It's too risky not to take every safety precaution."

"The net around him is growing smaller," Cooper added. "Should have had him today."

"Shoulda, woulda, coulda," Bobby chanted. "Forget it. We move forward and we do it smart."

Cooper played with his radio. "We need to figure out how to stop them."

"Sara showed me the tape of the hotel," Celina said. "It was definitely Valquis and Emilio."

Bobby backed up his wheelchair, swiveling it so he was facing a flat screen computer and keyboard. "I've got the video from the safe house and the hotel. Let's watch them together and do some brainstorming."

Cooper pulled up a chair for Celina, grabbed one for himself. The three sat in silence watching the scenes unfold. Over the next twenty minutes, they rewound, played, discussed, argued.

There were moments Celina had to look away from the screen. Look away from Valquis, who still lived in her nightmares. She gingerly touched the bandage on her collarbone. Rubbed her arm.

The alarm system alerted them a car was approaching the house. "Eliza," Bobby told Cooper. "I sent her for groceries."

As Cooper took three environmentally friendly bags out of Eliza's hands in the kitchen, Celina greeted her with a hug. "It's good to see you," Eliza said, gently squeezing Celina's arms as she looked her over from head to toe. Her kind eyes lingered on Celina's injuries. "How are you holding up?"

Cooper flipped a light switch and under-the-cabinet recessed lights came on. Eliza's long hair was pulled back in her signature braid. The tiny crow's feet in the corners of her eyes were visible even in the soft light, but Celina liked them. They reminded her of her mother, whose kind eyes and soft voice were always reassuring.

"I've had better days," Celina admitted, "but I'm not complaining."

Eliza offered another hug and Celina rested her cheek against the older woman's shoulder. "We're all so glad to have you back."

If Celina had closed her eyes, she would have fallen asleep in Eliza's embrace. She was that tired.

Eliza stepped back. "Let's put the guys on kitchen duty and you and I will get you settled in the guest bedroom, okay?"

Celina nodded. The guest bedroom.

"Put her in my room," Cooper said, and when everyone looked at him, he added, "The guest bedroom isn't a bedroom anymore." When no one moved, he said, "I'll sleep on the couch."

Eliza nodded, patted Celina on the shoulder, and helped her gather her camera and overnight bag, both of which Sara had returned to her. They left Cooper and Bobby in the kitchen.

Cooper's bedroom was all straight lines and clean surfaces

like the rest of the house. The bed was unmade, the black and tan comforter on the floor. Eliza picked it up, shook it out, and gave the bed a cursory glance before biting the inside of her cheek. "I'll find some clean sheets."

A dark-stained credenza of drawers ran underneath a bank of windows that looked out at the backyard. What yard there was, anyway. Twenty feet beyond the pool was a screen of thin-trunked trees and behind those, the cliff. Beautiful, but Celina barely registered the view.

Her gaze stayed fixed on the credenza where a framed photo was perched. A photo of a woman and a young boy.

The woman stared back at her with long sun-bleached hair and a wide smile, the boy hung over her left shoulder, his arm around her neck. He, too, was grinning at the camera. Carefree, happy. His eyes, his face, familiar. Small replicas of Cooper's.

Celina's legs went weak. When Eliza came back with a stack of clean bed linens, Celina sat on the bed, the photograph in her hands.

"That's Cooper's wife," Eliza said, and at Celina's horrified look, corrected herself. "Ex-wife, excuse me." She smiled sadly, setting down the sheets. "Her name's Melinda. Cooper never told you about her?"

Celina could no more than shake her head.

"It was a brief marriage when they were both very young. Only lasted a few years, but they had Owen. Isn't he mischievous looking?"

Celina's headed nodded yes of its own will.

"He's a good boy. Misses his dad a lot."

Celina gave her a questioning look and Eliza again smiled. "Oh, Cooper's a good dad, don't get me wrong. He spends as much time as he can with him, but his job..." Eliza shrugged. "It's demanding. And dangerous. He claims he doesn't see Owen enough because of his odd hours, but between you and me, I think Cooper worries about someone trying to get back at him by using Owen."

Celina returned the photo to the credenza and went through the motions to help Eliza strip the sheets off Cooper's bed and replace them with clean ones. Eliza chatted lightly about the weather, about Bobby's vices, about Cooper's good nature. Celina said nothing.

She'd known little about Cooper's past until that moment. He was a secretive person. No Facebook page or other social media, and his personnel files were off limits to everyone except the upper echelons of the DEA and FBI. Celina wasn't one to snoop anyway, and had convinced herself she didn't care what skeletons he might have in his closet. Everyone had a bony secret or two to hide.

But she'd never suspected Cooper had a son. An ex-wife.

He'd never mentioned them. No one on the SCVC taskforce had either during Celina's stint with them. Of course, her assignment with the group had lasted only a few months and most of that time was undercover, not in the office where the men and women discussed personal issues and gossiped.

When Eliza left her alone to unpack her stuff and use the master bathroom, Celina sat on the bed again and stared at the picture.

Cooper was a father. It was hard to wrap her mind around it.

CHAPTER TWENTY-SIX

Celina, standing in the open doorway, stared at the covered pool.

As Cooper walked by, he used the tongs in his hand to point at it. He was grilling dinner for them. "Do you want to swim? Or at least soak your toes?"

Winter in Southern California was balmy compared to what she'd left behind in Des Moines. The current high temperatures were record setting for this time of year. Still, the thought of stripping down and diving in, stepping out from the doorway of Cooper's fortress and out into the early evening made her feel exposed. "Too cold," she said, shaking her head. "And I don't have my suit."

"Pool's heated," Dyer said from behind her.

Cooper brushed by her on his way to the kitchen, stopped. "I've got some trunks you could use. Probably an old tank top."

Celina glanced back and forth between the two men. They'd both been watching her intently. Too intently. "Can't swim with this," she said, holding up her casted wrist.

"I can wrap it." Eliza set a stack of plates on the table. "We can put a plastic bag over it and tape the edges down to keep it dry. Might not be graceful, but you could at least get in and not worry about getting it wet."

Celina tucked her wrist against her stomach. It felt like a brick at the end of her arm. She couldn't stroke, that was for sure, but they were all so worried about her, so intent on helping her somehow, she felt the need to comply. She glanced back outside at the pool. Even with the cover on, it was sleek and inviting. Solar landscape lights dotted the edges of the patio. Fire leapt in the stone fireplace, the sound of sizzling meat reaching her ears as the steaks shed droplets of fat.

"You're safe here," Cooper said, suddenly beside her. His voice was barely above a murmur. Beyond the soft light of the pool area, the thin trees and cliff blended into a dark wall, surrounding the house.

I won't be safe until Emilio's dead, Celina thought. *Until Valquis is dead.*

"Okay," she said, wanting to please him. "I'll go for a swim."

Stroke…slap…stroke…breathe.
Stroke…slap…stroke…breathe.

Cooper's pool was a standard rectangle, perfect for laps. The water rushed past Celina's face and over her body like cold fingers. She closed her eyes and kept her pace as steady as she could with the brick on her wrist. It had taken her more than a minute to find her balance and a productive rhythm. Her heart now beat solidly in her chest and her mind cleared. For now, it was just her and the water.

Stroke…slap…stroke…breathe.

She lost track of her lap total and finally stopped when her muscles were on fire and her lungs screamed for relief. Instead of getting out, she floated on her back and stared at the sky. Flat gray clouds covering everything, threatening rain. She thought of the sky back in Des Moines where clouds like those meant snow. She thought of Forester and Sugars, who would never see clouds again. She let the tears she'd been holding back slide out the corners of her eyes and down into the chlorinated water.

Exhausted, she finally climbed out of the pool. The cool night air sent her scurrying for the stack of navy blue and white striped towels Eliza had set next to the lounge chairs. They smelled freshly washed and felt warm against her cold skin. With clumsy movements, she wrapped her hair in one and used another to dry her body. Then she grabbed two more, wrapped herself in them, and sank into the nearest lounge chair.

Cooper came out of the house carrying a platter for the meat. He moved some foil-wrapped potatoes over on the large stone grill and flipped the steaks. Then he stirred the coals underneath and flames leapt up for a moment before dying back down. He sprinkled seasoning over the steaks and took a swig from his nearby beer bottle. He swept a look at her and then disappeared into the house.

A minute later, he returned with a fresh beer and a fleece blanket. He offered her the beer, but she shook her head no. Setting it down on the nearby tabletop, he threw the blanket over her legs. It was winter white with blue polar bears. The blanket stitch around the edges matched the bears. Celina snuggled under its weight as he tucked it under her chin, over her shoulders, under her legs and around her feet. She tried to speak, to say thank you, but the words wouldn't come. Instead, mummy-like, she watched him take the beer and walk back to the grill. Content just to watch him, she closed off thoughts about Emilio, about the men he'd had Valquis kill because of her.

Cooper's sure movements as he cooked and replaced the pool's cover consumed her. His stillness as he watched the quiet woods next to the house and enjoyed his beer gave her relief. A rock steadiness that was better than pills at easing her pain, better than a high-tech security system, and trained SCVC taskforce members camped around the perimeter of the house. Contemplating this, she fell asleep.

CHAPTER TWENTY-SEVEN

The steaks were done and Cooper was ready to eat. Celina, however, was sleeping on his lounge chair. "If I leave the meat on the grill any longer," he said to Dyer as they watched Celina from inside, "it'll overcook. If I pull it off the grill, I have to wake her up."

Dyer seemed to find Cooper's predicament amusing. A small smile danced around the edges of his mouth. "What happened when she saw her chief's body?"

Cooper remembered the look on her face when she'd seen Forester naked and bloody. The numbness that had taken over her personality and the cold detachment she'd embraced to shut down her emotions was exactly what he'd told her to do. But it wasn't good. "She held up pretty well initially. When Navarrette discussed cause of death, bam. It hit her."

"What did Emilio say to her on the phone?"

Cooper felt his guts draw in. "Told her she was his and because of her betrayal she must be punished."

"And she challenged him."

"Yes." Foolhardy kid. "Val could have killed her right there."

"He could have killed her at her apartment. At the hotel."

Dyer didn't have to remind him. Cooper's brain now had an endless loop of worst-case scenes in it. There was the one of him stumbling back upstairs to her apartment, thinking about waking her for a continuation of their night, only to find her blood all over the floor, the bed, and the walls. Her vacant eyes staring at him.

Or the one of him seeing a body bag on a gurney leaving the entrance to the hotel. Men in dark jumpsuits loading the body into the coroner's van.

"Your steaks are going to be crispy," Eliza called from the kitchen sink. She was cutting up red peppers and onions.

Cooper lifted his chin to acknowledge Eliza's comment, lowered his voice to Dyer. "How soon until Valquis shows up here?"

Dyer shrugged. "A while. He doesn't know where you live and the manhunt is so intense right now, he'd be smart to lay low."

"Why is he helping Emilio? What does he get out of this?"

"Been wondering that myself. If law enforcement thought you were dead, wouldn't you start over? Build a new empire?"

"Suckerfish."

Dyer frowned. "What?"

Cooper pointed at his fish tank. "Suckerfish use other fish, like sharks, for food and shelter; sharks use suckerfish to stay clean. It's symbiosis. Same thing in the world of drug empires."

"Valquis is a suckerfish—Emilio pays him to terrorize people, which is his dream job. Emilio is the shark who doesn't want to get his hands dirty."

"Exactly." Cooper walked out on the patio. As he stopped at the grill, he watched Celina's eyes move under their lids, listened to her breathing. Her face was free of makeup. The towel wrapped around her hair had come undone and loose tendrils of brown tumbled around her face and down her neck. Her chest rose and fell, and he remembered her wet body climbing out of his pool, his old swim trunks sticking to her curvy legs, his white tank top melted to her breasts. He'd watched her dry the water off her legs and grown so hard he could have drilled holes in the kitchen tile. He'd gone to the fish tank and fed the fish to hide his obvious reaction.

Looking down, he suddenly realized he was growing hard again. Turning away from Dyer's ever-watchful gaze, Cooper made a lot of work out of taking up the steaks, checking the potatoes, dousing the flames. Fat drops of rain fell and he walked over to Celina and woke her.

Groggily she gathered up her blanket and followed him into the house. The smell of the steaks and the baked potatoes was strong. She sniffed and sighed deeply. "Smells good," she said before disappearing down the hall to the bedroom.

Cooper felt like whistling. A ridiculous reaction but there it was. When he looked up from unloading the potatoes on the four separate plates, Eliza was smiling at him. That pained smile she always got when she wanted to discuss his past life. "She knows, Cooper, honey. About Owen. And Melinda." At Cooper's blank stare, she added, "She saw the photo in your bedroom."

Cooper mentally kicked himself. He'd forgotten about the photo. Forgotten in a small way about his past. He set the steaks on the table, went to the counter, and poured Celina a glass of pinot noir. Took it to her place and set it there for her. He should go talk to her right now. Some part of him told him that.

But the steaks were already overdone, and Dyer and Eliza were there, and just like the other night, the timing was all wrong. "Let's eat." He pulled out a chair for Celina as she entered the room.

She accepted it without looking at him. As he sat at the other end, she kept her eyes on the table. Made polite small talk as Eliza forced conversation and cut Celina's steak for her. She ate awkwardly, but refused help with anything else, and complimented Cooper's cooking. She barely sipped at the wine.

Eliza shot looks at Cooper. Dyer, good man that he was, brought up photography, asking Celina's advice on a long-range lens for his new Canon Rebel digital camera. The hundred-mile stare left Celina's face, her eyes met Dyer's as she asked about the kind of shots he wanted to take. She sipped more wine, nodded her head, offered to take him shopping after their current situation was over.

"Why didn't you become a professional photographer, Celina?" Eliza asked. "Why did you become an FBI agent?"

Celina looked down at her plate, suddenly self-conscious, a small smile passing across her lips. "As a child, I wanted to be a painter like my aunt Colette. She painted oil portraits of children and they were so perfect, so lifelike. I wanted to do that." Celina chuckled softly, glanced around the table at them. "But my paintings were awful. Truly awful. Everyone else in my family, my mother, my brothers, all of them, could draw or paint or write. Even sing. But me? Nothing. Not a creative bone in my body. My brother John used to tell me I'd been left on the doorstep of the church and our parents adopted me. That I wasn't really part of the family."

"We told my little brother Austin a similar story." Dyer had an evil gleam in his eye. "Carl and I always told him we found him in the woods behind our house and Mom said we could keep him for a pet."

Celina smiled. "My brothers would like you."

Dyer held up his wine glass to her. "My brothers would like you too."

Eliza punched his arm and they all laughed.

"For my ninth birthday," Celina continued, "my grandmother Colette gave me a camera, and it was like opening the door to another world. I became fascinated with butterfly wings and antennas. The backs of children's hands. These micro-worlds that existed all around me. I could see pictures inside of pictures. Tiny stories that went with these tiny worlds. It was..." She shook her head, shrugged one shoulder, "all I wanted to do."

Cooper had stopped eating to listen to her. He'd never thought about Celina as a young girl. About her family. He'd thought her photography was interesting and he knew she was selling some of it through legitimate sources, but he'd never wondered why she'd chosen the FBI over her obvious passion. "So why'd you end up at the Academy?"

She looked at him, that small smile still in place. She was tired and scared and uncertain. Scared of Emilio and Valquis. Uncertain of her place in his house, but she was covering it all remarkably well. "My parents have a strong work and moral ethic. They believe in giving back to the community as well as pushing yourself to excel in your chosen field. My brother, Matt, is a cardiac specialist in Seattle. Mark is a public defender in Bakersfield. Luke's a marine biologist. Johnny, well, he's kind of the black sheep of the family. He writes graphic novels and illustrates them himself, but he sits on a board for a local children's hospital so Mom and Pop cut him slack for that. When it came to me," another shrug, "neither Mom nor Pop believed I could make a decent living off photography. My only other interest was being a cop, but I didn't want to work the streets. I saw a lot of bad stuff with cops growing up in Miami. I didn't want that, didn't want to be the one harassing people I knew, arresting people I grew up with. The FBI on the other hand seemed cool. I talked to a recruiter at school and she steered me in this direction."

"You have four brothers named Matthew, Mark, Luke, and John," Eliza said, eyebrows raised.

Celina laughed. "Yes, we're Catholic. Mom hoped for a full dozen."

"Why'd she name you Celina?" Dyer asked. "That's not biblical, is it?"

"My name is Celina Colette Maria Davenport. I'm named after both my Cuban grandmother, Celina, and my American grandmother, whose family is from Britain and Wales. Maria is, of course, in reference to the Virgin."

"Davenport sounds English," Eliza said.

Celina nodded. "My grandfather Davenport is English and Irish. My brothers, Matt and Mark are Irish twins." When everyone looked quizzical, Celina elaborated. "They were born in the same year. Matt was born in January. Mark, ten months later."

Eliza and Dyer laughed. Eliza said, "But you were the end of the line for your mother?"

"The four boys were quite a handful. Even before she had me, I think she'd given up wanting a dozen."

"I don't blame her," Eliza said, "and I can see why you're good at taking care of yourself. Having four older brothers makes you pretty tough, huh?"

Celina's smile faded and her hands went into her lap. "Tough enough," she said quietly.

CHAPTER TWENTY-EIGHT

While Cooper was in the shower, Celina moved her bags into the living room, fluffed the pillows on the couch and sat down to wait. She flipped channels on the TV and turned it off when not even a rerun of CSI kept her mind off Cooper standing naked under running water.

Bobby was still in the house, having sent Eliza home and declaring he would take first watch so Cooper could sleep, but he'd disappeared down the hall, holing up in the computer room. Celina knew he was giving her and Cooper space so they could talk.

She *was* going to talk to Cooper. She'd been thinking about what to say ever since she saw the picture of Owen. Cooper's son put a new perspective on things. He was Cooper's only real responsibility. And so Celina had her speech ready—the one about leaving so she wouldn't endanger Cooper—but when he emerged from the bathroom and sauntered into the living room in nothing but a pair of board shorts, his wet hair combed back, and the stubble still on his face, her breath caught in her chest and the words in her brain got all mixed up.

He took in her bags on the floor, her bug-eyed expression. "What's up?"

"I, uh." She closed her eyes, shook her head to clear it. "You take the bed. I'll sleep in here."

"It's no problem."

"I've had several naps today. I'm wound for sound." Standing up, she smoothed her shirt with her left hand. "I'm going to hang out with Bobby for a while. If I get tired, I'll crash on the couch."

He was too much of a gentleman to let her sleep on his couch. "Celina."

"Cooper," Celina mimicked his tone. "Take the damn bed."

She brushed by him, hoping fervently he would reach out and grab her, pull her into his bedroom and make wild, passionate love to her, but when he didn't, she went to find Bobby.

In the back room, Dyer was studying the security monitors. He glanced up at her when she entered, saw the look on her face, and went back to the monitors. "Tough day."

Celina flopped into a chair next to him. "The day from hell."

"Want to talk about it?"

"No. Yes." She shook her head, rubbed her temples with her fingers. Blew out a long sigh. "I can't stay here."

He was silent, frowning at the screens in front of him. "And your other option is?"

"I know, I know. I've got nowhere to go. Anywhere I land, I endanger other people, but that's the reason I can't stay here either. Cooper's got a kid. I mean…oh, hell." She leaned forward and dropped her head between her knees. "If he gets killed or injured because of me…"

She drew a deep breath, let it out slowly, "I can't live with that, Bobby. I can't."

"Hey, hey." He rubbed her back. "Nothing's gonna happen to Coop."

Celina set her head in her hands. "You can't say that. Sugars and Forester are dead because of me. Cooper's next if I stay here. Your life's in danger, too. Even Eliza."

"First of all, we're a team. We know how Londano and Valquis work. We've lived and breathed them for years. They can't surprise us like they did Forester and his agents. Second, *we're a team.* Do you hear me? We cover each other's backs.

Take care of each other 24/7. And third..." he trailed off, lifted his eyebrows for her to finish his sentence.

"We're a team."

"Exactly." He gently pinched her chin. "No one's gonna break us up. We're exponentially stronger and smarter if we're united. We stay together, work together, sleep together on occasion." He waggled his eyebrows.

Celina couldn't help but smile at his teasing. "It's too dangerous for all of you. I can't be part of the team this time."

"And, again, your option is?"

"I have to take down Emilio on my own."

He straightened, cracked his knuckles. "Don't take this the wrong way, Celina, but you're not capable of taking on Londano or Valquis on your own."

How can I not take that the wrong way?

"It's not because you're a woman or because your field experience amounts to a hill of beans. None of us, not one single member of the SCVC taskforce, no matter how intelligent or tough or experienced, is capable of taking on these two alone. The only way—are you listening?—the *only way* to succeed at taking them out, is if we work together. One united front."

"But Emilio only wants me. If I turn myself over, he'll stop killing the people around me. Then I'll figure out how to stop him."

"You can't be serious. You think Londano won't brutalize you? Kill you?"

"Not if I kill him first."

"What about Valquis? You gonna kill him too?"

"How else do I stop them?"

Bobby slumped in his chair. "You're serious."

Celina nodded.

"You'll die, and in the end, Val and Londano will still come after Cooper."

She didn't follow. "Why?"

"He's head of the SCVC. He's given them a lot of trouble

over the years. Coop and I talked this over. The night Val did this to me," he tapped the arm of his wheelchair, "he was sending Cooper a message."

A message. Like he'd sent her via Forester's body? "What kind of message?"

"Cooper messed with Londano's empire, pissed him off one too many times. So instead of going after Cooper directly, he sent Val after me. He knew that would do more damage to Coop's mental and emotional state than anything else."

"Like he's doing with me right now." Celina shifted, rubbed her temples again. "It's payback."

"Londano's keeping you totally freaked out and off balance." He checked the security screens. "If you walk out of here and Valquis grabs you, what do you think that will do to Cooper?"

Celina sat for a long moment, knowing exactly what it would do to Cooper. "But he's got a kid," she said, picking at the brace on her wrist. "That's his only real responsibility. Not me."

The two friends sat in silence, staring at the black and white images on the screens in front of them. Bobby turned his chair to face her. "You have to stay with Cooper, Celina. He's your only chance to walk away from this alive."

She thought about that, figured it was true. "You could keep me safe."

A disgruntled half-laugh escaped his lips. "Have you looked at me? In case you didn't notice, I'm in a fucking wheelchair, rookie."

"Oh, god," Celina said, putting her hand over her mouth. "I forgot."

Bobby's face took on a look of confused bemusement. "You forgot I'm stuck in this contraption?"

Celina put her head down. "That was rude. I'm so sorry. I wasn't thinking."

"Don't be sorry. That's the first time anyone's forgotten. It's actually nice."

Celina leaned over and hugged him. "Why did they get divorced?" she asked.

He didn't miss a beat at the change in subject. "Typical reason. Cooper worked a lot of long hours. Lots of holidays. Melinda was lonely. She got pregnant thinking that might turn Cooper into a homebody. It didn't. Don't get me wrong, Owen changed a lot of things for Cooper. He worked smarter, landed the taskforce unit's head position in order to keep him off the streets as much as possible while still being involved in drug enforcement. But he and Melinda, well, they fought a lot. She finally gave up. Divorced him."

"Is that why he doesn't want to get involved with me?"

"Cooper was nuts over Melinda when they got hitched. He was also twenty-four years old. Too young to know what he really wanted."

Twenty-four. The same age as her when she joined the taskforce. "And?"

"He knows how things change, how love can start out wild and passionate and get overcome by other stuff and go bad."

"That can happen at any age. Love is risky."

"That's true," he said, pointedly sizing her up. "So what are you going to do about it?"

What *was* she going to do about it? "I figure I have two options." She closed her eyes and leaned back in her chair. "I can go put on my Victoria's Secret lace peek-a-boo teddy, jump in bed with him, and hope the sex is mind blowing enough that he keeps me around until he realizes he can't live without me, or I can leave now and save face." She opened her eyes and stared at the ceiling. "Try to forget about him."

"Do you really have a Vicki's peek-a-boo teddy with you?"

Celina rolled her eyes. "What happened with him and Lana?"

Bobby's eyes narrowed. "Why do you ask?"

It was his tone that confirmed her suspicions. "Ah ha," Celina said. "I knew there was something going on between them."

"Trust me, there is *nothing* going on between Coop and Lana."

"But there was once, wasn't there?"

When he looked away, Celina sat forward. "What happened? Tell me."

"I can't. I'm sworn to secrecy."

"Did he sleep with her?"

"Oh, hell no." He affected a false shiver and made a disgusted noise like he'd drunk sour milk. "That's sick."

If it wasn't sex, than what was it? Celina grabbed the arms of his chair. "Then what?"

He shook his head *no*, kept his eyes on the screens. "I'll self-destruct if I say anything."

"Why does he lie about her?"

Bobby's gaze shifted to her. "What kind of lie?"

"He told me she benches something like two hundred and twenty pounds. That she's a black belt in karate."

His eyes shifted away. "Those aren't lies."

"I saw her today." Or maybe it was yesterday or the day before. Celina was losing track of time. "She's Dolly Parton on a power trip."

"Dolly Parton on steroids, maybe."

"You've personally been at the gym and seen her bench press that much weight."

"Me? No," Dyer said. "But I have it documented."

"Documented for what?"

He looked around the room. "I've already said too much."

"Why would you be documenting what Lana does?" Celina said it to herself more than to him.

A thought dawned. "You're keeping a file on her for Cooper." She stared at the DEA field officer-turned-techie. Saw his face flush. "Sounds like blackmail."

"No. Not anymore at least. I was keeping a file on her, but Cooper told me to destroy it when she went to the FBI, only I didn't because it was too risky. She could come back and Coop's problems could start over with her."

Problems? Now Celina was totally enthralled. In a flash of memory, she saw Lana eyeing Dupé. *Wants to snag the boss.*

"She wanted to sleep with Cooper," Celina said as the idea came to her. "When she was DEA. He was married to Melinda already. He wouldn't sleep with her. Pissed her off, didn't it?"

Bobby was humming under his breath now, something that sounded like the soundtrack to *Jaws.*

"She tried to get Cooper in trouble," Celina continued, as the thoughts kept morphing. "What did she do? Claim sexual harassment?"

His tune picked up tempo. "I hear nothing. I see nothing. I know nothing."

"She hit him with a sexual harassment charge."

The humming stopped. Bobby let out a long-suffering sigh. "She threatened him with it because he wouldn't play her game, but she never followed through once she found out I had a file on her. The only one being harassed was Coop and she knew I could prove it."

"Why didn't Cooper take the file and give it to someone higher up? Get Lana fired?"

"He said she'd move on and eventually she did. He was satisfied with that."

"And now she's after Dupé."

"You noticed that too, huh?"

Celina nodded her head. "Someone should bring this to light. Warn the director."

He was humming again and shaking his head. "Not me. I hear nothing. I see nothing. I know nothing."

"She has access to a lot of sensitive information, and Dupé trusts her. She could ruin him."

"Coop says Dupé's smart enough to figure it out on his own and he doesn't want that passed out in the light for everyone to know about. As far as Cooper's concerned, the file no longer exists."

That's crap, but now she understood Cooper's intense dislike of Lana. His comments about her. "Did he really punch her when you were in the hospital?"

"Punch her?" Bobby's eyebrows drew together in a frown. "Cooper would never punch a woman. Not even Lana..." his voice trailed off and he smiled. "But I bet he sure fantasized about it. I certainly have."

CHAPTER TWENTY-NINE

When Cooper woke, gray light and the smell of strong coffee filled his bedroom. His digital clock read 6:47. Damn, he'd slept all night. Why hadn't the alarm went off at two am like he'd set it for? He reached out and checked the switch, found it in the off position.

"I turned it off," a soft voice said from the corner. "You needed the sleep."

He rolled onto his side and pushed himself up on one elbow. Celina was backlit from the window, her features dark, but he could see her outline clearly as she sat crossed-legged on his credenza, holding a coffee mug with her left hand. Her gun was next to her, as was a second mug, and the two-way radio Dyer had given her.

He ran a hand over his face. His voice rough from sleep. "I had second shift."

"I took it, sent Bobby home, put Thomas and Nelson on outside duty. You didn't miss anything but a rangy-looking fox crossing the driveway around three-thirty."

She'd refused his bed and taken his couch so he could sleep in comfort. Turned off his alarm and taken his watch. He was supposed to be taking care of her, keeping her safe, and instead she was taking care of him.

God, he could hug her. But what the hell was she thinking?

He wished she were closer so he could see her face, but he stayed still, holding himself in a forced comfortableness, thankful for the sheet that still covered his morning hard-on. Wondering what she might do if he pulled her into bed and took her clothes off. "How long have you been watching me sleep?" His voice was still rough sounding, but he knew it was from the sudden image of Celina warm and naked under him.

"Awhile." She unfolded her legs and let her feet swing. "I didn't want Freddy to get you."

"Freddy?"

"Krueger." At his blank look, she smiled. "*Nightmare on Elm Street.*"

"Right." He sat up, pulling the sheet with him. Leaned back against his pillows and put one arm behind his head to prop it up, still trying to look comfortable.

Celina stopped swinging her feet, set her mug down, and slid off his credenza. She picked up her gun and shoved it into the backside of her waistband. Her hair was loose around her face and she was wearing one of his white t-shirts *sans* bra.

His heart did a skip as he stared at the points growing out of his shirt when she turned to pick up the coffee mug, and, then, *thank you, Jesus*, she walked over to the bed. She smelled good, like she'd just stepped out of his shower, and she was definitely wearing his shirt. "We survived the night," she said. "No one got hurt."

As she looked down at him and held out the mug, Cooper willed himself not to reach for her. To accept the coffee instead.

"I don't make coffee too often." She sat on the edge of the bed, one knee bent and touching his hip through the sheet. "But I know you like it strong so I doubled the amount the instructions listed."

Cooper sipped the coffee with her staring at him, her eyes big and soft in her face, waiting for his reaction. "Thanks," he managed.

Staring at her over the rim of the coffee mug, he waited. He wanted her so bad, his teeth were on edge, but he refused to make the first move. Her invitation was clear. Bringing him coffee, sitting on the bed braless, wearing his shirt. But still, he would wait. She'd been through an emotional few days. She was looking for comfort. Comfort he wanted more than anything to provide, so long as he wasn't misleading her like he had in Des Moines. Her crush on him would melt away after this was over and he knew that. He didn't want her to look back at this moment and think he'd taken advantage of her vulnerability in any way.

But damn, the way things were going this moment, this sweet moment with her sitting here like one of his fantasies come true, with her hair freshly washed and her voice soft and free of fear, might be the last one he had like this with her. Their future, both professional and personal, loomed infinitely dark, like a black hole in front of them.

Celina drew up her knees, hugging them, her bare feet resting on the bed. "Melinda called last night after you went to sleep."

Cooper gripped the mug tighter, his lower region softening at the name of his ex-wife. So much for taking advantage of the moment. He glanced at the nightstand and saw his cell phone wasn't there.

"I took the phone when I turned off your alarm. I didn't want anyone to wake you." She smoothed her hair with her left hand, pulled it over her shoulder. "Today's your day with Owen."

"Owen doesn't come until Saturday."

"Cooper, it is Saturday."

Damn, she was right. He set down the mug. "I'll call Melinda and explain the situation. Owen will understand."

"Owen will *not* understand." Her eyes were fierce. "Besides, I'm going to the L.A. office today. There's going to be a press conference. I spoke with Dupé, and he agreed I should be there. They're going to give out more details about what Emilio's done and expand the manhunt to include Valquis. I want to be sure Emilio sees me on national television. That he knows I'm not cowering or hiding from him. It may just be the trick to flush him out once and for all."

Cooper shifted so he was fully sitting up. He draped his arms over his knees. "I'll take you to L.A."

Her gaze dropped to his lips, rose to his eyes again. "Melinda said Owen's guitar lesson is at ten and then he's planning on you taking him to lunch. He's counting on you to spend the day with him, Cooper. You can't let him down."

How many times had Cooper heard those words from Melinda? "What else did Melinda say?"

Celina hugged herself tighter and looked away. "Nothing, really."

Her body language told him different.

An angry tension spread through his veins as he thought about Melinda and her razorblade tongue. He'd been cut too many times not to have a healthy distaste for it. Feeling incredibly protective, he reached out and touched the ends of Celina's hair. Its sleek weight felt like satin to his fingers. "It's all right. You don't have to tell me. I can imagine what she probably said."

"She saw the news about Londano. I explained that I was here because you felt responsible for me and were trying to protect me. I told her there was nothing going on between us."

Right? Her unspoken question hung between them, her eyes searching his again for a reaction.

His heart skipped and then settled into a hard thumping. He rubbed her hair between his fingers, watched her lips part. She'd taken on Lana, Forester, and now Melinda, all in an effort to keep him out of trouble, even after the way he'd squashed her hopes of having a relationship. Even after he threw her inexperience in her face constantly by calling her *kid* and *rookie*. "You always manage to surprise me, Celina. In a good way."

She tilted her head, smiled. "You better hold off on the praise. I'm pretty sure Melinda didn't believe me. She was pretty angry I was here. That I answered your phone and refused to wake you up to talk to her."

Cooper couldn't help but smile back. "Melinda has issues. They're with me. Don't take it personally."

"She's still in love with you."

A small chuckle escaped his throat. He so didn't want to talk about Melinda. "She's not in love with me, but she's still trying to make me into the man she thought she married. She wants me to be a good dad to Owen. Unfortunately, her idea and mine on that subject are different. Just like when we were married, she emphasizes quantity over quality."

Celina nodded. "Sometimes women use anger to cover up fear. She's no doubt scared something will happen to you. That you won't be around for her and Owen."

"You're very perceptive for someone so…"

Cooper stopped himself before he said it, but Celina finished the sentence for him. "Young?"

He grimaced. She smirked. "My mother and father had a strong bond, still do, so I never watched my parents go through divorce, thank goodness. But my best friend in middle school went through it. It was ugly. Her dad ran off with her mother's best friend. Tami spent a lot of time at my house. Her mother was very angry and it made Tami angry too, but what I realized was that my friend was mostly just scared. So was her mom. Their futures were uncertain for a while. To this day, Tami has trouble putting trust in anyone. Her dad ran away with her godmother. Talk about issues."

"So you took care of Tami," Cooper said, giving her hair a gentle tug. "And you took care of that old security guard's blood pressure, and Annie Richardson's kids." *And now you're trying to take care of me and Owen.* He sighed. "You're a nice person."

"You say that as if it's a bad thing."

"Don't jeopardize yourself trying to make things right for me."

"Thomas can take me to L.A. I'll be safe at FBI headquarters. You need to be here with Owen."

He did need to be there with Owen. He also needed to keep Celina safe.

And away from Thomas.

"No. I don't like it," he told her.

She studied him for a moment, a grin lifting one corner of her mouth. She let go of her legs, shifting so the one closest to him folded under her butt, enabling her to lean toward him. Close enough to kiss. "What *do* you like, Agent Harris? Besides logical women in short skirts?"

Damn. He liked *her*. More than he wanted to. He liked her in his bed wearing his clothes. He liked her turning off his alarm and bringing him coffee. "Are you trying to distract me so I'll give in and let you go to L.A. without me?"

The grin widened to lift the other side of her mouth. "Now would I do that?"

He ran his hand under her hair to the back of her neck and pulled her the half inch forward so he could kiss her. The moment his lips met hers, she sighed, deep in her throat, and Cooper's reservations evaporated like the steam from his coffee.

Her lips parted under his and her left hand came up and rested on his forearm, slightly hesitant, as he kissed her deep and long. She kissed him back, her lips not hesitant like her touch, but all out intense and consuming. She tasted sweet and dark like his French roast with a couple teaspoons of sugar.

Careful of her injured wrist, he placed his hands on her sides and lifted her gently on top of him, leaning back as he did so. She took his lead and straddled him, the thin cotton fabric of his shirt a teasing barrier between his bare chest and her hard nipples. As she lowered her weight, he steadied her with his hands and inhaled her with his mouth.

Cooper kept his left hand on her waist and let his right hand explore under the shirt. Celina broke away from his lips on a gasp as his fingers pinched a nipple. "Be nice," she murmured against his mouth.

So he massaged her instead, filling his hand with the heavy weight of one taut breast and then the other, wanting to follow his hand with his mouth. In order to do that, he needed her out of his shirt.

Both hands on her waist again, he raised her up, using his stomach muscles to pull himself up at the same time. Then he tugged the shirt up and off, still mindful of her injured arm. She helped as best she could, and Cooper stopped as the t-shirt fell to the floor.

A beautiful woman was sitting in his lap. A smart, beautiful woman. Her breasts were full and heavy from his fondling, her lips as well from his kissing. She was regarding him with that same wariness she seemed to wear on her face around him now. Seeking his approval, scared he'd shut her down. Wanting him to want her.

Want her he did, in this very physical way. He wanted to touch her everywhere, to keep her in his bed until he'd done everything he'd fantasized about doing and then made up a few new fantasies. But he wanted more than a fulfillment of his sexual fantasies.

He wanted to protect her. To spend his days and nights with her. And he wanted her approval too. Approval to be the man who could keep her safe and happy.

He touched her cheek with the ends of his fingers. Let them trail down her neck, over her collarbone that was half covered with white gauze and tape. Her skin felt firm and smooth as silk under his fingertips.

"I'm okay, Cooper," she said. "You don't have to baby me."

He smiled at her insistence. "I'm not babying you, Celina. I'm staring at your beauty."

She grinned. Placing her hands on his shoulders, she moved a centimeter closer, seating herself in his lap in the exact spot they both benefited from. The heat of her body in that spot, combined with her lush breasts brushing his chest, made him jerk.

"Jesus," he swore under his breath as she lowered her lips to his. He knew he should be up and out of bed, watching the monitors, figuring out how to balance Owen's schedule today with his own. Figuring out a way to capture Londano and Valquis and keep Celina safe. But all he could do was tug her closer, kiss her back. He'd never felt this way about a woman. Not even Melinda.

He rolled Celina underneath him, careful of her wrist, and withdrew the gun from her waistband. As he moved the gun from one hand to the other to set it on the nightstand, he dropped his lips to her neck and kissed the area around her bandage. He went lower to take her breast in his mouth and felt smug satisfaction when she inhaled sharply and pulled him closer.

CHAPTER THIRTY

The two-way radio on the credenza squawked. Thomas's voice filled the room. "Switchfoot, this is Crazy Clock. Come in."

Cooper released Celina's breast, laid his forehead on her chest, and blew out a sigh. "You've got to be kidding me."

Celina chuckled under her breath. "He told me to check in with him every hour on the dot." She lifted her head from the bed and peered at Cooper's alarm clock. "Seven-o-one. He's punctual."

"Switchfoot, this is Crazy Clock," Thomas's voice had elevated a notch. "Are you all right? Over."

Cooper rolled off Celina. She scooted off the bed, swept up the radio, and smiled at Cooper over it as she answered. "This is Switchfoot." While irritated with his partner's bad timing, Cooper enjoyed the swing of Celina's breasts as she paced back to the bed. "Everything's fine."

"Yeah, not quite," Thomas responded. "Melinda and Owen are on their way up the driveway."

"Ah, shit." Cooper threw back the sheet now tangled between his legs. "What the hell's she doing here at seven in the morning?"

Celina picked his shirt off the floor. "Roger that," she said calmly into the radio, then she dropped it on the bed and pulled on the shirt. Grabbing her hair, she slipped it out from beneath the collar and let out an exasperated sigh. "You hit the bathroom." She shoved her gun back in the waistband of her

223

shorts. "I'll answer the door and let them in."

He sat up, then stood, rubbing his hands over his face through his hair, and pulling on his running shorts. "I'm not sending you to the door to handle my ex-wife at seven o'clock in the morning."

"You're going to open the door looking like that?" She pointed at the tent between his legs.

Damn. Right again. He pointed at her nipples, still predominantly on display under his shirt. "You're going to greet them like that?"

Celina glanced down, crossed her arms over her breasts. "I'll throw on a sweatshirt."

She left the room and Cooper heard her bare feet padding quickly on his hardwood floors. He glanced at his bed, and even though he was in a pickle, smiled to himself as he too jogged across the hardwood to the bathroom.

———

Celina fought with her sweatshirt as she walked into the kitchen to open the door for Melinda and Owen. The tight sleeve of her right arm snagged on her cast and she had the shirt half over her head, half not, when Melinda opened the door and pushed Owen through it in front of her. Cooper's ex stopped at the sight of Celina and lowered her Gucci sunglasses an inch on her nose. The two women stood staring at each other.

Melinda was at least six inches taller than Celina, owing part of her height to a pair of embossed leather heels. Her natural blond hair was long and straight and pulled up in a partial ponytail, partial bun on top of her head with a set of polished black chopsticks embedded in it. The perfect weapon, Celina thought, to poke someone's eye out. Someone like the woman sleeping with her ex-husband.

"Hi," Celina said cheerfully as she shoved her left arm in the sweatshirt and snugged it down over Cooper's t-shirt. Melinda's dark brown eyes ran an accusatory lap from Celina's head to her feet. "You must be Melinda." Without thinking, she offered her right hand. "I'm Celina. We spoke on the phone last night."

Melinda regarded her hand and the accompanying cast. She didn't accept Celina's handshake.

Celina punched in the code on the security alarm by the door under Melinda's unwavering scrutiny. Then she smiled at the young boy with his guitar case standing beside his mother. He was older than the picture on Cooper's dresser. His hair was longer, curling on the ends, and blond like his mother's, but his other features matched his father's right down to the tiny cleft in his chin.

"And you must be Owen," Celina said, still forcing brightness into her voice as she came back to a spot in front of him. Using her left hand, she gathered her hair and pulled it out from under the sweatshirt's collar, and this time extended her hand to shake Owen's. "Your dad tells me you're quite a guitar player."

Owen nodded and shook her fingers, his eyes darting to his mother, back to Celina. "My friend plays too," he told her. "We're going to have a garage band this summer."

Celina smiled an honest smile this time. "That's cool."

"Where *is* Cooper?" Melinda looked past Celina with efficient dismissal in her tone and her body posture.

"He's in the bathroom," Celina said. "He *just* woke up."

Melinda pressed her red glossed lips into a tight line. "He *just* woke up?"

Celina felt her true smile fading. Fast. "Yes. As I explained to you on the phone, he's been working the Londano case all week. Last night was the first sleep he's had in the past seventy-two hours."

"I see," Melinda said, but the tone of her voice said she didn't buy it. "Owen, honey, take your guitar into the living room and practice that new chord Brian gave you last week."

The boy gave Celina a look that said *sorry* as if this was a cue he'd been given from dear old mom before and he knew what was heading Celina's way. He picked up his gig bag to clear out.

Once he was out of hearing distance, Melinda stepped forward, glaring down at Celina. "You spent the night here." It was not a question, not even a rhetorical one. It was a statement. The start, Celina knew, of an ass chewing.

"Yes," Cooper's voice came from behind Celina. She turned to see him sauntering into the kitchen, sport pants falling appropriately in all the right places. "She's under my surveillance at the moment. Why are you here so early, Mel?"

Melinda drew herself back, straightening her already ramrod stiff posture another fraction of an inch. "Steven and I are going to Vegas for the weekend. I told you that. We're flying out of LAX this morning. That's why I had to drop Owen off now."

"Dad!" Owen shouted as he flew back into the kitchen, drawn by the sound of his father's voice. Cooper opened his arms and the boy jumped into them. Cooper picked him up and gave him a bear hug.

"How y'doin', buddy?" Cooper held Owen in one arm, used his free hand to tousle the boy's hair.

"Good," Owen mimicked his father, running his own smaller hand through Cooper's short cut.

"We going to have fun today?"

Owen nodded. "Yeah."

"Did you practice *Dirty Little Secret*?"

Owen's head continued to nod. "I've got it down cold."

Cooper bear hugged him again. "That's my boy." He put Owen down and looked at Melinda over his son's head. "Let me talk to your mom a minute and then you can play it for me."

Owen shot Celina another of his knowing looks. "All American Rejects?" Celina asked him. "You can play a song by them?"

A tiny smile tugged at Owen's mouth and he glanced at his dad.

"He plays all kinds of alternative rock," Cooper said, acknowledging Owen's competence. Celina saw the boy swell with pride as Cooper winked at him.

Celina widened her eyes. "I love that song. Would you play it for me?"

When Owen nodded, Celina started for the living room, following him. She gave Cooper a supportive smile as she passed and he smiled back, gratitude in his eyes.

As Owen plugged his guitar into a small amp, Celina heard Melinda's voice, sharp as steel in the kitchen. "You promised me you'd never bring one of them here."

One of them. Girlfriend? Taskforce agent? Celina couldn't make out Cooper's reply, only the low sound of his voice, but Melinda's came through loud and clear again. "She shouldn't be here. I won't have her here. She's a danger to Owen. To you."

And then the rest of the conversation was lost as Owen placed his fingers on the strings, the first chords of *Dirty Little Secret* filling the room.

Thirty minutes later, the smell of cooking filled Cooper's nostrils as he opened the bathroom door. Bacon, eggs, toast, onion, and pepper scents made him breathe deeply. The sound of a pan banging into another, a piece of silverware hitting a bowl, echoed down the hallway. *Homey sounds,* he thought. *Like someone lives here besides me.*

He'd showered, shaved, and tried to figure out what he was going to do with Owen and Celina both.

Worst-case Scenario One: he let Celina go to L.A. with Thomas and Valquis snagged her.

Worst-case Scenario Two: he kept her home with him and Owen, and Valquis snagged Owen.

Cooper's gut hurt at either thought. He couldn't keep them together without risking Owen's life and that was one thing he would never do.

Celina was at the stove, moving a spatula around in a pan of scrambled eggs. Her back was to him as she stared down at the food in front of her, but she wasn't standing at the stove alone. Thomas was leaning one elbow on the counter, his body open toward her as he stared up at her face, smiling. He was entirely invading her personal space, talking in a soft, low voice, and waiting expectantly for…what? Was he trying to coax a smile out of her?

Worst-case Scenario not involving Petero Valquis or Emilio Londano: Celina fell for his partner.

And they lived happily ever after. Right under Cooper's nose.

"Hey, Dad." Owen sat at the kitchen bar, scooping scrambled eggs into his mouth, a crispy slice of bacon in one hand. He had a tall glass of orange juice in front of him as well as a second glass full of milk. A milk mustache was growing on his top lip.

And that's when Cooper knew he really had no choice. It would be just like Valquis, the bastard, to target an innocent child. He'd done it before and Cooper had seen the results.

Cooper was all Owen had standing between him and a cruel psychotic killer. Celina, while vulnerable because of her injury, was still a trained FBI agent with a host of her Fed counterparts and the entire SCVC taskforce trying to protect her. She didn't need Cooper. She had Thomas.

"Hey, buddy." Cooper gave Owen's head a rub as he walked by him.

Thomas nodded at Cooper but didn't give up his stance next to Celina. She turned from the stove and smiled at Cooper. "Are you hungry? I made breakfast."

"Smells good." Cooper set his empty coffee mug on the

counter and refilled it from the pot. His cutting board was out with a sloppy pile of diced tomato, onion, and pepper sitting beside a chopping knife. A loaf of bread was open, the toaster humming as it did its thing.

"Thomas, pour Cooper some orange juice," Celina ordered and Thomas blinked at her. He straightened up slowly when Celina waved the spatula at him before she flipped a pile of hash browns over in a second skillet.

The younger man gave her a half-salute and ignored Cooper's smile. Cooper joined his son at the breakfast bar, watching Celina cooking at his stove. He liked seeing her there. Liked having someone in his kitchen fussing over him. It had been a long time and only now did he realize how he'd missed spending these little everyday moments with someone. He wished he could stop time at the moment and just enjoy it.

And he wished like hell Thomas would fall over and die.

While he was at it, he'd throw in a wish that Londano and Valquis would go straight to hell and stay there.

Five minutes later, Cooper was scooping up scrambled eggs topped with the tomato and onion mixture. The bacon was crisp, the hash browns were perfectly browned, and the juice was cold.

But Owen was now off in the living room watching cartoons and Thomas was sitting next to Cooper, eating his own pile of eggs and hash browns, and sending Cooper distinctive male posturing messages.

Cooper ignored his younger partner and focused on his food.

"Hot sauce," Celina said, plunking a bottle on the bar next to Cooper's plate. "I figured you'd want some on your eggs."

She stood on the other side, munching toast and casting furtive glances at Cooper's plate to see what he was eating. He caught her gaze and held it. "Thanks, but it doesn't need any. It tastes delicious just the way it is."

He winked at her and she blushed.

His cell phone rang; caller ID saying it was Dyer.

"Navarette found GHB in Forester's blood," Dyer said without preamble.

"The date rape drug?"

"Yep. Probably how Valquis got him in the laundry cart and out of the hotel without a fight. Navarette believes he was only tased afterwards, like after the drug wore off."

Switching gears, Cooper lowered the phone from his mouth and said to Celina, "You ordered room service that night at the hotel, right?"

"Forester ordered a pizza," she said.

"He drink anything with it?"

"A Coke."

"You drink any?"

Celina shook her head. "I drank the Dew you brought."

Cooper raised the phone back to his lips. "Is it possible Val meant the GHB for Celina?"

"Anything's possible. Navarette said there was a significant amount in Forester's blood. If Valquis intended it for Celina, he meant for her to die."

Cooper stared at Celina across the counter, a white-hot rage poking at his gut. "Make sure Carlsbad PD checks the remains from the food service tray to see what they can find."

"Already called Sam. You going to L.A. for the news conference?"

"No," Cooper said, hating the word. "But you are. The conference is scheduled for eleven o'clock. Thomas and Celina will pick you up in thirty minutes."

Cooper saw Thomas stop eating out of the corner of his eye. Give him a look. There was a slight pause on the other end. "Coop, you know I'd do anything for you. I'd give my life for Celina. But I can't protect her from Valquis if it comes down to it."

Turning the bar stool, he faced Thomas. "Val isn't the one that worries me," he said softly and saw understanding flash in Thomas's eyes. Saw the grin tweak the corners of his partner's mouth as he tried to hide it behind his glass of milk.

"Thirty minutes," Cooper said into the phone. "Be ready."

"Where are they going?" Owen said from the doorway. Everyone turned to look at him as Cooper ended his call. Owen moved his gaze from his dad to Celina. "Can I go too?" he asked her.

"It's a news conference at FBI headquarters in Los Angeles," she told him. "Boring stuff for a kid."

"What's it about?"

"It's about a fugitive. A bad man who escaped prison and is hurting people. Your dad and Thomas and I are trying to stop him."

"Uncle Dyer too?"

"Yes. Uncle Dyer too. A lot of people, FBI, DEA, and some others are all working together to stop the bad guy."

"The news conference," Cooper told Owen, "is to let everyone know what this bad guy has done and to warn them to stay away from him and call the police if they see him."

"I saw his picture on the news last night." Owen pointed at Celina's wrist. "He's the man who hurt you, isn't he?"

Celina nodded.

"Can kids come to FBI headquarters?"

"No," Thomas said in unison with Cooper.

The truth was, kids could and did often come to FBI headquarters to the daycare services on the fifth floor while mom or dad worked. Cooper knew if Celina called Dupé, she could get permission to bring Owen, but she wouldn't do it, even if Cooper wanted her to.

From the way her eyes avoided his and the set of her lips thinned to a tight line, Cooper knew she was about to leave him, whether he liked it or not.

He definitely did not like it.

CHAPTER THIRTY-ONE

Owen needs a dog, Celina thought. A big-hearted Golden Retriever who would follow the boy around, lie down beside him, and listen to him talk. A silent but kind friend who would give him undivided attention and never send him out of the room or make him feel uncomfortable.

It was easier to think about Owen than her own predicament. Easier to conjure images of Owen and a dog chasing each other in Cooper's yard, jumping in the pool and sleeping in front of the television. It was easier to imagine Owen burying his face in the soft fur of a lovable dog than to watch Cooper's stiff posture and damning stare as she climbed into Thomas's hybrid car.

It had to end here, with her walking away. Being around her made Cooper and Owen easy targets, and she loved Cooper too much to go on endangering him, endangering his son's future. She'd known she'd have to leave him, stop their relationship even as she sat on his bed seducing him that morning.

A desperate sadness welled up inside her. This was it. Taking a deep breath, she straightened her spine, preparing to leave Cooper behind as Thomas started the car. She shut her eyes against the sun, against Cooper's glare. Deep inside, she wanted him to knock on the window, stop Thomas from pulling away, and beg her to be careful. Anything. A gesture to let her know he loved her.

As the car made its way down the long, sloping drive, there

was no knock on her window, no shout telling Thomas to stop. In her mind, Celina called up Owen's face again, a smile breaking over it as he ran with the imaginary dog through his father's backyard. He was safe. Cooper was safe. That was all that mattered.

———

"Don't lose her," Cooper said to Dyer on his cell phone. He stood in his driveway watching Thomas's car drive out of sight.

"Of course not," Dyer replied, his voice edged with impatience. "Did you tell her how you feel?"

Cooper moved the phone away from his mouth, blew out a tight breath. Returned the mouth piece to his lips. "Of course not."

"Why the hell not?"

"None of your damn business."

"Jesus, you're a jackass. You just blew what is probably your only chance to tell her you love her."

"I don't—" Cooper stopped himself. Could he honestly say he didn't love her?

He could say it, but he'd be blowing smoke. Dyer wouldn't believe him.

"Save the denial. You're in love with her and she'll be going home with Thomas after the news conference. Or maybe she'll come back here with me. But I guarantee she will not come back to you."

Cooper squinted at his now empty driveway. "What are you talking about?"

"The table has turned, my friend. Celina now feels responsible for you. She told me she was leaving you because she didn't want to cause you problems. Not with Melinda. Not with Owen. And especially not with Londano."

From the moment she'd told Owen no, that he couldn't come to FBI headquarters, Cooper had known Celina's intentions. Maybe even before that. In his bedroom, when she'd told him she was going to the news conference...maybe then he knew it. Felt it in his bones. "She can't possibly believe—"

"Hell, yeah, she does. She believes in you and she believes in happy endings. Only, I think you've finally convinced her there will never be a happy ending for you and her."

"I couldn't lead her on. We don't have a future together."

"Like I said, you're a jackass."

"Why is it other people disagree with you, they're blockheads, but with me, I'm a jackass?"

"Because you are."

"Anything new on the investigation?"

There was a slight pause as Dyer gave up the inquisition and shifted gears. "Londano's right-hand man south of the border made an impromptu move last night. Allende's been on holiday in Cozumel for the past two weeks. He came rushing back home to Mexico City last night."

"Boss is back in town?"

The clicking of computer keys echoed in the phone. "My guess."

Cooper kicked a rock. "Think Valquis is with him?"

"Nope. Two lieutenants under one roof. Gets messy."

Messy. An understatement if ever there was one for what Londano's men could do to each other. "It's good if Emilio is out of the country, but is Val still after Celina?"

"Worst-case scenario? Yeah."

His lungs felt tight. "Don't lose her, D."

"Don't worry. I have a plan."

"What plan?"

"Everything's under control. If you weren't thinking with your dick, you would have already thought of this."

"I am not," Cooper protested.

"Look, you've been too busy trying to figure out how to keep her from leaving. You forgot to figure out what to do if she *did* leave."

He was right and Cooper knew it. Thank God, one of them had their head on straight. "Tell me the plan."

"The gang's all here," Dyer said. "Gotta go."

"Be careful. Check in hourly."

"You're welcome and I love you too."

Cooper lowered the phone, stood another minute looking at his empty driveway but seeing Celina's face, eyes closed to him, as she'd rode away in Thomas's car. He should have told her to be careful. Should have told her to keep her guard up. Should have told her he loved her.

"Dad?"

Owen watched him from the doorway. "What is it, son?"

"How do you know if a girl likes you?"

Owen's gaze lowered, suddenly finding the cement beneath his feet interesting.

Smiling to himself, Cooper caught the boy around the shoulders and directed him back inside the house. "Let's talk."

CHAPTER THIRTY-TWO

At Bobby's house, the drill went fast. Thomas pulled the hybrid into the garage, the door shut. Celina moved from the car to the house under Bobby's direction, gave her newspaper boy hat to Sara, and watched as the FBI fugitive apprehension agent pulled her hair back in a ponytail and donned the hat, sliding in next to Thomas. The door went up, the hybrid started to back out.

It didn't go far. A white service van wheeled in and blocked the drive.

Celina's heart banged hard inside her ribcage. Bobby drew a weapon, moving Celina behind him with his wheelchair at the same time. Thomas shoved the car in drive and jetted back into the garage, the door already coming down.

The commotion was for nothing. Lana and Quarters exited the van, Lana waving her hand at Bobby and raising a brow at his raised weapon.

He lowered the gun, but didn't put it away. Celina stayed near his chair.

"What are you doing here?" he demanded.

"We had just arrived at Cooper's house when we saw Thomas take off with Celina." Lana said. "Dupé wants us to bring her to L.A. for this morning's conference. But she and Thomas took off before we had a chance to synch up the plan with Cooper."

Bobby looked nervous. "Let's get inside."

They filed into his kitchen, gathering around the table. Lana looked at the group with a weird smile playing over her lips, as if they were children making a big deal out of nothing. "What is with all the cloak and dagger stuff? Emilio and Valquis can't get back in the country."

Thomas folded his arms over his chest. "You can't guarantee that. Londano's been a step ahead of us every move we make."

"He's running for his life right now." She glanced at Sara. "And you should be joining the manhunt in Mexico, not wasting time and resources on hiding Celina."

Bobby frowned, setting his jaw. If Sara was annoyed, she didn't show it. She removed the cap, tightened her ponytail. "My orders are to—"

"Your orders have been changed, Agent Rios."

At the same moment, Thomas's cell phone rang, followed by Bobby's landline. Each man glanced at their displays, then exchanged a guarded look.

Lana smiled. "SCVC taskforce has been ordered to join the manhunt in Mexico. I suggest Agent Thomas and Agent Rios grab their bags and head out."

God, she was so full of herself. Celina waited for the men to answer their phones and confirm it was true. Each moved to different sides of the room, nodding and "damn"-ing about the news. Sara, who'd also been watching them, checked her phone. It rang in her hand, her dark-eyed gaze rising to meet Celina's as if to say she was sorry. She excused herself from the room to take the call, and finally, it was Lana and Celina facing off across the table. Quarters hovered near the back door.

At the sink, Bobby cursed under his breath. "Eliza can pick up Owen on her way home from her friend's, Coop...nah, it's okay. She won't mind."

A nervous humming started low in Celina's stomach. Cooper was leaving too? Well, of course. The Beast had to lead the team, and if the team and Sara were all in Mexico, she was a sitting duck.

In actuality, what Lana claimed might be true. Emilio and Valquis might be too busy running for their lives to come after her, but Emilio had friends and minions everywhere. One call and another assassin could be on Celina's trail. Maybe one already was.

"We should get moving." Lana said. "Wouldn't want you to be late for your press conference."

"*You're* taking me?"

Sara filed by, raising a hand in a small wave. "I'm wanted in San Fernando. There's been a spotting." She shot a cold glance at Lana, a warmer one at Celina. "Call or text if you need anything."

Celina tried to control her nerves, now buzzing like bees. "I will. Be careful."

Thomas hung up and tucked his phone away, looking pained at leaving her. Bobby disconnected his call with Cooper and shook his head.

"I'll be all right," she said to all of them. None of them believed her. She straightened her back. "I'm not a rookie any more, and you can't guard me for the rest of my life. I can handle this."

A minute later, Thomas and Sara were gone. Bobby pulled her aside. "You don't have to leave with that bitch. You can stay here with me."

"And put you and Eliza in danger?" Celina patted his arm. "Thank you, but no. I have to do the press conference in L.A. and see what happens."

"Cooper doesn't like it."

"Cooper doesn't like anything."

He started to say something, stopped and shook his head again. "I don't like it either."

Lana interrupted, tapping the expensive watch on her wrist. "Tic toc, Agent Davenport. Time to move."

Leaving Bobby with a hug and a promise to be safe, Celina climbed into the back of the van. The second row seats were utilitarian bucket seats, the windows blacked out. She wondered why Cooper hadn't called her to tell her about the change in plans. She got why he'd called Bobby, but it would have been nice to hear the news straight from Cooper's mouth. To hear his voice, period. She could call *him*, of course. But it didn't feel right. Not after the way he'd glared at her when she was leaving his place. Besides, he'd be busy preparing to leave for Mexico.

Fighting off the bitterness that threatened, Celina buckled her seat belt and ignored the covert glances Lana shot at her from the passenger seat as they backed out of the drive. Closing her eyes, she recalled Cooper's face that morning in his bedroom. Felt his lips on hers. Remembered the paths his hands had taken. How gentle his touch had been.

A smile curved her lips and she held those memories close as the van picked up speed.

This is it. No more Miss Nice Guy.

Slipping her good hand under her jacket, she fingered her gun in its holster against her ribcage. It was in the wrong spot for her left hand, but at least she was armed.

Armed or not, she didn't need Cooper or the SCVC team to protect her. She would go to L.A., do the press conference, and see what resulted with Londano. Lana may have been a bitch, but she was right. Emilio and Valquis were on the run in Mexico. And if they weren't? She was ready for them.

CHAPTER THIRTY-THREE

Cooper didn't like distractions. Wild goose chases even less. SCVC's latest orders seemed like both.

A targeted manhunt was only successful when the perp was known to be in a certain area. Londano was in Mexico, but where in Mexico? The agents already down there were working with the media and local law enforcement to find a trail—any trail—of Emilio and Valquis. So far, they'd had a dozen different reports sighting one or the other. None in the same location and all from the public. Respectable citizens doing their job to stop a couple of no-good lowlifes.

Except Cooper knew these "respectable citizens" from Tijuana to Mexico City were phoning in reports to throw the Feds off the real trail. Probably every one of them was on Londano's payroll or had been terrorized by his henchmen.

Sending the entire team down there was pointless until someone had an actual lead, but that's exactly what he'd been ordered to do. Take his team off protection duty and put them on a plane headed south.

Leaving Celina in Lana's hands sat like day old chilies in his stomach. Dupé would listen to none of Cooper's concerns, however. The old man insisted Celina was in capable hands, perfectly safe without the SCVC agents playing bodyguards, and they would proceed with the press conference. One way or the other, the FBI would nail Londano in the next twenty-four hours.

Cooper's gut niggled with doubt. In his career, there had been plenty of wild goose chases, but this one felt more and more like a distraction. Who was pulling the strings on this? Lana? Dupé? Someone higher up?

Cooper had called five different contacts looking for more info and came up dry. The big wheels in the FBI and DEA were keeping details close to their vests. It smacked of Lana setting up a game behind the scenes, insinuating in the process that someone on his team was leaking information. Back at the hospital, Sara had insinuated the same, but then they'd found the tracking device. He knew his team and knew none of them would betray a fellow agent. But Lana would love nothing better than to prove Cooper was ineffective at his job, and she'd probably do anything to make herself the hero.

He glanced at the clock beside his bed as he shoved a pair of shorts in his open duffel bag. His plane left in forty minutes and a driver was waiting outside to speed him off to the airport. Even if they left this second, they wouldn't make it in time. But Dupé, or whoever, would make the plane wait.

Instead of finishing his packing, he dialed Dyer again. The man answered on the first ring. "You were right," Cooper said. "Don't let her leave until I get there. I need to talk to her."

"I'm always right, you moron." Cooper heard the whine of the electric wheelchair in the background. "And you're too late. Lana and her henchman swooped in and grabbed her before I could put my plan in play."

"Shit." Cooper looked up at the ceiling. This day, like the previous ones leading up to it, had gone to hell so fast his head swam. He'd screwed up with Celina and Owen both, shuffling the kid off on Eliza as soon as word came down about the Mexico manhunt. The boy's eyes had filled with disappointment and hurt...the same look Celina had given him before Thomas had whisked her off. "Tell me you got a tracking device on Lana's car."

"Why? What's going on?"

"I gotta a bad feeling about what Lana's up to. I'm going to follow her."

Computer keys clicked. "Already ahead of you. Lana's too good for me to sneak a tracking device onto her vehicle, but I got the license plate, make, and model of the van she and Quarters were driving. I'm tracing it via traffic cams right now. I lost them outside of Carlsbad, but picked them up again in Oceanside. Once they hit the freeway alongside Pendleton, I'll lose them until the webcam in San Clemente."

"What about Pendleton's security cameras?"

"Sure, no problem. I'll just break into Pendleton's secure server and access their cameras along the freeway perimeter, and this time tomorrow, you'll be visiting me in prison."

"I'll bail you out."

"Comforting. You know they only have a few cameras, and those are at the access points to the grounds. They won't pick up much freeway traffic. You need satellite surveillance images."

"Can you get those?"

"Not in the time frame we're dealing with. It would take hours for me to hack a government satellite."

Cooper glanced at the clock again. "I'll catch up with Celina eventually, but do what you can to keep eyes on that vehicle."

"I'll send the picture I snapped of it in the driveway to your phone."

"Roger that. I'll check in with you in half an hour or so."

"You got it."

They disconnected. Cooper thought about telling the rookie Fed outside waiting for him to take off, but explaining why he wasn't going to the airport would only start an avalanche of trouble. The rookie would call his boss, who would call Cooper's boss, and the shit would hit the fan. Arguing would take too much time and he was flat out of that.

Quietly exiting the house from a side door, he stole around back, uncovered his Yamaha motorcycle, and eased her into the alley before he hopped on, gunned the motor, and took off for L.A.

CHAPTER THIRTY-FOUR

Celina woke with a start, her head canted to the left, and a crick in her neck. Her temples pounded. How had she let herself fall asleep?

Too many days with not enough sleep had finally caught up with her. She rubbed her eyes as the van left the freeway and now bumped over sand dunes, coming to a stop behind a grove of scraggly trees where a red pickup truck waited.

"You sure the Marines won't use us for target practice?" Quarters asked Lana, amusement in his voice.

Lana glanced at the red truck. "I cleared it with them."

The overhead sun reflected off the truck's back window, a sharp glare that hurt Celina's eyes and blinded her from seeing the driver. "What's going on?" she asked, sitting forward and squinting.

"Vehicle switch." Lana unbuckled and reached for the gun holstered under her jacket. She looked over her shoulder at Celina. "Security measure. I asked Agent Someran to meet us here for a quick exchange."

A man stepped out of the truck. Head down, he walked toward them, a cap on his head, boots on his feet. A sudden gust of wind made him grab his cap to keep it from blowing away.

"Gonna be a tight squeeze with three of us in a pickup." Quarters shifted the van into park. "Wouldn't the Bureau spring for something bigger?"

Lana laughed, incredulous. "I won't be riding in that thing."

Someran approached and Quarters hit the button to roll down his window. "You're not going with us to L.A.?"

"Oh, I'm going to L.A., but you're not."

Quarters unbuckled and turned slightly toward her. "Why not?"

Someran was at the driver's side window. Celina caught site of his jawline, nose, and thin lips as he raised his gaze to Quarters'.

Valquis. "Look out!" she yelled as Valquis pointed a large black gun at Quarters' head.

Celina lunged, shoving Quarters forward just as the gun went off. The noise was deafening; the bullet ripped across the backside of Quarters' skull, spraying Celina, Lana, and the car with blood. His forehead hit the steering wheel and he went limp. Lana's gun came up and another earsplitting sound erupted, causing Celina to flinch back.

But Lana didn't shoot Valquis. She shot the dashboard.

Valquis had disappeared. Celina dropped to the floor in the back of the van, scrambling for the door. There was nowhere to run, except open desert and the freeway. She'd be easy pickings. But, better out there where she had a chance, than trapped inside the van.

In the back of her mind, she knew Lana had misfired. She'd meant to hit Valquis, missed because of the tight quarters and shock.

Or had she?

Didn't matter. Celina had to get out.

Grabbing the door handle, she jerked hard. Nothing happened. It was locked.

Reaching back, she tried the other handle. Valquis was on that side, but she yanked it anyway. It moved loosely in her hand but didn't open the door.

Lana *tsked* from the front seat. Celina glanced up and saw the section chief looking down at her, wiping blood off her face with a tissue. "Child locks. Handy little things when keeping a troublemaker inside the car."

Oh, god. What the hell was she doing? Celina darted a glance at the driver's side window, out the front of the windshield, and at the passenger window. No Valquis. She fumbled to unbutton her holster. "Where did he go?"

Lana waved the tissue at the blacked out rear windows and raised her voice, seeming to want him to hear. "He's outside waiting for you." Then she smiled and lowered her voice to barely above a whisper, "He thinks we're working together."

What? Celina's ears rang from the gunshots. Surely, she hadn't heard Lana correctly. She got the holster unbuttoned, but couldn't get the gun out. She needed to remove her jacket.

Lana's eyes had a scary brightness to them. Her smile was downright deranged. Celina scooted back between the second row's bucket seats, putting distance between herself and Lana's gun. "What have you done?" she whispered back.

Lana used the end of her gun to point at her chest. "I flushed him out. Me! Using you as bait. He thinks I'm going to hand you over to him."

In a flash, everything became clear. "You're the leak."

Lana shook her head. "No, unfortunately, I'm not, but I thought the idea was a good one. Work with the enemy to draw him out." She grinned like they were in agreement about her plan. "Perfect."

"Are you kidding me?"

Lana shushed her. "Just climb out of the van and do what he says."

"You think you can take on Valquis alone? You're crazy."

"Not crazy." She tapped her temple with the gun. "Smart. I'm taking this monster down and you're going to"—

The bullet came out of nowhere, shattering the passenger window, and hitting Lana in the back. She bent forward, a startled expression on her face, pausing for a split second before her eyes rolled up in her head, and she pitched forward. Her gun landed at Celina's feet.

Valquis' face appeared in the empty window, his thin lips parting in an evil grin. "Hola, chica. Miss me? Ah, I know you did. We're going to get reacquainted soon. Take a little drive to see Emilio."

"I don't think so," Celina said and dived for Lana's gun.

CHAPTER THIRTY-FIVE

Lana's gun was unfamiliar, but the adrenaline pumping in her veins didn't care. Gun, hand, trigger.

Good thing she could shoot with either hand. Bad thing, the safety was on.

Flicking off the safety, she scrambled behind the second row seats, raised the gun, and fired at the window.

As always, Valquis was a step ahead of her. Her shot hit nothing, flying out the window and into the desert.

Celina resumed her cover behind the seat. Valquis wouldn't shoot her. Hurt her, yes, but she was sure his orders were to take her to Emilio. Shooting her would be too messy. He'd smack her around, knock her out, tie her up. Easier to transport.

Trapped in a van. A killer outside. No one knew where she was.

Call Cooper.

Retrieving her phone, however, would mean putting down the gun. No way was she doing that.

"Come on, chica. Don't make this harder than it has to be."

Valquis' voice came from the area around the rear right panel of the van. He was taunting her. He couldn't see in, but if she squinted, she could make out his form through the dark windows.

She raised the gun, aimed.

The shadow moved, disappeared.

Keeping the gun trained on the general vicinity of the rear windows, she used her bandaged hand to grope for her phone.

Her wrist was immovable, but her fingers landed on the cool plastic of the cover and she breathed a sigh of relief. The damn wrist splint limited her hand's ability to grip anything, though, and the phone slipped through her hand and dropped to the floor of the van.

The air in the van was hot and sticky. Sweat trickled between her breasts. Distant car noises drifted in through the open window. Camp Pendleton seemed like the ideal place to find help, but the base covered over a hundred-thousand acres of Southern California terrain. Acres of nothing but desert, scrub trees, and hot sunshine beating down on her.

The freeway and its traffic was a better bet. If she could get to the freeway, she could get help.

Or I can end this. Right here, right now.

Making up her mind, she firmed her hold on the gun. "I'm coming out!" she yelled. "Don't shoot."

———

Cooper gunned the bike on the freeway, didn't slow down through Oceanside, weaving in and out of cars, scaring pedestrians and picking up a patrol car in the process. He had to get to Celina. Never should have let her leave his house without him.

Another patrol car joined the chase, but after a minute, Cooper realized they weren't trying to pull him over, just keep up with him. Dyer had come through, no doubt, calling the locals for backup in case Cooper needed them.

He hoped he didn't. He hoped he'd have to apologize and get his ass kicked by Kipfer and Dupé for causing trouble. He hoped he was totally wrong about Lana.

When had he ever been wrong about her?

Swearing into the wind, he revved the motorcycle's engine even harder.

CHAPTER THIRTY-SIX

The side van door would slide open; the back ones would swing outward. Choices, choices.

Celina slid over to the back double doors. If she could make a claw with her injured hand, she could ease it open without having to lower her gun...

"Throw out your gun first, chica," Valquis commanded.

What would he do if she didn't comply? If she just stepped out, gun in hand, and confronted him face-to-face?

She jerked on the handle, ready to do just that. The door wouldn't budge.

Damn. The child locks.

"I'm unlocking the doors," she called out. "The child locks are on."

No reply. Celina picked her way to the front, checked for pulses on Lana and Quarters. Both were weak, but there. She shrugged off her jacket, padded Lana's bleeding chest. There was nothing she could do for Quarters without more time.

She didn't have time. Maneuvering her arm over the front seat, she hit the unlock button. A soft click resonated through the interior. Glancing down, she closed her eyes against the sight of Quarters' bloody head. His body still leaned against the steering wheel, arms down at his sides.

Wiping sweat from her forehead with her arm, she glanced out the front and side windows, keeping an eye out for Valquis. She spotted part of him in the side view mirror on the passenger side. He stood, waiting, every muscle tense, but confidence radiating off of him. He knew he had her.

Keeping her eye on him, she laid down Lana's gun, removed her holster, and laid it on the floor. Taking her gun, she stuck it in the waistband of her pants at the small of her back. Then she dug out her phone.

Valquis stepped closer to the van, raised his gun. "Ándale! Get out here."

His gaze caught hers in the side mirror. Celina froze, letting the phone slip back into her pants pocket. Her holster and Lana's gun still lay on the floor at her feet. He couldn't see it, so she kept her eyes steady on his as she covertly used her foot to slide the gun backwards and out of sight in case he came to the window. "I can't get through the dead bodies, thanks to you. I'm coming out the back."

Without waiting for a reply, she slid into the darkened interior, grabbing Lana's gun and feeling the solid weight of her own weapon in her waistband.

Easing one of the back doors open, she held out Lana's gun, then dropped it to the ground. "I'm unarmed."

He lowered his weapon, motioned at her to come out.

She opened the door the rest of the way, climbed out with her hands in the air. The sun hit her with its hot glare. The air shimmered with mid-day heat.

Valquis smiled. "That wasn't so hard, was it?" He pointed the black barrel of his gun at her, motioned for her to walk. "Move."

She had to make her stand here. If she turned her back on him, he'd see the hidden weapon. If he got her in that truck, she was dead.

"I'm not going anywhere with you."

He came at her like a tiger pouncing on a gazelle. He shoved her against the second van door, still closed, and put his face in hers. She let him think he had the upper hand, allowing him to press his body against hers. His smelled like day-old body odor and his breath reeked. "Always so cocky. I will cut that out of you."

God, that smell. *Don't throw up, don't throw up...* "You can try."

Her challenge only made him grin. "We are going to have lots of fun together."

"You can't hurt me. Emilio ordered you to bring me to him, didn't he? You stashed him well. He's not in Mexico, either, I bet. He's here. Somewhere close."

"He's nearby. Where do you think a man like him would hideout? He's still head of the cartel, still has deals to make with his friends. Mexico has some nice getaways, but America is his home."

His home. Celina had been to the Londano estates several times during the undercover op. The government had confiscated that house and property, but Valquis was right. Emilio had a lifestyle to maintain, expectations he wanted fulfilled. Where would he find a place similar to his own house?

She needed more info. "Why go to all this trouble to get revenge on me?"

Valquis snorted. "You put him in prison, chica. Cut into his very profitable business dealings and cost him dearly. If he doesn't make you an example, he will be a laughing stock. Others will try to hold it over his head that he was bested by a pretty woman. His street status used to exalt him over everyone. He needs to restore that."

"Getting revenge on me won't restore his street cred."

"You don't give yourself enough credit." Valquis ran a finger down her cheek, pinched it. "I am very much looking forward to making you an example."

The threat should have put the fear of God in her. But she would never let it get to that point. "I look forward to it. I'd rather have you than Emilio, so why don't we blow him off and go our own way? Together. Partners. I'm tired of the FBI game."

The odd statement threw him off. He hesitated. "What?"

It would be great if the cavalry came right now. A jeep full of Marines, investigating the cars and the gunshots, racing in with guns raised and dust flying. The spot they were in was too far from the main base, though. No one would have heard the shots, and gunshots and explosions were hourly occurrences around a military base. No one would investigate a few measly handgun pops.

All she wanted to do was put as much space as possible between her and Valquis, but Cooper had taught her to charge forward in situations like this, rather than rearing back. She shifted her hands and lightly placed them on Valquis' chest. "You. I've always wanted to be with you. I like it rough, you know."

He believed her for half a second, but half a second was all she needed. In one fluid movement, she slid her hands down to his waist, pulled him in hard, and at the same time, jammed her knee up toward his balls.

Valquis hadn't become Emilio's second in command by being an easy target. A split-second before her knee connected, he shifted, and her knee merely grazed his precious parts, slamming instead into the inside of his thigh.

He shoved her hard, but she hung onto him, keeping him off balance. They both fell to the ground, Celina kicking his shin with the heel of her shoe. He grabbed her by the ponytail, yanked her head back. She slammed a fist into his nose, felt bone snap underneath it.

He grunted and rolled away, striking her head with the butt of the gun. Pain exploded behind her eyes and her vision blurred. Gaining his feet, he kicked her in the ribs, lifting her body from the ground with the effort. She landed against the wheel of the van.

Although her ears rang, Celina heard the sound of a motorcycle. No surprise, since the freeway was only a few hundred feet away. The thing that caught her attention was that the sound was growing louder, the cycle coming closer. Had someone seen them? Was an innocent bystander coming to help her?

Valquis would kill whoever it was. She knew it. No way was she letting one more person die at his hands.

He was getting ready to kick her again when the motorcycle did indeed roar around the stand of trees and fishtail to a stop a few yards away. Valquis stopped in mid-kick and turned. Celina caught a brief glance of the man on the bike and sucked in a breath. Cooper?

Hot damn. The cavalry's here.

Her vision swam, creating three of Valquis as she sat up, but her hand was steady, finding the butt of her gun in her waistband and yanking it free.

"I've got…" she called to Cooper, feeling sick again. *This*, she finished mentally.

Cooper yelled something that was lost in the sound of a dozen sirens as a squadron of police cars arrived, lights flashing and sirens blaring. Valquis crouched, running for the truck and raising his weapon to fire on Cooper.

Focusing on the middle version of his crouched and running form, Celina popped the trigger…once, twice, three times.

All three versions of her target arched in unison, staggered, and fell.

CHAPTER THIRTY-SEVEN

"Celina!"

Cooper's heart slammed against his ribcage so hard he thought he might be having a heart attack. After nailing Val, Celina had slumped sideways. Her eyelids drooped, her hand released the gun. She was too pale and sweating profusely.

He knew Val was dead without checking for a pulse. His fiery rookie had shot the man three times in the center of his back. The coroner would find his heart and lungs shredded from her accuracy.

Cooper lifted her from the hot, sandy ground and moved her to a shady spot under the trees. As the cops Dyer had alerted went to work securing the body, reporting the crime, and checking for survivors in the vehicles, he eased her down to the ground and checked her for fresh injuries.

There was a slight swelling on the side of her head. Nothing else he could visibly see. One of the cops handed him a bottled water and told him they'd found bodies in the van. Both had sustained gunshot wounds. Both were still alive. Barely, but there was hope. Cooper told him who they were as an ambulance siren sounded in the distance.

"Celina." He gently patted her cheek. "Wake up, sweetheart, and drink some water."

Her eyelids fluttered open. Her brown eyes slowly focused on him. He cradled her head and she sipped some of the water he offered.

"Did I get him?" she asked.

"Bull's-eye to the back."

She sat up fully, whisked a few strands of hair away from her eyes. It seemed to take her a minute to find her balance. "Where's the gun?"

"It's been confiscated by the police for evidence. Why?"

Locking onto Valquis' body, she leveraged herself to a standing position using the nearest tree trunk. "Give me your gun."

"For what?"

"I'm going to shoot him again."

She was delusional from the heat. "He's dead, sweetheart. You don't need to shoot him again."

"I *want* to shoot him again. A bullet for everyone he killed or hurt." She held out her hand, wiggled her fingers. "Give me your damn gun."

Not delusional. Just vengeful.

He liked it. "You need medical care, and the cops need a statement."

"Screw that. I owe him."

"Save that anger for Emilio. He's still on the run."

That got her. Her gaze swung to his. "Then let's go get him."

"We can head for Mexico after you see a doctor."

"Emilio's not in Mexico."

Cooper checked her pupils to make sure her head injury wasn't messing with her logic. They looked normal, her eyes simply determined. "Then where is he?"

She headed for the bike before he finished speaking, staggering slightly. "Right under our noses."

One of the wet-behind-the-ears cops rushed over to her with a fresh bottle of water and a healthy stare. She waved off the water, and patted his cheek. "No, thanks."

He looked flustered and Cooper shook his head and sent the guy away. "Did Val tell you where Emilio was hiding out?"

"Londano's house in the hills is still vacant, isn't it?"

"Yeah." Cooper wasn't following. "As far as I know, nothing was done to it after he went to prison. Too much red tape tying things up. Everyone from the FBI to Homeland and the Mexican *Federales* want their cut, so it's sitting empty while the courts figure out who gets what. Why?"

"Something Valquis said. The way Emilio lives—what he *needs* to live and operate his enterprise. His house fits the bill in a way nothing else can. It was specially designed for him. Lana may have even known he was there. She made a deal with Valquis to draw him out. That's how he knew to meet us here." She sighed heavily. "And that deal cost her her life."

"She's not dead. Not yet, anyway."

A look of surprise mixed with relief flashed over Celina's features. "Quarters?"

"Still breathing. Ambulance is on its way."

"Lana wanted to be the hero. She thought she could blackmail Valquis and save the day. Think about it, Cooper. This type of score would have catapulted her career into the stratosphere."

He stared at her for a moment, pulled out his cell and speed-dialed Dyer.

"You catch up with her?" Dyer said by way of greeting.

"Everything's cool. She killed Valquis."

"No shit. Really? How's she holding up?"

"Time will tell. I need you to assemble the team and send them to Londano's house in San Diego."

"He doesn't have a house anymore."

"His former place. The one the Feds confiscated. Celina thinks he may have holed up there."

"Nah. Lana had it under surveillance. We would have known if he tried to move back in. He's still in Mexico."

"Like Val was? I'm looking at Val's dead body right now. Everything points to Emilio being here too."

"Put an extra round in Val for me. Make sure he's good and dead."

Celina was quiet, staring at the cops administering basic emergency care to Lana and Quarters. Her eyes were flat, her arms crossed tightly over her chest as if holding herself together.

"Lana was running her own game behind the scenes," he told Dyer. "Which may have involved cutting deals with Emilio and Valquis. Celina and I are heading to the house now. Send the rest of the team."

"The team is off to Mexico, remember? I'm all you've got."

Damn. He'd forgotten about the manhunt. The wild goose chase. It had been one damn good distraction after all. "Lana sent everyone to Mexico while she stayed here to capture Valquis and Emilio." He shook his head. "Damn woman. I knew she was ambitious, but this takes the cake."

"I'll call Dupé. Some of his other agents can meet you at Londano's."

"No. No FBI. I don't know who we can trust at this point. Sounds like Lana was working alone, but we still may have a leak in the ranks. Word goes out we know where Londano's hiding, and he's in the wind again."

"If he's even there."

"Yeah, *if.* It's our best lead, though."

"You shouldn't go alone."

"We'll recon the place to start. I see anything suspicious, I'll call Kipfer or Dupé."

"I don't like it."

Seemed like they were both saying that a lot these days.

He didn't like it either. Taking Celina to Londano's was poor protocol. Not calling for backup was as asinine as Lana cutting a deal with Valquis. The whole situation went against his training and experience, but what choice did he have? He needed to follow Celina's instincts. She hadn't been wrong yet. "I'll check in as soon as I have something to report."

He disconnected and climbed on the bike, ignoring the

shouts from the lead police officer. "Hold on," he told her over the noise as he gunned the engine.

Her arms went around his waist. For the first time in a long while, breaking protocol felt right. Like it had in Des Moines. In fact, nothing in his world felt more right at that moment than her hands wrapped securely around him as she sat on the back of his bike.

Leaving the scene in a hail of dust, he took off for San Diego.

CHAPTER THIRTY-EIGHT

"How many fingers am I holding up?" Cooper yelled at her over the roar of the motorcycle as they zoomed down the freeway.

Celina leaned her head against his strong back. "Two, and I'm fine."

Her ribs hurt. Her head throbbed. The vibration of the bike echoed loudly in her ears.

But it also soothed her tired body. Or maybe it was Cooper's presence. Even though they flew through the Southern California afternoon at eighty miles an hour, weaving around traffic and heading for the one place she was scared to go, he was a rock to hold onto. The one solid thing in her life.

Tucking in even closer, she closed her eyes and held on tight.

The drive that should have taken them an hour only took forty minutes. Cooper parked the bike at the bottom of the hill where Emilio's estate loomed over them. He took out binoculars and scanned the area.

Emilio's house, an elegant gated Spanish number, had an elevated view of Coastal San Diego. Over seven thousand square feet with five bedrooms, six baths, a theatre, and wine cellar, it also contained an underground firing range and weapons room.

Although the house had sat empty for the past year, from what Celina could see, the grounds had been cared for, groomed. The house didn't have the distinctive air of abandonment.

She shivered. A storm was moving in from the west, darkening the ocean. The temperature had dropped and a gusty wind teased her hair. "Anything?" she said, rubbing her arms.

"Nada. If he *is* here, he's laying low."

No surprise. If Emilio was hiding, he wouldn't exactly be flaunting it. "We need to get closer."

"I'll take a walk around the perimeter. You stay here."

"There are a dozen or more security cameras. He'll see you."

Cooper handed her the binoculars. "I know where they are. I'll avoid them."

She started to argue, saw the set of his jaw and knew it would be pointless. "I can't just stand here and do nothing."

He patted her shoulder. "You're the backup this round, rookie. You see anything funny, call it in. Otherwise, stay out of sight in case Londano is hanging around." He handed her his weapon—hers had been confiscated at the crime scene with Valquis. "Shoot first, ask questions later."

"I'm shocked you'd consider leaving me alone."

"Val was our biggest threat and you handled him like a pro."

There was more to it than that. She could see it in his eyes. "And you don't believe Emilio is here."

He looked away without answering. The argument burning her tongue came out, but before she could say anything, Cooper grabbed her and drew her to him. His lips shut off her complaint with firm, warm kisses.

She melted against his strong body. The kiss deepened, wet and hot. She no longer felt any pain, had no fear of the coming moments. All she could feel was Cooper's powerful hands holding her up, his warm, urgent lips caressing hers.

"I'm sorry," he murmured against her lips. "About this morning. About everything."

"Shh," she murmured back. "We're together now. After we nail this guy, you'll have years and years to make this up to me."

"Years, huh?"

"Decades."

"You're going to put up with me for decades?"

"That's what you do when you love someone."

Love. It scared him. She could see it in his eyes. But she wasn't letting him off the hook. "Just admit it. You love me too."

The fear left his eyes. He chuckled. "You ever do anything half-assed?"

"No, and neither do you, remember? So stop finding excuses not to be with me, and accept the fact I'm sticking around, Beast."

He kissed her again, and held her tight for long moments, trailing his hands up her spine, down to cup her ass, pulling her into his groin where a serious erection had grown.

Celina chuckled. "My, my, you're breaking a lot of rules today, Agent Harris."

"Yes, I am." He cupped one of her breasts through her shirt. "And it's all your fault."

"I'm a bad influence?"

"The baddest. But if we don't nail Londano, all this rule-breaking will be for nothing."

In other words, they had a job to do. So even though they wanted to continue their make-out session, it would have to wait.

Celina wished they had comm units to keep in touch. She waved her phone in front of him. "Text me every few minutes, okay?"

He nodded, and with one final kiss, he slunk off into some overgrown shrubbery ringing the gated estate.

Celina sighed and watched him go. Then she tucked herself out of sight from the road and the house. Her head felt better, although the lump Val had given her courtesy of his gun was sensitive to the touch. Her ribs were the same. Maybe it was the adrenaline pumping through her body from Cooper's kisses, but all in all, she felt stronger, ready for what was about to happen.

Cooper may not believe Emilio's here, but I do.

As the minutes wore on, the adrenaline faded. Restlessness set in. No word came from Cooper and anxiety flooded her system. She didn't hear any sounds from the house or the grounds, but it was a huge place that had sat empty for a long time. Maybe Cooper was right and it still was empty.

She got up, paced, snatched up the binoculars, and scanned what she could see of the area. Nothing moved except palm trees blowing in the wind.

Another five minute passed. Fumbling with her phone, she texted Cooper.

No reply.

Fumbling with it some more, she managed to call Bobby. "Cooper's gone to reconnoiter the place, but he hasn't checked in for twenty minutes. I haven't heard any shouts or gunfire, but I'm worried. If no one was here, why isn't he back?"

Bobby said some curse words under his breath. "I'm calling in backup."

"What should I do?"

"Sit tight."

He hung up.

Sit tight? Hell with that. Just because she hadn't heard sounds of a struggle or fight didn't mean Cooper wasn't lying in a pool of blood or knocked unconscious.

Lightning flashed over the water, the storm moved closer. Thunder boomed, its echo ringing down the hill. She tried Cooper's phone again, calling this time. The call went directly to voice mail.

If Emilio was indeed here, the only way to end this was to face him head on. Emerging from her hiding spot, she climbed the hill, heading for the front gate. There she rang the bell. If nothing else, she could distract Emilio from whatever he might be doing to Cooper.

The house sat quiet, the large windows empty. No one answered her summons, and soon she started tapping her foot and ringing the buzzer over and over again.

Nothing happened. Frustration took over. She tried the gates but they were locked. The only way in was up and over.

She was strong but not strong enough to haul herself up the ten-feet of iron gate with only one hand. Still, she gave it a try, only to land with her butt on the ground.

The clouds overhead began dropping rain. Standing up, she dusted herself off, and tried to remember the backyard area. More gates, a pool and a large patio. But maybe she could find an easier way in, a service entrance or something. Maybe even find Cooper was safe and sound and simply on his way back to tell her Emilio wasn't there.

A crash of thunder rumbled over the hills. Celina headed off the way Cooper had disappeared, fighting off the tangle of shrubs and bushes just as the storm finally cut loose.

CHAPTER THIRTY-NINE

The backyard was equipped for hosting large parties. A private courtyard looked out over the hills and olive trees. The patio stretched for yards on either side of the main house, an infinity pool looking out over the water to the west. Two large stone fireplaces and an outdoor kitchen flanked the east. As Celina snuck around the outside gate, she saw a man sitting under the covered terrace in a chair facing the hills. He was spinning a golf club in mindless circles in his hand. Emilio.

"Welcome," he said without turning to look at her. "I've been waiting for you."

Of course he had. Smart ass. Well, she could smart-ass, too. "I rang the bell. Why didn't you answer?"

He stood slowly, stretching, and keeping his back to her as he watched the rain pour down. He was dressed in an expensive suit and his favorite pair of Gucci shoes—the same ones he'd worn the night she'd arrested him.

He appeared unarmed, except for the golf club—a prized driver he'd had imported from Ireland while she was 'dating' him. "I was otherwise preoccupied. Practicing my swing, you see. Prison doesn't allow for such luxuries."

"And here I figured you were waiting for Valquis to return with me in tow."

"I assumed he would be with you." Finally, he faced her, letting his eyes scan the area behind her and to each side. Looking for his second-in-command, or perhaps he thought she'd brought other agents?

As usual, he sported a goatee and a confident smirk. "But it seems you have escaped my lieutenant."

"I did more than escape him," she said through the iron bars of the gate. "I shot him three times in the back, just like he deserved. He's dead."

Emilio's dark eyebrows rose half an inch. "You're lying."

Celina raised her hands and motioned around them. "Do you see him anywhere?"

There was a moment of silence. "And now you've come for me?"

Where was Cooper? She prayed he wasn't on the other side of the compound. *Charge forward and do the unexpected. Keep him off guard.* "I've come to surrender."

"Surrender?" he laughed.

His whole pursuit had been psychological. Like a commander of an army, he'd done the strategizing and sent his soldier, Valquis, to do the physical dirty work and terrorize her. Now it was her turn to get into his psyche.

Play the part. She gripped the bars, rested her forehead against them. Took a deep breath and sighed as if in resignation. Why not give him what he'd wanted all along—to destroy her life, like she'd done to him?

"You've taken everything from me, Emilio. Hurt and killed people I care about. I can't do it anymore. I don't want anyone else to be hurt because of me. I just want this over, so I'm here, alone. To surrender."

He stayed put, eyeing her with suspicion. He wouldn't take the bait.

She held his gaze, forcing herself to appear sincere.

Still he didn't react. Didn't say a word. Testing her.

The predator waiting for his prey to make the next move so he could pounce. Waiting...waiting...waiting...

Damn. She held steady even though her pulse was triple-timing it. Now what?

Cooper and Emilio were diametric opposites, but there was one thing they had in common. One little chink in their armors she could exploit. She hadn't done it intentionally with Cooper in Des Moines—she'd thought he was already gone when she'd let herself cry on the apartment stairs—but the tears had worked anyway. And now she bet she could use them against Emilio with equal success.

Forcing tears would kill her chances, though. She needed real emotions to carry this off.

Thunder boomed overhead. The rain drenched her.

Sadness and dismay weren't hard to dig up. She was exhausted, in pain, and grieving for all the lives damaged and destroyed by the man in front of her. Ronni, Forester, the others who'd been hurt and killed...the thought of each one brought the ever-present raw, aching grief to the surface.

Her eyes burned with unspent tears. She drew on the pain; let a few tears slip down her cheeks, mixing with the rain on her face. "My friends are gone. My career ruined. Working for the FBI was my dream, the only thing I ever wanted. Now, they've kicked me out." A lie, yes, but she hoped he didn't know otherwise. "Killing Petero Valquis won't change that. My professional and personal lives are a complete disaster. I have nothing left."

Sliding down the bars, she acted like a woman barely holding on. "Do what you want with me, Emilio. I'm a failure. A loser. I have no fight left."

Hugging her knees to her chest, she turned so her back was to him. As she let herself cry softly—overdoing the dramatics would only backfire—she heard the faint sound of his leather shoes on the wet patio. A moment later, he stood on the other side of the iron bars hovering over her. "How does it feel? To have your life ruined? The empire you built with your own hands, destroyed?"

Come on, Cooper. Where are you? If she kept Emilio distracted long enough, Cooper and/or the cops Bobby was calling in would show. Just a few more minutes...

She hitched her breath, fake crying a bit more and letting her body language suggest she truly had nothing left. She was weak, broken.

At his mercy.

The predator sensed his advantage. The next thing she knew, he reached through the bars, grabbed a section of her wet hair and yanked her head back. The bars bonged as her skull smacked against them.

His voice was low but self-assured as he murmured in her ear through the gate. "You are mine, bitch. All mine."

"I don't think so," a familiar voice said from behind Emilio.

Emilio whipped around, releasing her at the same time. The sudden shift made Celina pitch forward, but not before she saw Cooper take a swing at Emilio's head with the golf club.

There was the sickening sound of crunching bone as the club connected with Emilio's nose. He cried out, staggered against the bars. Celina jumped up, wrenching his right hand through the bar spacing and pinning it behind him. Cooper took a second swing, this one at Emilio's kneecaps. Jammed against the gate, blood pouring from his nose over his wet silk suit, the cartel leader cried out again, cursing both of them.

Celina didn't release his arm, even as he sank to the ground, howling over his broken kneecaps. If anything, she pinioned it tighter. No way was she letting go. "Shoot him," she told Cooper.

A police siren echoed in the valley. A second one joined it. Cooper, soaked and smiling, acted like he was taking a practice swing at Emilio's head. "Not necessary."

"It is *too* necessary. Shoot him."

"Killing him is too easy. He needs to suffer."

"Exactly. Start with his balls and work your way up."

"In prison. He's got a death row stint waiting for him."

Emilio stirred, tried tugging away from her. His voice sounded muffled, thanks to his broken nose. "I never committed murder."

Cooper took another practice swing. "We have your prints on the knife used to carve up Chief Forester, Londano, as well as all the lovely conspiracies to commit murder charges on multiple Federal agents. The death penalty is definitely on the menu."

Celina's arm was shaking, trying to hold Emilio in place, even though she was sure he couldn't walk with two broken kneecaps. Didn't stop him from lunging at Cooper. "You're lying."

Cooper winked at her, wrestled Londano over onto his stomach, and handcuffed him. Patted him on the back of the head. "A word of advice. Stay in prison this time. You ever set foot out in the free world again I *will* shoot you. Right between the eyes."

Stepping over Emilio's body, Cooper sidled up to the gate.

"How did you get in?" she asked.

"Climbed the fence. How else?"

"I tried that. One-handed doesn't work."

"Nice act with Londano. I saw the whole thing. You certainly know how to use your feminine wiles against unsuspecting men."

She stood and smiled up at him. "They do tend to work better than the tough federal agent act. I haven't quite gotten that one down, but I'm getting better."

His eyes searched hers for a moment. "I love you, Celina."

She had to grip the gate bars to keep her knees from buckling. "Finally giving in, are you?"

"Yeah." He reached through and touched her face with his fingers. "I'm giving in. You make me loco, but I've never wanted a woman more than I want you."

Police cars were pulling in the drive now. The squawk of radios mingling with the sirens.

Kissing Cooper through the bars wasn't easy, but she'd never signed up for easy. His lips were wet from the rain, the angle of their heads all wrong. He still managed to capture her mouth perfectly, teasing and seducing her to the point she nearly climbed the gate, regardless of her immobile hand, and attacked him right there in front of Emilio and the officers pouring onto the scene.

"Hands up!" one of the officers called.

Celina and Cooper both raised their hands, but didn't stop kissing.

"DEA," Cooper said around her mouth.

She giggled, broke away from his lips. "And I'm FBI. We're on the Southern Cal violent crimes taskforce."

Cooper flashed his badge, appeasing the officers, and went to find the security panel to open the gates.

The policeman nearest Celina pointed a stubby finger at her. "Hey, ain't you that gal who was on the front of *Time* magazine a while ago? The new face of the FBI?"

Celina brushed wet hair from her eyes, and stared at Emilio lying on the ground. The *Time* magazine article seemed like a lifetime ago. She wasn't that woman any more. She wasn't that agent. "You must have me confused with someone else," she said. "That agent is a rookie. I'm not."

CHAPTER FORTY

Carlsbad Beach
Two days later

Cooper stood near the rock outcropping, watching the familiar curvy form of a certain Fed jog the beach. Her dark hair was pulled high in a ponytail, and her gait was purposeful. She'd had surgery on her hand hours after arresting Londano for a second time and the prognosis was good. Given time, a bunch of physical therapy, and a return to gun training exercises, the accuracy in her right hand would return to one hundred percent.

Forester's body had been released and flown home to Des Moines. His funeral was scheduled for the following Monday, and Celina and Cooper had already booked plane tickets so they could attend.

Ronni Punta was out of the hospital, and Mary, the safe house agent, had already returned to work. Dawn McBroom was still hospitalized, but improving daily. Agent Quarters and Lana Custov were also still in the hospital. Pending Celina's testimony, Lana would be facing a full investigation and criminal charges for her actions once she'd recovered.

Celina caught sight of him waiting for her and slowed, a curious look on her face. She was sweating and out of breath, but her color was normal, and the cloud that had hung over her for the past week had lifted.

She came to a stop, sized up his clean shirt, nice jeans, and shaved jawline. "What is that in your hands?"

"Starbucks. Iced coffees."

"Thought you didn't do Starbucks."

"I don't drink Mountain Dew, either, but for you?" He shrugged and handed her one of the paper cups. "If it makes you happy, I'll concede once in a while."

She took the cup and he clinked his against it, giving her a smile. She eyed him, taking a healthy swig. "What's wrong with you?"

"Wrong with me?"

"Yeah, you seem…happy. Did Londano slip on a bar of soap in prison and break his neck or something?"

"What? I can't be happy watching my girlfriend jog down the beach on a beautiful California morning?"

"You're The Beast. You don't do Starbucks. You don't do happy. Your words, not mine."

Small beads of sweat glistened on her upper lip. He wanted to kiss them off. "I got the dog."

Her eyes brightened. "You did? You found Thunder?"

He nodded. "Wasn't easy tracking him down, but he was still with the gal who trains dogs for government work. Bomb sniffers, drug sniffers, and dogs like Thunder, who help with undercover work. I officially adopted him this morning. I took Owen out of school and he and Thunder are in the car. Apparently, Chihuahuas like Starbucks too."

Her smile was contagious. "You're a good dad."

A kind of pride he hadn't felt in a long time rose up inside him. "It was the least I could do for the little fellow since he helped nail Londano last year. And you're right. Owen needed a friend."

Celina looked out at the ocean. "It is a beautiful morning, isn't it? Wish I'd brought my camera."

Her camera was at still at his place with the rest of her stuff. "How about you, me, and the boys go home and grab it?"

"Home. Hmm."

"What?"

"I don't really have a home at the moment, and my job is in flux. I'm on medical leave, but I still have paperwork to do and depositions to give. And all I really want to do is stay right here and enjoy the view."

"Dyer will do the paperwork for you, and Dupé can wait for his deposition. I'm taking the day off, and I say we grab your camera and have a picnic."

She laughed and shook her head. "I really am a bad influence on you."

He pulled her close, careful of her drink and wrist brace. "Not true. You're the best influence I've had in my life in a long time. Come home with me, Celina. Make it your home. Owen needs that dog, and I need *you*."

She melted against him, and then looked guilty. "I want to pursue photography full time."

"Leave the Bureau?"

"I don't want to do undercover work anymore."

"Okay…" But he worried there was something else behind this decision. "You're not just bailing because of me, right? Because of the potential conflict with our jobs?"

She shook her head. "I'm still going to work for the FBI, but I'm going to be a forensic photographer once I'm off medical leave. I've already signed up for the certification course."

No more undercover work. No more worrying his balls off that she was in danger. He couldn't keep the relief off his face. "If that makes you happy, I'm ecstatic."

"Dupé said they can use me in both the San Diego and L.A. offices, so I guess I can go home with you and live here, if the offer still stands."

He dropped his cup, grabbed her, and twirled her around. She laughed out loud, throwing her head back, and dropping her cup too. For Cooper, it was better than the rush from his first bust, and he hoped it outshined hers as well.

She lifted her hands and let him swing her around. People stopped and stared. A few clapped and whistled. When he put her back down, she was still laughing, carefree and happy. "I think I'm up for the picnic now," she said.

He kissed her, once, twice, three times. Quick kisses, each a promise for their future. "I think I'm ready to make you happy for many, many decades."

"Decades. I like the sound of that. I love you, Cooper Harris."

"I love you, too." He picked up their cups and tossed them in a nearby garbage barrel. Then he took her good hand and led her toward his truck. "Let's go home, Celina."

She squeezed his hand, waved at Owen in the truck, the little dog standing on his lap and wagging furiously. "Yes, let's go home."

ABOUT THE AUTHOR

USA TODAY Bestselling Author Misty Evans has published fifty novels and writes romantic suspense, urban fantasy, and paranormal romance. She got her start writing in 4th grade when she won second place in a school writing contest with an essay about her dad. Since then, she's written nonfiction magazine articles, started her own coaching business, become a yoga teacher, and raised twin boys on top of enjoying her fiction career. When not reading or writing, she enjoys music, movies, and hanging out with her husband, twin sons, and two spoiled puppies. A registered yoga teacher and Master Reiki Practitioner, she shares her love of chakra yoga and energy healing, but still hasn't mastered levitating. Get free reads, all the latest news, and alerts about sales when you sign up for her newsletter at www.readmistyevans.com.

Printed in Poland
by Amazon Fulfillment
Poland Sp. z o.o., Wrocław